MR. PRESIDENT

HE'LL RULE HER
LIKE HE'LL
RULE THE COUNTRY.

KATY
EVANS

NEW YORK TIMES & USA TODAY
BESTSELLING AUTHOR

Copyright © Katy Evans

All rights reserved, including the right to reproduce this book or portions thereof in any form whatsoever. For information contact the copyright owner above.

First paperback edition: October 2016

Cover design by James T. Egan, www.bookflydesign.com
Interior formatting by JT Formatting

10 9 8 7 6 5 4 2 1

Library of Congress Cataloguing-in-Publication Data is available

ISBN-13: 978-1539407140

To the future

TABLE OF CONTENTS

PLAYLIST

"Hall of Fame" by The Script
"Close" by Nick Jonas
"Make Me Like You" by Gwen Stefani
"Talk Me Down" by Troye Sivan
"If I Had You" by Adam Lambert
"Something In the Way You Move" by
Ellie Goulding
"Tear in My Heart" by Twenty One Pilots
"Come Down to Me" by Saving Jane
"Secret Love Song" by Little Mix
(featuring Jason Derulo)
"Forbidden Love" by The Darkness
"Perfect Ruin" by Kwabs
"You're Beautiful" by James Blunt
"The Reason" by Hoobastank

AUTHOR'S NOTE

Although I tried to stay true to what happens in politics and on the campaign trail, this is ultimately a love story between Matt and Charlotte. This is a work of fiction; therefore I took some liberties with the political world so that I could craft the story that I craved to tell you. This is not a political book, but a love story born in the world of politics. I hope you are as swept away with these two as I am. So settle in, take off your shoes, and step inside ....

YOUR NAME IS MATTHEW

Charlotte

We're in a suite at The Jefferson Hotel where Benton Carlisle, the campaign manager, is smoking his second pack of Camels by the open window. Exactly eight-tenths of a mile from here, the White House stands all lit up for the evening.

All of the televisions inside the suite are set on different news channels, where the anchors continue reporting on the ballot-counting progress of this year's presidential election. The names of the candidates are being tossed around in speculation—three names, to be exact. The Republican candidate, the Democratic candidate, and the first truly strong independent candidate in U.S. history—the son of an ex-president and at barely thirty-five, the youngest contender in history.

My feet are killing me. I've been wearing the same clothes since I left my apartment this morning, headed to the polling station, and cast in my vote. The entire team that has been campaigning for the past year together met here at noon—at this suite.

We've been here for over twelve hours.

The air is thick with tension, especially when *he* walks into the living room after taking a break and heading into one of the bedrooms to talk to his grandfather, who's been calling from New York.

His tall, wide-shouldered frame looms in the doorway.

The men in the room stand, the women straighten.

There's just something about him that draws the eye—his height, his strong but unnervingly warm gaze, the polished ruggedness that only makes him look more male in a business suit, and his infectious smile, so real and engaging you can't help but smile back.

His eyes pause on me, visually measuring the distance between us. I left for an errand and just came back, and of course he notices.

I try to stay composed. "I brought you something for the wait." I speak as smoothly as I can and head into one of the bedrooms with a tightly closed brown bag meant to appear to be food. He follows me.

He doesn't close the door—I notice that—but he pushes it back so that only an inch remains open, giving us as much privacy as possible.

I pull out a crisp men's black jacket and pass it to him.

"You forgot your jacket," I say.

He glances down at his jacket, then the most beautiful dark-espresso eyes raise to mine.

One glance. One brush of fingers. One second of recognition.

His voice is low, almost intimate. "That would've been difficult to explain."

Our eyes hold.

I almost can't let go of his jacket and he almost doesn't want to take it.

He reaches out and takes it, his smile soft and rueful and his gaze perceptive. I know exactly why that smile is rueful, why it is soft with tenderness. Because I'm barely hanging in there tonight and there is no way that this man—that this man who knows it *all*—doesn't know.

Matthew Hamilton.

Possible future President of the United States.

He sets his jacket aside and makes no move to leave the room, and I glance out the window as I try not to stare at his every move.

Through the open window, a breeze that smells of recent rain and Carlisle's cigarettes flits into the room. D.C. seems quieter tonight than usual, the city so still it seems to be holding its breath along with the rest of the country—along with me.

Quietly we head into the living room to join the others. I'm careful to take a spot in the room that's nearly opposite his—instinct. Self-preservation maybe.

"They're saying you've got Ohio," Carlisle updates him.

"Yeah?" Matt asks, quirking a brow, then he glances around the room, whistles for Jack, his shiny black German Shepherd Lab mix, to come. The dog darts across the room and leaps onto the couch, setting himself on Matt's lap and letting him stroke the top of his head.

"... *that's right, Roger, the Matt Hamilton campaign pulled off an impressive feat this year until, well, that incident ...*" the anchors discuss. Matt grabs the remote and turns it off. He glances at me briefly.

One more connection, one more silent look.

The room falls silent.

In my experience, guys love talking about themselves and their accomplishments. Matt, on the contrary, avoids it. As if he's sick of rehashing the tragedy of his life's story. The story that has been the center of the media's attention since his campaign began.

You can note varying degrees of respect in a person's voice when they talk about a particular U.S. president. For some presidents, the degree is nonexistent, the tone more like contempt. For others, the name is turned into something magical and inspiring, filling you with the same feeling you're supposed to get when you look at a red, white, and blue American flag: pride and hope. Such was the case with the Lawrence Hamilton presidency—the administration started by Matt's father several terms ago.

My own father, who until then had supported the opposite party, soon became a staunch Democratic supporter, swayed by President Hamilton's charisma. The man's incredible connection with people spread across not just the nation but overseas, improving our international relations. I was eleven when I was first introduced to Hamilton's legendary charm.

Matt Hamilton, in his late teens when his dad began his first term, had everything, his future bright. I, on the other hand, was still very much a girl, with no idea who I was or where I was going.

Over a decade later, even now I struggle with the sense of failure of having not lived up to something important. A meaningful job and a guy that I loved, those were things I wanted. My parents wanted more from me, politics. I went into social services instead. But no matter how many people I've helped, how much I've told myself that being an adult only means that

I will be in my prime to really make a difference, I cannot help but feel like I not only didn't live up to what my parents wanted for me. But what I wanted for myself.

Because at this very moment as we wait for the next President of the United States to be announced, both of those dreams of mine hang in the air—and I'm afraid when the results come in, they will both vanish my hopes into nothing.

I wait silently as the men create conversation, Matt's voice reaching me occasionally.

Ignoring him feels impossible, but it's all I can manage today.

The suite is grand, decorated to appeal to the tastes of those who can afford rooms that cost a thousand dollars a night. The kind of hotel to offer mints on your pillows and they have been extra hospitable to us, because Matt's a celebrity. They've gone as far as to send up yogurt pretzels, after the press made sure everyone knew they're his favorite.

There was even a bottle of champagne being chilled. Matt asked one of the campaign aides to remove it from the room. Everyone was surprised, they all felt that it meant Matt thought they'd lost the election.

I know that's not the case, instinctively. I simply know if the results are not what he hoped for, he won't want that cool champagne sitting there, a reminder of his loss.

Leaving Jack on the couch, he restlessly stalks across the room and takes a seat beside his campaign manager by the window, and he lights a cigarette. Memories play in my head. Of my lips circling the same cigarette that was on his lips.

I watch Jack, his warm puppy eyes and lightly wagging tail, to avoid looking at *him*. The dog raises his head on alert as Mark walks into the room, breathless, eyes wide, as if he cannot believe whatever it is that just happened—or *is* happening. He informs the room that the count is in. And as he announces the name of the next President of the United States of America, Matt's gaze locks with mine.

One look.

One second.

One name.

I close my eyes and duck my head upon hearing the news, the sense of loss overwhelming me.

AND MATTHEW IS
HOW I'VE THOUGHT
OF YOU FOR YEARS

Charlotte

Ten months earlier ...

E ver since I started working full time, my days seem to have gotten longer and my evenings shorter. As I've grown older, big gatherings have lost much of their former appeal, while letting loose among small groups of friends is something I now very much enjoy. I'm having a birthday today, and our booth holds my best friend Kayla, her boyfriend Sam, myself, and Alan, a sort of a friend/suitor and the one who insisted I celebrate at least for a little while tonight.

"You're twenty-two today, baby," Kayla says as she raises her cocktail glass in my direction. "I hope now you will finally drag your ass out to vote in next year's presidential election."

I groan, the options so far nothing to get excited about. The current struggling and unlikeable president who is up for a second term? Or the opposite party candidates, some who are just too hard to take seriously considering the radical ideology they're embracing. Sometimes it feels like they're just saying the craziest thing that comes to mind to snatch themselves some airtime.

"It'd be exciting if Matt Hamilton stepped up," Sam adds. My drink sloshes over my sweater at the mention of him.

"He has my vote on automatic," Sam continues.

"Really?" Kayla quirks a saucy eyebrow and keeps on hitting the tequila. "Charlotte knows Hammy."

I scoff and quickly wipe away the damp spot on my sweater. "I do *not,* I really do not," I assure the guys, then shoot a scowl Kayla's way. "I don't know where you get that."

"I got that from *you.*"

"I … we …" I shake my head, shooting her an evil eye. "We've met, but that doesn't imply I know him. I don't know the first thing about him. I know as much about him as you all do and the press is hardly reliable."

God! I don't know why I told Kayla the things I did about Matthew Hamilton … at an age when I was young and clearly very impressionable. I made the mistake of declaring to my best friend that I wanted to marry the guy. But even then, I at least had the wits to extract a promise that she'd never tell a soul. Kid promises always tend to seem so childish when we're adults, I guess, and she doesn't mind hinting at it now.

"Come on, you *do* know him, you crushed on him for years," Kayla says, laughing.

I watch her boyfriend give me an apologetic look. "I think Kay's ready to go home."

"I am so not, so not drunk enough," she protests as he eases her out of the booth.

She groans but allows him to pull her to her feet, and then turns to Alan.

"How does it feel to compete with the hottest man in history?"

"Excuse me?" Alan asks.

"*People* magazine's Sexiest Man Alive, you know ..." Kayla recounts. "How does it feel to compete with him?"

Alan sends Sam a look that definitely says *yeah, she's ready to go home, man.*

"She's so wasted," I apologize to Alan. "Come here, Kay," I say as I wrap my arm around her waist while Sam lets her lean on his shoulder. Together, we help her outside and into a cab Alan has hailed for her, sending them on their way.

Alan and I jump into the next cab. He gives the cabbie my address then turns to me.

"What did she mean?"

"Nothing." I glance out the window, my stomach caving in on itself. I try to laugh it off, but I feel sick to my stomach thinking of people actually knowing how infatuated I was with Matt Hamilton. "I'm twenty-two, this happened ten, eleven years ago. A little girl's crush."

"A crush that's been crushed, right?"

I smile. "Of course," I reassure him, then turn to stare out at the blinking city lights as we head across town to drop me home.

A crush that's been crushed, of course. You can't seriously crush on someone you've only seen like, what? Twice? The second time was so fleeting and at such an overwhelming moment in time ... and the first ... well.

It was eleven years ago, and I somehow remember everything about it. It's still the most exciting day I can recall even though I don't like the effect that meeting President Hamilton's son had on my teenage years.

I was eleven. We lived in a two-story brownstone east of Capitol Hill in Washington, D.C. My father, my mother, a tabby cat named Percy, and I. We each had a daily routine; I went to school, Mother went to the Women of the World offices, Dad went to the Senate, and Percy gave us the silent treatment when we all got home.

We didn't stray far from that routine—as my parents preferred—but that day something exciting happened.

Percy was sent to my room, which meant that Mom didn't want him causing mischief. He curled up on the foot of my bed, licking his paws, not interested in the noises downstairs. He only paused to occasionally stare at me as I peered through a tiny slit in my doorway. I'd been sitting there for the last ten minutes, watching the Secret Service walk in and out of my home.

They spoke in hushed tones into their headsets.

"Robert? One last time. This one? Orrrr this one?" My mother's voice floated into my bedroom from across the hall.

"This one." My father sounded distracted. He was probably getting dressed.

There was a pregnant pause, and I could almost feel my mother's disappointment.

"I think I'll wear this one," she said.

My mother always asked Dad what to wear for special evenings. But if he didn't pick the dress she wanted, she wore the one she'd *hoped* he'd choose.

I could picture my mother putting away the black one and carefully setting the red dress down on the bed.

My father didn't like it when my mother got too much attention, but my mother loves it. And why not? She has stunning green eyes and a thick mane of blonde hair. Though my dad is twenty years older and looks it, my mother looks younger by the day. I dreamt of growing up to be as beautiful and poised as she is.

I wondered what time it was. My stomach growled as the scent of spices teased my nostrils. Rosemary? Basil? I got them all mixed up no matter how many times Jessa, our housekeeper, explained which is which.

Downstairs, the chef from some fancy restaurant was cooking in our kitchen.

The Secret Service had been preparing the house for hours. I was told the president's food would be tasted before it was served to him.

The food looked so delicious I'd gladly taste every morsel. But Father asked Jessa to bring me back upstairs. He didn't want me to attend because I was "too young."

So what? I thought. People used to get married at my age. I was old enough to stay home alone. They wanted me to act mature, like a lady. But what was the point if I never got to act the part they'd been grooming me for?

"It's a business dinner, it's not a party, and god knows we need things to go well," Dad grumbled when I tried to plead my case.

"Dad," I groaned. "I can behave."

"You really think Charlotte can behave?" He shot my mother a glance, and my mother smiled at me. "You're not eleven until next week. You're too young for these events. It'll be nothing but talk of politics. Just stay up in your room."

"But it's the president," I said with so much conviction my voice trembled.

My mom stepped out of her bedroom in that glorious red dress that tastefully draped over her figure and spotted me eagerly peering down at the excitement downstairs.

"Charlotte," she said, with a sigh.

I straightened up from my crouched position.

She sighed again, then walked to her bedroom, picked up the phone on her nightstand, dialed an extension, and said, "Jessa, can you help Charlotte get dressed?"

My eyes widened and, miraculously, Jessa suddenly swept into my bedroom, smiling gleefully and shaking her head. "Girl! You'd cajole a king out of his crown!"

"I swear I didn't do anything. Mother simply saw me peeping and must've realized this is a once-in-a-lifetime opportunity."

"All right then, let's put your hair into a nice long braid," Jessa said as she started pulling open the drawers of my vanity. "Which dress are you going to wear?"

"I only have one option." I showed her the only dress that still fit me, and she helped me carefully slip it on.

"You're growing too fast," she said fondly as she ushered me to the mirror. She stood behind me and brushed my hair.

I looked at my reflection and admired the dress. I liked how blue the satin fabric was. I imagined standing next to my mother in her red dress and my father in his perfectly tailored suit. Entering my parents' forbidden, mysterious world was exciting—but nothing was more exciting than meeting the *president*.

When the president arrived, a group of men trailed in after him, all of them in suits. They were tall and handsome, but I was too busy looking at the young man directly beside the president to notice much.

He was gorgeous. His hair was the color of sable, and although it was combed back, it was unruly at the ends and curled at the collar.

He was an inch taller than the president. His suit seemed crisper, more tailored. He was staring at me, and although his lips weren't moving and his expression revealed nothing, I could swear that his eyes were laughing at me.

President Hamilton shook my mother's hand before greeting my father. I pulled my eyes away from the young man next to him and saw the president's lips curl a little as he looked down at me. When it was my turn, I took his hand.

"My daughter, Charlotte—"

"Charlie," I corrected.

Mother smiled. "She insisted on not missing the fun."

"Smart girl." The president grinned at me, gesturing to his side with obvious pride as he drew the young man beside him forward. "My son, Matthew. He's going to be president one day," he said conspiratorially.

The man that I couldn't stop staring at laughed quietly. It was a low, deep laugh, and it made me blush. Suddenly, I didn't want to shake his hand. But how could I avoid it?

He took my hand in his—it was warm and dry and strong. Mine was soft and trembling. "Absolutely not," he said and winked at me.

I smiled at him shyly and realized my parents were watching us carefully. "You don't look like a president," I blurted out to President Hamilton.

"What does a president look like?"

"Old."

President Hamilton laughed. "Give me time." He pointed at his shiny white hair and slapped Matthew's back then let my parents lead him into the dining room.

The adults focused on talking politics and bills, while I focused on the delicious food. When my plate was clean, I summoned the waiter and quietly asked about seconds.

"Charlotte," my father warned.

The waiter looked at my father, wide-eyed, then at me, just as wide-eyed, and I tried to very quietly repeat the question.

The president regarded me with interest.

Feeling worried, I wondered if it was bad manners to ask for more before they all finished.

Matthew had a serious expression on his face, but his eyes seemed to be laughing at me again. His gaze didn't leave me as he said to the waiter, "I'll have seconds too."

I shot him a grateful smile, then started feeling nervous again. His smile was so powerful. I could feel it piercing my heart.

I glanced down at my hands resting on my lap and admired my dress. I hoped Matthew thought I looked pretty. Most of the guys at school did. At least, that's what they told me.

As my parents talked with the president and Matthew, I fiddled with my braid, placing it on the side of my shoulder, then behind my back. Matthew's attention returned to me, and when his eyes sparkled with more quiet laughter, the pit in my stomach returned.

The waiter brought us both new plates full of stuffed quail and quinoa. My parents still looking at me as though it was too bold of me to ask for seconds in front of the president.

Matthew leaned over the table and said, "Never let anyone tell you you're too young to ask for what you want."

"Oh, don't worry, sometimes I don't ask."

This earned me a very nice laugh from Matthew. The president frowned at him, then winked at me. As Matthew turned his attention back to the group, I noticed his eyes appeared a shade lighter than black, like chocolate.

I sat there, trying to absorb everything, knowing that that moment, that night, would be the most exciting experience of my life.

But like everything in life … it wouldn't last forever.

I watched with disappointment as the president rose from his seat and began to thank my parents for dinner.

I got up as well, my eyes fixed on Matthew. The way he stood, the way he walked, the way he looked. I started to wonder what he smelled like, too. I followed the group quietly toward the foyer. The president turned and tapped his presidential cheek. "A kiss, young lady?"

Smiling, I rose up on my toes and kissed his cheek. When I dropped back down, my gaze caught Matthew's.

As if on automatic, my toes rose again. It seemed only natural that I give him a farewell kiss too. When my lips grazed his jaw, it was hard and it tickled with a little bit of stubble. It was like kissing a movie star. He turned his head and kissed my cheek in return, and I almost gasped out loud from the surprise of feeling his lips on my cheek.

Before I could compose myself, he and the president walked out the door, and all the hustle and bustle of the day turned to dead quiet.

Hurrying upstairs, I watched them leave from my bedroom window. The president was ushered into the back of his shiny black chauffeured car.

Before he got in, the president slapped Matthew on the back and squeezed the back of his neck in a friendly gesture.

The pit in my stomach grew into a ball as they disappeared into the car.

The car started and drove down our quiet neighborhood street, little American flags flapping in the front. A trail of cars followed them, one after the other.

I shut my window, closed my drapes, then took off my dress and hung it carefully. I then slipped into my flannel pajamas and eased into bed as my mother walked in.

"That was a lovely evening," my mother said. "Did you have fun?"

She smiled as though she was laughing to herself about something. I nodded honestly. "I liked listening to the conversations. I liked everyone."

She kept smiling. "Matthew is handsome. You noticed, of course. He's also smart as a whip."

I nodded in silence.

"Your father and I are writing a letter to the president to thank him for spending his evening with us. Do you want to write him too?"

"No, thank you," I said primly.

She raised her brows and laughed. "Okay. You sure? If you change your mind, leave it in the foyer tomorrow."

Mother left my room and I just lay in bed, thinking about the visit, about what the president had said about Matthew.

I decided I'd write Matthew a letter, just because I couldn't stop feeling awestruck and amazed by the visit. What if I not only ended up meeting one president tonight, but two? That had to take the cake of meetings, for sure.

I used the first page of the stationery my grandmother sent me for my birthday, and in my best handwriting, I wrote, "I want to thank you and the president for coming. If you decide to run for president, you have my vote. I'd even be willing to join your campaign."

I licked the seal and closed it firmly, and set the letter on my nightstand. Then I flipped off the light switch and got under my covers.

I lay in bed and in the dark. He was everywhere. On the ceiling and in the shadows and on the duvet.

And I wondered if I'd ever see him again and suddenly the thought of him never seeing me grown up felt like an ache in my chest.

I'm so lost in my thoughts I had not realized Alan was studying my profile.

"A crush that's been crushed, right?" he asks again.

I turn to him, startled to realize we've already pulled over in front of my building. I laugh and get out of the cab, peering inside. "Absolutely." I nod more firmly this time. "I'm focused on my career now." And I shut the door behind me, waving him off.

ANNOUNCEMENT

Matt

I was never the sort of kid tempted to try on my father's shoes. Too clean, too classic, too big.

But, oddly, his shoes are what I remember most clearly about him—pacing a perfect circle around his desk during a tense phone call. Me, at his feet, building a puzzle.

My father strived for perfection in all things, including his appearance. From his impeccably tailored suit, to his smoothly shaved face and his tightly cropped hair.

While I, young and clueless, dreamed of freedom. Freedom from the privileged life my father's success gave my mother and me.

A thousand times, my father said I would be president. He told his friends, his friend's friends, and he often told me. I'd laugh and shake it off.

The seven years I spent growing up in the White House were seven years I spent praying to get out of the White House.

Politics interested me, yes.

But I knew my father rarely slept. Most choices he made were wrong for a certain percentage of the population, even when they were right for the majority. My mother lost her husband the day he entered the White House.

I lost my father the day he decided that being president would be his legacy.

He tried juggling it all, but no human in the world could run the country and still have energy for his wife and teenage son.

I focused on my grades and succeeded in school, but forming friendships was hard. I couldn't casually invite anyone over to the White House.

My life, as I imagined it after the White House, would be focused on work, perhaps on Wall Street. I'd have the freedom to do all the things I never could under America's watchful eye.

Father ran for reelection, and won.

Then, three years into his second term, an unhappy citizen put two bullets in him. One in his chest, the other his stomach.

It's been thousands of days since. Too many years spent living in the past.

Now, as I secure my cufflinks and smooth my tie, I think back to those shoes and realize that I'm about to step into them.

"Ready, sir?"

I nod, and he pulls back the curtain.

The world is watching. They've been speculating, hoping, wondering.

Will you, won't you … Please do, please don't …

He'll win if he runs …

He doesn't stand a chance …

I wait for the noise to settle down, lean into the microphone, and say, "Ladies and gentlemen, it is my pleasure to announce that I'm officially running for President of the United States of America."

THE NEWS

Charlotte

The morning after my birthday, I notice the light on my answering machine is blinking. I press play, half listening as I lie back in bed, trying to shake my grogginess away.

"Charlotte, it's your mother—call me."

"Charlotte, answer your cell."

After a third similar message, I get up, put coffee on, and return my mother's calls. "You heard the rumor?" she asks in place of a greeting.

"I've been asleep for the past ... seven hours." I squint. "What rumor?"

"It's on national television! And we've been invited to his campaign inaugural, Charlie, you *must* come. Time for you to get your feet wet in politics."

My first thought is the same I've had for years. That I don't want to be in politics. I've seen and heard too many things being the daughter of a senator. I've lived through much already.

"It's time for you to make a difference, take steps in embracing your own personal power ..." my mother continues, and while she rambles on, I turn on the television. Matt's face flashes before me.

His sun-bronzed, slightly-stubbled, perfectly symmetrical, hot-as-hell face.

He stands behind a podium, a place he's never been photographed before. The paparazzi have caught him unaware on dates, on the beach, everywhere, but never, as far as I know, behind a podium.

A black suit and crimson tie cover a body fit for a *GQ* cover, his suit so black that the suits of the men surrounding him seem gray in comparison.

He's been known to be an outdoorsman who loves physicality, who keeps in shape by experiencing every adventure and sport nature has to offer. Swimming, tennis, hiking, horseback riding. His lean, athletic build, clearly defined beneath the fitted suit, is certainly a testament to that. A full, rather seductive mouth curves into a smile as he speaks into the microphone.

Beneath him, a black line scrolling across the screen says:

BREAKING NEWS: MATTHEW HAMILTON HAS CONFIRMED HIS INTENTION TO RUN FOR PRESIDENT

I read the line again. I also vaguely listen to his voice on the TV. He has such a delicious voice, it's making the little hairs on my arms stand at attention.

"… running for President of the United States of America."

Something inside of me somersaults; I'm hit by a series of emotions—shock, excitement, disbelief. I fall back on the couch and press a hand to my stomach to keep the winged things inside of it from moving. My mother continues telling me how much my father and she would love my company, but I hardly listen.

How can I, when Matthew Hamilton is on TV?

He is so gorgeous I bet every woman watching wants him to father all of her babies, put those lips on nobody but her, and use those eyes to look at nobody else ...

This god.

The prince of America.

Has decided to run for president?

He speaks from a place of confidence and strength.

I know firsthand that politics are not for wimps. I know what my father has gone through to reach and keep his seat in the Senate. I know the kind of sacrifice, patience, and discipline that serving the people requires. I know that despite doing his best, criticisms have kept him awake at night more times than he'd care to admit. I know that being president cannot be easier than being senator. And I know that Matt hadn't really wanted this.

But after his father was murdered, our economy went to shit. We're all basically at the point of reaching out for lifesavers, and the situation is so dire that there are probably not enough to go around.

So he's doing it?

Stepping up?

"So there's really no excuse for you not to come!" my mother continues.

"Okay."

"Did you just agree, Charlotte?" My mother sounds so shocked that I smile at having managed to surprise her.

Hell, even I'm surprised that I'm not singing my same song. Blame it on my birthday and another year spent waiting for a big neon sign to point me toward my ideal life path that has yet to appear.

Another year spent waiting for that "this is who you are, this is what you are meant to do" moment. When I remember the night the Hamiltons came for supper, I felt like I was touched by something exciting, historical, and meaningful. That moment branded me in so many ways. You cannot express in words the awe, honor, and complete amazement of being faced with the President of the United States. It makes you want to do great things too.

Maybe seeing Matt again will bring me clarity. Or at the very least, I might actually get to know him and see what he is made of. See if he really is capable of living up to the Hamilton name.

I'm curious.

I'm … intrigued.

Maybe I'm even a little bit in need of convincing myself that my infantile crush has, indeed, been crushed.

Or maybe, like the rest of the world, I'm just excited. That there's finally a man who can really earn the respect of both parties, cut through the red tape, and get serious work done.

"I'll go with you," I agree, much to my mother's delight. "When is it?"

STILL THAT GIRL

Charlotte

I 've moved into my own flat close to the offices of Women of the World. One bedroom and a sizeable closet. My wardrobe is filled with more power suits than anything, they're a must for hunting down sponsors and job opportunities for our women ... new opportunities that inspire them to be better.

But there's a short row of dresses in the crammed closet of my new apartment. I might not have dozens of options to choose from, but the night of the kickoff party, I have more picks than the one dress I had when I was eleven.

Kayla is dying of jealousy, and Alan and Sam have been hinting on being willing to escort me to the event—in case I needed an escort. I've declined, since I'm going with my mother. My father, as a current Democrat, is not really up to coming to support an Independent candidate. But my mother has a mind of her own, and when it comes to anything Hamilton, it seems so do I.

I wonder what sort of man Matt Hamilton has become, and if he's the player he's made out to be through the years as the fascination of the press with him has continued to grow.

I end up going for the yellow dress with an open back.

I comb my red hair down my back, add a shiny crystal clip to hold it back from my forehead, and head downstairs, where my mother waits in the Lincoln Town Car.

The last time I saw Matt, it was two years and eight months after that dinner at my parents. I'm taller then, officially a woman, and like my mother, I'm wearing a black dress. He's dressed in black as well, standing next to his mother, who looks tiny and beat up as he puts his arm around her.

He's older, a little thicker, a lot more masculine, and his eyes don't shine on me anymore when I follow my father and mother to give him my condolences. And then I sit in the back, trying to hold back my tears as I watch Matt bury his father.

His mother cried softly, delicately, and the country cried; he stood there, strong and proud, the boy his father raised, the one trained to weather catastrophe and go on.

White decorations peppered with silver and blue surround us.

I'm a little bit outside of my comfort zone when I follow my mother into the ballroom. Walking through the doors is like opening the pages of a living encyclopedia full of important names—politicians, philanthropists, heirs and heiresses, along with people in positions at the top of the country's best schools, Duke, Princeton, Harvard.

And suddenly all the artists and writers and poets …

Pulitzer and Nobel prize winners and faces you see in the blockbuster films of the year …

They somehow disappear with Matt Hamilton sharing this same room.

He's at the far end, tall and broad-shouldered, his hair dark and gleaming under the lights. He's wearing a perfect black suit and a tie the color of platinum, his shirt crisp white and contrasting against the gold-kissed hue of his skin.

My mouth dries up and my body seems to start working a little harder to pump the blood through my system.

It's not easy to lose track of Hamilton, he's the darling of the media.

From the rebellious teenager, to the private college guy, to the man he's become. The youngest contender in history who turns thirty-five by Inaugural day, my mother says he represents the golden years his father gifted us with—growth, jobs, peace. I want that. Every one of the thousands of supporters here tonight wants that.

As we wade through the glittering crowd, the air scented with the most expensive perfumes, I greet some of my mother's acquaintances, all dressed to impress. The famous always gravitated toward the Hamiltons, their presence silent endorsements. It's been nine years since the last time I saw Matt, give or take. (I actually know the exact time, but I want to pretend I didn't count so religiously.)

He's taller than he even seemed on TV, looming over the others by a good few inches.

And god.

He's *all* man.

Sable hair. Espresso eyes. A Greek god's body.

Confidence streaks out of every pore.

Even the black suit he wears is perfect.

If there was ever a man with an air around him of privilege and success, Matthew Hamilton is it.

The Hamiltons have been influential since they were born. Bloodlines dating back to English lords and ladies. They called him prince when his father was alive, now he's about to take the king's throne.

When *People* magazine called him "the Sexiest Man Alive," *Forbes* called him the "Most Successful Businessman." He disappeared for a few years after law school—quietly building, expanding his family's real estate empire. Judging by the amount of press vans outside the inaugural party ballroom, the world is being taken by storm with his return.

Every headline today had the name Hamilton on it.

I've never seen so many important people together in one place in my life.

I can't believe all of them came out in support.

The enormity of Matt's reach hits me, and I'm suddenly awed that I could even snag an invitation to his kickoff party in the first place.

In Women of the World, we assist women going through rough moments in their lives—divorce, health problems, and trauma. The spirit of the organization is helpful and humble. Here, it's along the same lines—everyone united for a common cause—but the air here is extraordinarily powerful.

The people here are the movers and shakers of the world. And tonight, their world revolves around Matthew Hamilton.

Matt is suddenly enveloped by an actress. She's doting on him and wearing the skimpiest dress to flash her toned muscles and perky ass and breasts.

My stomach twists around in part envy, part awe. I have no idea what I could talk to that woman about, but I'm starstruck all the same.

"He's so handsome," my mother whispers as we head his way.

My nervousness increases. There are already too many people around him, waiting for an introduction. I watch him shake hands, the firmness of his grip, the way he makes eye contact. So ... direct.

The knot in my stomach keeps tightening.

"I think I'll just take a seat over there," I whisper to my mother and point to a sitting area with the least number of people milling about.

"Oh, Charlotte," I hear her say.

"I've already met him, let the others have their chance!"

I don't let her protest anymore and instantly cut to my secluded spot. From there, I scan the crowd.

It's so easy for me to strike up conversation with people at work, but this crowd would intimidate anyone. I spot J. Lo in a designer white dress at the corner of the room. I look down at my yellow-gold dress and wonder why I chose such a stand-out color when it would be better to blend in. Maybe I thought "fake it till you make it" would work. That I would look as sophisticated as everybody else here and soon feel that way.

I move my gaze back to the cause of all the buzz today.

Everyone wants to greet the Hamilton prince and I can see it is going to take a while for my mother to succeed, especially when men keep trying to pull him away from the line.

I scan the ballroom for the restrooms and spot them at the far end. Easing to my feet, I keep my gaze straight ahead as I walk past the line, past the gorgeous Matt among a group of politicians, and toward the ladies', where I slip inside and check my makeup and freshen up.

Three women are gushing as they primp in front of the mirrors.

"I want to wear him like a fur," the cougar woman purrs.

I laugh inwardly and yet pretend I'm not amused by their fawning—especially when they're old enough to be his mother.

Once I exit, I'm headed straight down the hall, toward my table, when I step on the hem of my dress as I enter the carpeted ballroom area. I glance down at my shoes and lift my dress up an inch, never slowing my stride, when I bump into a large figure.

An arm flies out to steady me by the waist.

My breath catches and I freeze, registering the hand on my waist, the side of my breast pressing into a bulging forearm. And I look up, up at a flat, flat chest, the length of a platinum tie, up a tanned throat, and stare straight into Matt Hamilton's dark eyes.

I gasp. "Mr. Hamilton!—I'm sorry. I didn't see you, I was …" His grip is warm, and noticing that he's slowly releasing me as he realizes I've got my balance makes me stutter. "I was having dress trouble," I rush out. "I shouldn't have worn this dress."

I'm completely overwhelmed by his presence. Lean and athletic. Larger than life. Face so chiseled and beautiful. All of him so hot my eyes hurt.

I hate that my toes are curling under his stare. "I truly didn't see you. For the record, I'm not some crazed fangirl. This isn't an attempt to get your attention, not at all."

"And yet you most definitely have it." His voice is rich and deep, but his tone is playful and his eyes are twinkling.

It's hard to swallow all of a sudden.

His lips start curving and they are gorgeous and plush.

Lips to kiss.

To swoon over and fantasize about.

Gosh, his smile is lovely.

Even if it lasts only a second.

"Again, forgive me." I shake my head, exhaling nervously. "I'm Charl—"

"I know who you are."

Although his lips aren't curved into a smile anymore, his eyes are sparkling even brighter—if that's possible. I can hardly take this exchange. This guy is the closest thing to a god in our country. "I'm pretty certain I still have your letter somewhere," he says, low.

Matt Hamilton knows who I am.

Matt Hamilton still has my *letter*.

He was in college then. Now the man before me is fully matured, seasoned to perfection. And goodness, I can't *believe* I wrote *him* a letter.

"Now I'm doubly embarrassed," I whisper, ducking my head.

When I raise my eyes, Matt just keeps looking at me with a direct gaze I'm sure hugely impacts everyone it ever lands on. "You said you'd help me if I ever ran."

I shake my head in consternation, laughing lightly at the idea. "I was eleven. I was just a girl."

"Are you still that girl?"

"Matt." Some guy taps his shoulder and calls him over.

He nods at the man, then simply looks at me as I stand here, puzzled over his question.

"You're busy. I'll just go …" I say, and I dip away, taking a few steps before I glance past my shoulder.

He's watching me walk away.

He looks at me as if he's a little bit intrigued and a little bit laughing inside, or maybe I just made it up? Because the next instant he turns around, his broad back tapering down to a small waist providing a gorgeous visual as he heads back to greet his excited supporters.

"I cannot believe you were able to say hello before I did—that line is a killer." My mother is suddenly at my side. "The big rollers keep pulling him aside. I'll be back."

She heads back to the line while I take my seat at the table once more, chatting for a while with one of the couples there.

I'm still reeling from the encounter.

"Oh, Senator Wells's daughter—a pleasure. I can't say I know him, but he's a good man. He voted against—"

"Hugh, really," his wife interrupts, stopping the elderly senator. "Let's go say hello to Lewis and Martha," she says, coaxing him away.

I'm relieved when they head off, dreading to say anything to embarrass myself. I'm still reeling because of my encounter with Matt Hamilton and I can't seem to focus on anything else.

I watch as my mother waits patiently as six people before her greet him, until finally she hugs him, and she looks tiny and feminine in his tall, muscled form. When they release their embrace, I'm shocked to notice her pointing in my direction.

My stomach caves in on itself when his gaze follows the direction of her finger.

Ohmigod, is my mother pointing at me?

Is Matt looking at me?

Our gazes meet—and for the flash of a second, there's something in his eyes. He nods, as if he's telling her he's said hello already.

As they talk, his gaze stays on me.

I'm briefly aware of the curiosity of the room as they collectively wonder where their new candidate is looking, but I can't pull my eyes away long enough to verify who exactly is staring.

God. He even *stands* like untitled American royalty.

He's grown up to be the most delicious mix of polished and earthy, and somewhere beneath that focused gaze I can see a unique primitiveness that pulls at me.

A passing woman leans over to my ear. "He's as hot, smooth, and rich as a lava cake. And he makes politics thrilling," she says.

I glance at her, then move my gaze back to the smoldering Matt Hamilton as he continues greeting the line. He's almost done, but I'm sure it won't be for long. A shadow falls over half of his face, but I can see his attention is now focused on an elderly couple, his smile barely there, but still so sexy and gorgeous it makes my lungs work a little extra hard.

Once he finishes speaking to the couple and he's able to pull free, he starts adjusting his cufflinks.

And starts heading in my direction.

He is heading in MY direction.

The *hottest guy in the room is heading in my direction*, and my heart just flipped over a thousand times in one second inside my chest.

I glance around the room in an attempt at *la-dee-dah* nonchalance, but I'm not that good an actress.

I'm afraid to look into his gorgeous face and know that he knows the effect he has on me. It takes a moment to gather my courage, wary to see the expression he's wearing. Even warier to find him looking straight.

At.

Me.

He's not looking at me.

Someone stopped him to chat.

I exhale.

But before I can release the tension in my shoulders, Matt pats the middle-aged man on the back, shakes his hand, and starts in my direction again.

I sit here, struggling with these feelings I can't suppress.

I want to talk to him. I want to pick his brain. I'm curious and professionally thirsty, and maybe I want to accidentally press myself against him one more time.

So I can smell him.

No, definitely not that last.

Anyway, I'm certain that with a drink, I'll be a little less nervous. But it's too late for drinks now!

Before I can stand to greet him once more, Matt—Matt fucking *Hamilton,* the complete American *candy bar*—sinks into the seat behind me, eyes coming level with mine as he shifts forward. "For the record, I'm not some crazy stalker man just attempting to get your attention." His voice is so close that it feels like he just ran a fingertip down my spine.

And the timbre is just like sex on silken sheets.

His scent is a prelude to sex.

Even his warm, dark espresso eyes seem an invitation for sex.

I laugh, flushing.

His lips twitch, and his smile? It is pure, wicked foreplay. The kind girls like me only watch on TV. The kind that sneaks in unnoticed until your panties are everywhere except where they belong.

Oh god. He is the hottest thing I've ever seen.

I'm struggling to suppress a little shiver from inside. "Don't worry, I know who you are too."

"That's right. But I bet you don't know how serious I am about getting an answer."

"Excuse me?"

He just smiles and surveys my face, taking me in in silence. I can't help but do the same. His features are even more chiseled now, one thousand and one percent *male*, and every visible inch of skin on his body seems to have been kissed recently by sunlight.

I notice the luster of his gorgeous hair and eyes and the way he smells like expensive cologne. The space his body occupies and the warmth emanating from every athletic inch of him makes me feel hot all over.

He's really here. In front of me.

My stomach flips, and I laugh self-consciously and nervously run my hands down my dress. "At that time you were dead-set on not running. How was I supposed to know? I mean. Look at you now," I say, signaling to him. To Matt freaking *Hamilton* sitting right next to me, obviously feeling vastly entertained by my nervousness.

"I know what you're thinking," he warns me, his expression sober but with a playful glint in his eyes.

That you're gorgeous? I wonder.

That I don't know how you have this effect on me and why I still after all these years want you?

"Trust me, you don't," I whisper, flushing.

He shifts forward and grabs a strand of my loose red hair, tugging it and watching me lick my lips in nervousness. "You're wondering why I ran."

"No! I'm …" *wondering why you're here talking to me.* I don't say that, I just trail off and watch him curl the strand of my red hair around the tip of his index finger, then slowly release it, watching me as he uncurls his finger very, very slowly and lets it fall.

"So how are you?" he asks, his voice deep.

"Good. Not as good as you seem to be," I say. Gosh, am I flirting? Please don't be flirting, Charlotte!

"I doubt that. I thoroughly doubt that," Matt says, his voice still so deep and the smile still in his eyes—but not on his lips.

He seems so focused on me that it's like he doesn't realize everyone is glancing in his direction.

I'm nervous in his presence, but at the same time, I don't want him to leave.

"You know, I've met you three times and realize I don't know anything about you other than the occasional story I hear," I blurt out. "They're so contrary I don't even know which to believe."

"None of them."

"Oh, come on, Matthew!" I laugh, then I realize I called him by his name. "I mean … Mr. Ham—"

"Matt. Charlotte. Unless you'd still like to go by Charlie."

"God, no! Are you dead-set on embarrassing me today?"

"Not really. Though I can't deny I find the pink on your cheeks quite charming."

His lips curve sensually, and there's a flutter in my stomach when he winks at me.

I shyly glance down, and I realize that the hard little points of my nipples are popping out against my dress.

Mortified, I lift my arms to fold them in front of me, but not before I catch his eyes noticing too. He slowly lifts his gaze to mine, his expression revealing nothing as he pulls his attention back to the crowded group.

"I should get going. But I won't say goodbye." He raises one sleek eyebrow in meaning. Pushing his chair back and standing to his full height.

His words leave me confused. I can't manage to answer quickly enough, so he simply smiles at me and leaves me to ponder them the rest of the night.

I have no idea how long my mother and I stay there, really, but I know exactly three times that I glanced in Matt's direction, he turned to meet my gaze—as if he has some sort of radar or simply sensed me watching him.

My stomach went crazy each of those times, and I jerked my eyes away.

When we're ready to leave, my mother takes the time to say her goodbyes. I consider grabbing Matt's attention to wish him good luck before heading out, I just really wish that we hadn't been interrupted when we were and that we'd been able to talk some more. But he is busy when I search for him through the crowd, and I don't want to interrupt. As I follow my mother to the door, one of her old congressman friends stops to say goodbye to us both. I smile and nod, and past his shoulder, I see Matt's eyes meet mine and realize he'd been watching me leave.

He smiles at me, and cants his head in the barest of nods, and there's something about that smile and that nod that fills me with an odd sense of anticipation.

For what, I just don't know.

I ride in the back of the town car with my mother, sort of unable to stop replaying the things Matt said to me when he came over. Sort of hating the fact that I still can't control the things he brings out in me. "He's going to win," my mother says softly.

"Do you think so?" I ask her.

The wanting for him to win suddenly hits me with so much force, it almost overwhelms me. Sitting there talking with him, I sensed a genuine quality in him and a strength that makes you want to cling to it. Which is silly, really, but don't you want a strong president? You want someone who can keep his head in a crisis, someone confident, and someone real.

"Well, his announcement caused quite a stir. But the Democrats and the Republicans won't let go of the presidency that easily," my mother says, and I press my lips together.

As I start to get out of the car, my mother says, "Charlotte, you know how much I hate you living alone here ..."

"Mom," I groan, shaking my head with a chiding frown, then wave her off and shut the door behind me.

That night is not the first time in the past eleven years that I dream about Matt Hamilton again, but it's the first one where the guy in the dream looks exactly like he did tonight.

THE NEXT MORNING

Charlotte

'm still thinking about the previous evening as I head to Women of the World. I've been working with my mother since I was eighteen, winging both my studies in Georgetown and social service hours here. I help run the organization and my days are usually a combination of fundraising, job hunting, and supportive talks with the women we take under our wing. I've just gotten off a phone call when a tall man with a full head of salt-and-pepper hair appears at my office door and knocks.

"Hi, Charlotte. Good morning." He speaks with the familiarity of old friends.

I recognize his face, but I can't pinpoint where I know him from.

"Benton Carlisle …" He extends his hand, which I promptly shake. "Unfortunately we didn't get the chance to be introduced last night. I'm Matt Hamilton's campaign manager."

My heart skips, regardless of me wanting it to or not. "Oh, of course—Mr. Carlisle, I'm sorry. I haven't had coffee yet. Please, sit down."

"I won't be staying long. I'm simply here on behalf of Matt."

"Matt?" I question.

"Yes. He wants to formally extend you an invitation to join his campaign."

If seeing Matt's campaign manager in my office wasn't shock enough, this certainly is.

"I …"

"He told me you were the first in line to help and he'd hate to refuse his first offer."

My eyes widen. "Mr. Carlisle—"

He laughs. "I admit I was taken aback. Most of our recruits have experience, something which you have nothing of. And yet here I am, first thing in the morning." He looks at me as if wondering what I did to deserve this and I don't like his possible assumptions.

"I agree that I have no experience. I appreciate the offer, but I'll have to decline."

"Fair enough."

"But please send my best wishes to Mr. Hamilton."

"I will." He leaves his card. "In case there's anything we can do for you."

We shake hands, and I watch the man depart as elegantly and soundlessly as he came in. When he is out of view, I sag in my seat, stunned.

The rest of the day I focus on busywork, but when I head home to my apartment, I sit on the couch, my precious cat Doodles perched on my lap, and I wonder why I declined the offer. I've been wanting to do something important on my own, out of my parents' shadows. Working on a campaign, wouldn't that be thrilling? Exciting? Why didn't I leap? I wonder if my fear has to do with the same reason it would be thrilling and exciting. Because it would involve Matthew Hamilton, and he is both what inspires me to agree and makes me crave to keep a safe distance.

That evening, I watch a TV show where one of the candidates is discussing purely incendiary things about poor immigrants, poor refugees, and how he'll raise taxes so that we can become the world's greatest army again.

He makes it sound as if refusing to help those who are suffering is the only way we could ever return to our golden days.

I press my lips together and turn off the television.

Maybe I can help. I believe in him. I believe he's better than any of the options they've been tossing around on TV.

I grab Carlisle's card and call him. "Mr. Carlisle, this is Charlotte Wells. I've been thinking about the offer … and yes. I want to help. I'm ready to be used in any capacity and I'm ready to start Monday."

There's a stunned silence, then, "Matt will be pleased."

He sends me the address where I should present myself on Monday, then I hang up and stare, wide-eyed, at my phone. *Holy shit!* I just signed up to work on Matthew Hamilton's campaign.

FIRST DAY

Charlotte

My eyes are fixed out the window of the back of the cab as I ride to the seat of the Matt Hamilton Presidential Campaign.

It's a clear February day.

D.C.'s quiet strength seems a permanent reminder of this being the home of the country's powerful executive seat. Sweeping monuments, carpets of green, politicians swarming its cafés and streets, Washington sits proudly and strongly as the most elegant city in the nation.

There's nowhere I'd rather live. If there is something beyond here … it's just a temporary fling.

My pulse is in D.C.

The pulse of the nation is in D.C.

If New York is the brain, Los Angeles is the beauty, D.C. is the heart, the very soul vibrating in our monuments, each one of them a testament to the strength and beauty of the American experience.

So the cab takes me through the heart of it all, past the labyrinth of the Pentagon, along the Potomac, and by the Lincoln Memorial, the pristine white walls of the White House, and the dome of the Capitol.

I don't know why I'm here.

What possessed me to want to leave my job at Women of the World?

The TV has replayed his announcement endlessly, and I've replayed the inaugural party in my head just as endlessly.

No, I *do* know why I'm here. Because he asked me, maybe. And because I want to take a little part in history.

I get out of the cab and rummage through my purse as the two-story building, seat of the Matt Hamilton campaign, looms before us.

I pay the driver, and the moment my strides start eating up sidewalk, I feel recharged with hope and anticipation.

I'm led inside by a middle-aged woman with a crisp voice and an even crisper walk. "He's ready to see you." She signals to the main area of the second floor, where a group of people hover anxiously around Matt—six feet plus of natural athleticism, brains, and hotness to the extreme clad in gray slacks and a black shirt—all of them staring down at a long table.

Matt's arms are crossed, he's frowning at some of the slogans he's being shown.

"I'm not wild about this one." His voice is deep, and it hums with thoughtfulness as he taps a finger to something he doesn't like. "Reeks of bullshit, and that's not what we're about."

We, as in he and *his team.*

He seems like the most down-to-earth, unpretentious guy, even when he's easily the most famous.

"Charlotte."

He lifts his head and sees me. And he gets that laughter in his eyes I remember so well, and I can't see what he finds so funny about me. But I smile nonetheless, his smile infectious.

As he eats up the floor toward me, he's wearing that easy charm that makes everyone want to be his best friend. Or his mother, or better yet, his wife. He *does* have that thing a reporter once said that "suggests to the easily suggestible he needs some loving." A sad tilt to his eyes makes him all the more handsome.

He's the man his father groomed and that a nation has waited for.

Hamiltons inspire loyalty more than any other family ever has who's been in executive power.

His hand clasps mine.

"Mr. Hamilton."

"Matt," he corrects.

His hand is warm, big. All-engulfing. I feel it slide over mine, I shake it and try to hold his gaze. But it feels as he squeezes me in his grip that he's squeezing my whole body. I'm nerve-wracked, and I blame the twinkle in his eyes and that handsome love-me, take-me-home, mother-me-or-fuck-me face.

He drops his hand at his side and shoves it into his pocket, and I glance at it for a second and wonder if he felt that electric rush that I felt when he touched me.

He glances down at my hands too, as if realizing how small my hand is compared to his too. "Settling in all right?"

"Yes, sir. I'm absolutely thrilled to be here."

"Matt …" someone calls.

He nods at the guy who hands him a phone, reaches out with his free hand and sets it lightly on the back of my shoulder as he nods at me. "We'll catch up, Charlotte."

He squeezes me—the lightest bit—and the touch sears me—it's a little unexpected—and though it lasts just a second, it sends a frisson of heat shooting down my body. My toes curl in my shoes.

I can't help but follow his retreating back as he lifts the cell phone to his ear and retreats to his office to take the call.

God, I'm in so much trouble.

Focus, Charlotte!

Nope. Not on his ass.

I tear my gaze free and paste a smile on my face as I'm led toward my cubicle.

My first day consists of a basic rundown of my duties as a political aide.

"Why did he run? He's been fiercely trying to protect his privacy for years."

Two young women talk by my desk, one dark-haired and the other with a sporty, short blonde bob.

"True. But only for as long as he chose to be," the blonde tells the brunette.

They glance at him. I resist the urge to do the same.

Matt is stepping into the limelight after years fighting for his privacy from obsessed reporters. The resourceful press would find itself filtering into Harvard when he began college, and every event where he was enlisted to help promote, he'd end up being the headline rather than the cause he was so generously trying to push.

It annoyed him.

"When he offered the job, I asked him, why me? And he said, why not you?" the blonde then shares. "*Because you're so hot no woman can work around you and think straight,*" she answers herself, laughing.

I smile and pull my attention back to organizing my desk.

My office is perfection, with a view of the city. Outside this building it feels serene, the country on track, as always, but there's a hum inside this building, in my coworkers, in me.

After settling in, I head into the small kitchenette for coffee. With a full cup, I turn the moment I hear footsteps behind me, but I miscalculate how close the newcomer is. I start when I bump into her and slosh coffee all over her shoes.

I'm mortified. *Dammit, Charlotte!* I pry my coffee-stained fingers from the cup and set it aside and grab napkins. "That didn't just happen. Your shoe." I start to bend but the blonde with the sporty bob bends too, getting it before I do.

"Hey, it's fine. A little excitement never hurt anybody." She smiles. "I'm Alison." She puts her hand out, and I take it. "The official campaign photographer."

"Charlotte."

"Charlotte, I know how you can make it up to me."

She waves me after her and we head into Matt's office as she carries her camera and stands inside. The instant I realize this is Matt freaking Hamilton's office I'm walking into, I run my fingers nervously through my hair—spotting his broad shoulders and hot self in the chair behind the desk, all gorgeous and busy as he reads some papers.

As he reads, my finger gets stuck on a small knot in my hair and I quickly try to smooth it out.

When I finally do, I summon the courage to look at him, and he's watching me, a frown on his face. "Do you want to be in the shot with me?" His voice is low and terribly deep.

I stare in confusion. "God, no. Absolutely not."

"All that effort and you won't let the world enjoy it?" he asks, his expression unreadable as he quirks an eyebrow, signaling to my hair.

Oh god.

I'm blushing. They say Matt enjoys life, he enjoys life so much he wants to change it. I smile, a little too nervous, and just stand aside as Alison sets up the camera. "Here, Matt?" she asks.

"Why don't we do something more natural?" His dark gaze remains on me as he crooks a finger, luring me forward. "Charlotte, want to hand me one of those printouts behind you?" he asks, his voice a bit rough.

Feeling a knot of nervousness in my throat, I grab one and walk up to him, aware of him watching every step forward that I take when I hear the consecutive clicks.

"Lovely," says Alison.

Matt takes the folder with lazy grace, his gaze still holding mine, his voice still terribly deep and unnerving. "See? I knew there was a reason I brought you on. You make me look good," he says approvingly. His lips curl just a tad.

I lift my brows; he lifts his too, as if challenging me. Heat crawls up my neck and cheeks. Really, there's nothing that can make him look a little better than he already does.

By the time I go home I'm beyond embarrassed. *Go ahead and look like a crushing fool, Charlotte,* I chide as I head to my apartment.

When I get home, I'm thinking of the most somber outfit I have. No matter if I'm petite and have a childlike face, I want to be taken seriously here. My feet are killing me, my neck is killing me, but I don't slip into my pajamas until I pull out a soot-black power suit, slacks and a short black well-cut little jacket for tomorrow. I spread it out on the chair that sits by my window and eye it judiciously. It's smart and crisp, exactly how I want to look tomorrow.

Matt Hamilton is going to take me seriously if it kills me.

My parents are proud.

Kayla has been texting nonstop, and she wants the details.

I spend a while texting her back, alone in my apartment.

I hadn't realized how lonely it would be to sleep in my apartment on my own. *You wanted to be independent, Charlotte. This is it.*

The light of my answering machine is blinking, and I play back the messages.

"Charlotte, I'm really not happy about you being there in that little apartment, especially now that you're doing this. Your father and I would like you to come back home if you're serious about embarking on a year of campaigning. Call me."

I groan. *Oh no, Mother, you won't.*

We had discussed that I'd be able to move from home and carve my own path at twenty. Mother, not happy when the date approached and I was still in college tempted to be foolish, pushed it to twenty-two. Now, a month after my twenty-second birthday, I've paid my dues, stood my ground, and refused for her to push the date farther.

She insisted the building was relatively unsafe—with only one man at the door. If any of the inhabitants summoned him upstairs, the door and lobby would be unmanned. It was small and uncomfortable and not safe.

I thought it was perfect. Well situated, the right size to keep clean and tidy. Although I haven't met anyone except two of my neighbors, one a young family, the other an army veteran. And I do feel, at night, that things creak and croak and keep me awake. This was the first step of me carving my path on my own.

So I lie in bed and set my alarm for tomorrow. I'm physically exhausted, but my mind keeps replaying the day.

I think of the campaign and of Matt and of President Hamilton's assassination. I think of our current president and my personal hopes for our future president.

Every person that I know, every person conscious of themselves and their potentials ... we all want to make an impact, a contribution, to work on something that matters to us. I'm on a new path that I'm carving on my own. I'm young and a little insecure, but I'm making a difference, even if small.

THE TEAM

Matt

The thing about presidential campaigns is that you don't just need the right candidate. You need the right team. I eye the dozens of folders strewn across my desk. I'm on my sixth cup of coffee, and I take the last sip as I consider the latest addition to my team.

"Women of the World, Charlotte Wells. She's almost an intern—no experience. You certain about this?" Carlisle asked.

I decided all this over a box of donuts, veggie wraps, soda cans, and bottles of Voss water.

You can't say Charlotte is beautiful, she's too stunning for that. You just don't forget a face like hers.

Red hair like a flame falling down her shoulders. And that spark in her eyes. She's energetic, unapologetic, exquisite. Despite being raised as a senator's daughter, she's so far been untouched by political scandal—untouched by the sometimes seedy dealings politics are paired with.

She's more right for the job than Carlisle believes. I'm aware of his reluctance, but more than certain Charlotte will prove herself in spades.

Rather than bring in the experienced political allies from my father's era, all too willing to back me up, I'm bringing in people who want to make a difference. Who've made it a habit of thinking of others before themselves and their pockets.

I'm determined to have her on my team.

Even before setting eyes on her at the kickoff party, I'd planned to have Carlisle pay a call to that girl I'd met, the one who cried an ocean and a half at my father's funeral. The one whose letter I skimmed, for some reason, the day my father died.

After the kick-off party ... let's just say, she's been on my mind, and not only because she's gorgeous and in another life, I'd have liked to slip my hands under her dress and feel her skin, lean my head and kiss her mouth for a hell of a long time. No, not because of that, but because she loves the presidency—and she always has.

And now she's been confirmed on my team, thanks to Carlisle. Carlisle is my campaign chairman and manager. We've already recruited our media advisors, chief strategist and pollster, communications director, CFO, media consultant, press secretary, spokeswoman, digital director, and official photographer.

Having them all together under the roof of the campaign bunker gives me a sense of satisfaction. We've assembled a team that will take us smoothly toward this year's election.

I'm ready to call it a day, so I pat Carlisle on the back of the head, saying, "Trust me," grab my car keys, and head out.

Home is a two-bedroom bachelor pad near the Hill. A far cry from the 132 rooms and endless acreage of the White House, it's modern and the perfect size for me to own it—not for the thing to own me. I'm also three blocks from my mother. Though she has a busy social schedule and a new boyfriend that has for five years tried to get her to marry him without success, I like to keep my eye on her.

My German Shepherd Lab mix is barking when I insert the key into the lock. He's sleek black, and the media calls him Black Jack. He's more famous than the Taco Bell dog. He's got eyes nearly as black as his fur and is thankfully past the phase where he would gnaw all my shoes to dust. He is at the door, barking three times. I open and he leaps.

I catch him in one arm, shut the door with the other, and set him down. He pads next to me to the kitchen. I adopted him once I did a showing to raise awareness of adopting. Jack was a puppy then, the mother found on the streets, curled up on him and his two dead sisters.

The White House is going to be a far cry from where he started.

I press the play button on the answering machine.

"Matthew, Congressman Mitchell. Congrats—you can count on me."

"Matthew, Robert Wells, thank you so much for the opportunity you're offering my daughter. Of course you can count on the family's support ... Let's do lunch sometime."

"Matt." A random female voice comes up next. "I hope you get this message. I'm ... I'm pregnant. My name is Leilani. I'm pregnant with your babies ... they're twins. Please, they need their father."

I pull out a glass-bottled Blue Moon beer from the fridge and a plate from the warming drawer.

I delete the messages, turn on the TV, prop my feet up, and start eating as I wait for Wilson.

He wanted to meet and I told him 10 p.m. was the earliest I could do.

He lets himself in and grabs a beer, then drops down on the couch to my right. He's pushing fifty. Still single, he tags his nephew on his off days from the Secret Service.

Surprising that he hadn't reached out to me after I dropped the presidential bomb across the country.

He eyes me for a moment, steepling his hands as he looks me square in the eye. "So here we are."

"Here we are." I grin and take a swig.

Wilson looks as if he never expected to say that, a fact I find slightly amusing.

"Saw the announcement. Never thought I'd hear you say it, dammit." He drags a hand over his bald head and drops it, eyeing me as if waiting for an explanation.

I just lift my beer in toast.

"Why?" he asks.

"Nine years, a lot of time to think about it. It was always there ..." I turn a finger, symbolizing the wheels in my head.

"Some say you should have waited another term, until you're a little older."

"Yeah, I don't think so. America can't wait anymore. Day off?"

"I quit."

Lifting the beer to my lips, I pause midway.

"You're going to need me," Wilson says. "And I want in."

I'm shocked to silence. Then I push myself to my feet as Wilson rises (habit, I suppose), and I shake his hand. "I'll get you back in the White House."

"No, *I'll* get you there. In one piece. I know many ladies who will be grateful for that. And your mother, too."

"She hired you?" I ask, torn between laughing and groaning as we settle back in our seats.

"No. I'd made my choice. But she did call. She's worried."

"I stayed in the shadows to appease that fear of hers, Wil. I can't stay there anymore." I shake my head, then study him in curiosity. "When do you start?"

"Tomorrow," he says.

We're so used to each other, we're not for greetings or goodbyes, that he stands and leaves.

I grab the remote to change channels when the anchors begin discussing my team selections.

"That's right, Violet, it seems Matt Hamilton is more interested in bringing fresh blood to the campaign than experience. We'll have to see if the method proves effective as we head into election year ... We have a dozen or more names confirmed as part of the campaign team. One of the youngest signed on as political aide, ex-Senator Wells's daughter ..."

Nothing I don't already know. A picture of Charlotte flashes on the screen. She's wearing my father's pin on her lapel. I lean forward in my seat and simply look at her, the smile on her face, the look in her eyes, and I can't fucking believe how gorgeous she is.

"A puzzle as to her inclusion in the permanent staff and speculation on why Matt Hamilton chose her ..."

"Gut instinct," I tell them, sitting back once the image disappears, raising my beer and taking a swig.

"She seems to have a solid Catholic background and a penchant for helping those in need. That angelic face will definitely not gain any haters ... "

"Plus she's pure and untouched by you," I say, setting my beer aside and watching the pictures of her flash across the screen.

It's been nine years since my father's funeral, but I still remember the way she cried, as if my father had been hers.

"We have a snippet of her in Matt Hamilton's arms at the funeral of President Hamilton. Think there's any romantic entanglement?"

"Not yet," I mumble. Whoa! Did I just say that?

Not happening, Hamilton. Not now.

Fuck.

I finish my meal and carry the plate to the kitchen, dropping it into the sink. I frown and lean on it when her face filters back into my mind. Charlotte, in that shimmering yellow dress. Carlisle's confirmation that she'd agreed to join the campaign. I'm confused by how much that affected me. How much I want her around.

I head back to the living room to hear the rest.

"Not really. Hamilton has been very careful with that, a very discreet man."

"It's true that since his abrupt departure from the White House he's been amassing the public's sympathy and support—the amount of fans he's gained so far is unprecedented for an Independent and donations are reportedly pouring in before the fundraisers begin. It'll be interesting to see what this team of rather young but impressive people do. Original

and inventive strategies to reach the public and a massive online campaign are expected."

I rub the back of my neck and turn off the TV.

I'm used to the attention. My mother never approved of my father's willingness to use me for publicity. She tried to fiercely guard my privacy, and I guess, before this, so did I.

But my father taught me the press didn't have to be foes, they could be friends, or tools to aid his administration. Those White House years, we were always swarmed by an armada of press and resourceful photographers. The only respite was found at Camp David where they were out of bounds. Yet, we rarely went there, no matter how much my mother loved the vacation spot. Dad felt as if he belonged to the people, and insisted on being as open and available as possible.

"I spend so much time away, I want you to know me," he'd tell me.

"I do."

I'd walk him out to the South Lawn as he boarded Marine One. As always, I was a teen with a fascination with all things military.

"What do you think?" he'd ask of anyone, with the paternal pride of any American parent. "He'll be president one day," he'd say.

"Ahh, no," I'd laugh.

He would have loved to see me try.

Instead, he's been gone for nine years.

My mother got the call from a U.S. senator when it happened.

My granddad saw on TV that his son was dead.

All I remember of the funeral is my mom kissing the top of his head, his fingers, his knuckles and his palms, putting her wedding ring in his hand, and taking his in her own.

The vice president sent my mother a letter, and one for me.

Matt, I know the phenomenal man and leader your father was. He won't be forgotten.

The letter was a kind reminder that my mother and I were homeless for the first time in our lives.

After the state funeral, we packed up as the new family established itself in the White House. I looked at the oval office one last time, the walls, the desk, the empty seat, and walked out, never imagining how determined I'd be to walk back in two terms later.

THE FIRST WEEK

Charlotte

I have restless dreams about the campaign, wondering who'll win the primaries for the main political parties, and flashbacks of the day Matt's father was killed.

It's still dark when I wake. I take a hot bath, but I'm not that tired even though I didn't sleep well. I'm still running on adrenaline from the excitement—stumbling half-naked around my kitchen, dressing while having breakfast.

I wear a khaki skirt, a plain white button-down shirt, and a pair of tan open-toed shoes with sensible three-inch heels. My hair is pulled back into a practical ponytail, not too tight, but tight enough that no wayward strands can escape.

The excitement in the room is palpable when I arrive at the building. Keyboards are clicking, phones are buzzing, people are maneuvering past the small halls, getting quickly from one place to the next. There's respect in the air, gratitude for being here.

We want our candidate to win.

Matt asks us what we all desire for our next president, what we desire for our country. As the group mulls his questions over, that ridiculously sexy stare locks on me. "If you had a genie that granted you three wishes, what would they be?"

Every word he says is like an indecent proposal.

The women around me look a bit like perspiring.

I wonder if they're all thinking of sleeping with him as their first wish and marrying him their last, like I am.

A woman raises her hand. "Jobs, health, and education. What every person wants. To feel validated, busy, like they've got something to offer. Love is impossible to grant, but if you make us busy, feel useful and validated, you give us self-love."

"I'll be your genie. You're right; love is not something in my power to grant. But for those first three wishes, I'll be your genie for everyone who knocks on my lamp." He knocks on the table, and then he leaves us with all the things to do. Twittering with inspiration.

We all want to impress him. We all want to feel like we did something for this campaign. If Matt Hamilton is elected president, we'll be making history.

I watch people putting together the slogans.

Hamilton is change

A new vision

Predestined to lead

The change we need. The voice we deserve

For the future

Slogans to capture what he represents.

Leadership for the people

The right man for the job

My favorite: *Born for this*

I settle in during the morning, and I'm happy to report that I'm settling in just fine.

The phone starts to ring more viciously from noon onward, and it doesn't stop ringing from then on.

I answer so frantically I almost drop it. "Matt Hamilton Campaign headquarters."

"Matt, please," a male voice demands.

"May I ask who's calling?"

"His father, Law."

I was warned of this by the other aides, of course. It's still hard to remain unfazed after a statement like that. "I'm sorry, state your name please."

"This is George Afterlife, and I'm a psychic medium and his father is using me to communicate a message. It is imperative I talk to him now."

It's hard to ignore the sound of impending doom on the other side of the line.

"Mr. Afterlife, if you'd like to leave a message I will be sure he gets it."

"Matt, it's your father!" the man starts yelling, changing his voice.

"Matt is unavailable, but if you'd leave a message ..."

"I must talk to Matt—I know the conspiracy behind my murder."

For the next ten minutes I try to get the man to leave a message, and all he leaves is a number. I jot it down.

The phone rings again, and I have a mini heart attack.

"Yes? Matt Hamilton Campaign headquarters?"

A breathy voice says, "Matt. I need to speak to Matt."

"Who's calling?" I take my notepad out to jot down her info.

"His girlfriend."

I hesitate. *Girlfriend?* My heart sinks a bit, but I ignore it.

"Your name, please."

"Look. He knows my name—I'm his girlfriend." At this point, I'm feeling suspicious. He doesn't have a girlfriend. Does he?

"And this is in relation to ...?"

"God, *fuck you!*" She hangs up.

Wow. I hang up too.

I stay until midnight, alternating between taking phone calls and working down the pile of letters.

It's been less than a week, and I've already started getting silent phone calls and weird notes on my email from his "sister" and "wife" and his father from the "dead." How does Matt sleep at all?

Am I really cut out for this?

Two days later, Carlisle calls a meeting.

It's dog-eat-dog in this political race, and the competition is already taking a nip out of Matt.

It turns out President Jacobs is already taking stabs at him.

"He's threatened?" Matt smiles and covers his expression with his hand when Carlisle summons us all to the TV room and rewinds a recording of the same day.

We watch a popular news channel interview the president about Matt's candidacy.

I watch his body language, and it's hard to tell anything with him looking so lifeless and stoic. "How can he effectively run the country without a First Lady?" He signals to his elegant First Lady, who's smiling demurely.

The next day Matt Hamilton appears, on the same channel, looking even more presidential than the president did.

"I find it laughable that President Jacobs believes a single, independent man cannot effectively run the country." He looks at the camera soberly, with a light smile on his lips and those strong but playful dark brown eyes lasering in on the camera lens. "The term and official role as First Lady wasn't even properly coined when Lady Washington served in Mount Vernon during George Washington's office. I have a wife"—his lips curl higher—"and her name is the United States of America."

The flood of calls is unprecedented. Carlisle the campaign manager is hecticly getting new slogans to be produced.

Committed to you
Made in America
All American

Hewitt, Matt's campaign press manager, is quoted during the week: "Matt Hamilton's sole obligation is to you, the United States of America. We need it to be clear. His First Lady is his country."

"I've got to say, the way Matthew Hamilton is representing America, it feels good to be American again," a TV news anchor jokes with her male co-anchor the same evening.

The effect this is having on women voters is almost naughty.

Primaries aren't over until a few months from now, but I can already tell that his most formidable adversary will be the current president. On the other hand, the leading Republican candidate is so radical and people are so sick of things, he's gaining traction too.

From one fundraising political event to the next, Matt is fielding two hundred to five hundred speaking invitations a week.

Today, we're all sitting at Matt's round table, and the tension in palpable. Matt's creative design and marketing people have been pitching ideas, hoping to answer the big question on the docket for the day: "How should we market Matt's campaign?"

The basics have been nailed down by Carlisle, who said simply that the efforts of the campaign should center around Matt's strengths: his father's successful presidency and his incredible popularity as president, Matt's popularity among the people (especially those ready for real change), and Matt's singleness.

However, the campaign has yet to come up with a real campaign strategy to bring Matt's ideas for change to the public.

Matt looks exasperated, running his fingers through his dark hair and rubbing his knuckles across the slight stubble on his chin.

I want to speak up, give a suggestion, but the silence is intimidating ... *he* is intimidating. His unreadable expression seems to make everyone in the room shift nervously.

He raises his gaze and sweeps it across everyone, meeting each and every gaze. "We can do better."

His gaze only passes me, but it definitely connects, and for that second, suddenly I'm eleven again, awed and confused by the effect he has.

I bite my lip, and I think about the letter from a young boy. I've been able to answer every letter, even some pretty crazy ones proposing marriage, but I can't figure out what to tell this one fan. Every time I think of him I ache, but I don't have the courage yet to go directly to Matt and ask him about it.

"Come on, guys." He sighs. "Is this really all we have?"

Papers shuffle and I can hear an awkward cough or sigh every now and then. We all look at each other, silently pleading with our eyes for someone, *anyone*, to speak up.

I feel myself itching to dare and pitch my idea, but Carlisle beats me to it, and I feel my heart sink in my chest.

Carlisle suggests that Matt market his campaign as the "next step" or "continuation" of his father's presidential plan. Calling it a Hamilton 2.0 of sorts, the new-and-improved Hamilton plan.

Matt immediately shoots it down. "I want the people to know that I will continue my father's legacy, but that I also have ideas of my own."

Carlisle sighs and exasperatedly raises his hands in defeat. "Does anyone else have any ideas?"

Matt looks at us all and his piercing gaze settles on me. I feel my breath catch in my chest. He quirks an eyebrow at me, silently beckoning me to speak up. To take a risk and speak my mind.

Unable to take his unsettling gaze anymore, I clear my throat, and immediately everyone looks at me.

"What do you guys think of something that brings home the fact that we are working on everything—down to the fundamentals?" I nervously begin. "We can call it the alphabet campaign. We're fixing, working, and improving everything from A to Z in this country. Arts. Bureaucracy. Culture. Debt. Education. Foreign relation policies ..."

The table is quiet. I turn to Matt and I see his eyes shimmering in approval.

Carlisle is the first to speak up, cracking a smile and turning to Matt. "That's actually really good."

Matt doesn't turn to look at him, just keeps his gaze on me. "It is," he says simply. He nods and stands, buttoning his jacket. "We're doing that. I want to have a full alphabet of campaign issues tomorrow first thing," he announces as he keeps walking. Immediately, everyone leaves the table, relieved to have something to do now that Matt chose an idea.

An idea that just so happened to be *mine*.

I turn to join them, a deep sense of pride bubbling up inside me and warming my chest. I keep walking but before I get to my cubicle, Matt speaks again.

"Charlotte, come to my office, please."

I swallow the lump in my throat and manage a "Sure" before following Matt there.

He sits down and gestures for me to take the seat across from him.

I sit down and start to twist the rings on my fingers.

"You did well in there, Charlotte," he says, looking at me with warm eyes. I can't tell if he wants to pat me on the back and tell me "good game" or kiss the hell out of me and tell me "come for me."

I shake my head, because that thought brought warmth between my legs.

"Thank you." I smile.

He smiles back and rubs the stubble on his jaw, saying more to himself than me, "I knew I brought you on this campaign for a reason ..."

I cock my eyebrow at him. "And what reason would that be?" I ask.

He looks me up and down, a devilish smile on his face. "Your looks, of course."

I laugh, and he laughs with me, but his laughter fades. "I brought you on because something told me you are just as passionate about this country and about real change as I am."

I feel myself blush. And he eyes me curiously.

"I didn't think you would say yes, you know," he confesses to me, and then prods, "Why did you?"

"Why did I what?" I ask, lost by the look in his eyes, and how I feel like the only woman in the world when they are looking at me so intently.

"Say yes."

I pause and think about his question. Actually think about it for a moment.

Why did I say *yes* to him?

I feel my mental wheels turning and before I know it, I'm answering him confidently. "I couldn't let my chance to do something great pass me up."

He stares at me. I stare back.

And in that moment, I feel the air shift. I feel like I just earned something Matthew Hamilton does not give out easily or frequently: admiration.

"If you don't need my help anymore—I should get to work myself," I say.

He nods.

Nervous about the connection I feel, I hurry off and get back to my desk. The phones haven't stopped ringing, the piles of letters distributed on my and Mark's (another aide's) table mounting by the second.

THAT DOG OF YOURS NEEDED A LEASH

Charlotte

The next morning, my alarm goes off at five o'clock. Before joining Matt Hamilton's campaign, I'd exercise at seven and be at work by nine. Now I need to be at work by seven thirty, and because I want a head start, I rise early, wash my face, get on my jogging pants and long-sleeved T-shirt, grab my phone, earbuds, and jacket, and head out.

The sun peers through a couple of gray clouds as I follow my favorite running trail—one that passes the Washington monuments. The day is too gloomy to admire the view, and I almost wish I'd stayed in bed.

I see a flash of movement out of the corner of my eye and from around a corner in the distance emerges a dog, happily trotting my way. He barks at me, then sits before me, all at attention and excited. Being a cat person, my relationship with dogs has been nonexistent, so I don't know what to do with the creature except try to get him to settle down. As I grab the end of his leash, something dark catches my attention, and I lift my head.

I stand in the middle of the trail, blinking my eyelashes, struggling with the shock of seeing Matt Hamilton walking toward me in a red running shirt and navy-blue shorts.

His face shows a combination of a frown and a smile. He looks both surprised and amused to see me, and I'm shocked.

His shirt molds to his skin, revealing the lovely definition of his chest. He's so rugged and at the same time so elegant, it's hard to think straight.

My heart beats a thousand beats a second. "Fancy seeing you here," he says.

"Fancy that." I smile, my throat dry as he stops before me.

And then we start walking, together, and he's eyeing my profile as the sun kisses every inch of his face.

His dog happily trails beside him, and I find it amusing to see the way he looks up devotedly at Matt. Matt turns toward me. "I see you've met Jack."

"Jack," I repeat, smiling at the dog.

"He has the bad habit of saying hello to anyone we meet at the park."

"I bet those people end up terribly excited when they find out who the dog's owner is."

His brows fly up. I can't freaking believe I said that out loud. I start to laugh and quickly say, "I have a cat. Doodles. She's not like Jack; she hates strangers. I hope she won't consider me one too one day—she's staying with my mother because I'm hardly home."

We continue walking in comfortable silence—well, not *that* comfortable, I suppose. I'm too aware of him. How tall he is compared to me.

"So what made you go to Georgetown? And become an advocate for women?" he asks me.

I'm surprised by how genuinely interested he sounds. By the attentive way he looks at me as he waits.

"I want to make sure women's rights are known." I shrug. "What about you? I know you went to law school to run your empire."

"Really. Where did you hear that?"

"The press."

He gives me a smirk, then chuckles and shakes his head in reprimand. "I think you know better than to listen to them." His smile fades, and he falls sober and adds, "No, really. I admire the fact that you went into public service. What inspired you to change the world?"

"I don't know," I begin, thoughtful. "Every summer during college, I went on mission trips. I loved getting to know all these people and I loved helping. Especially women: it's hard to imagine when you live in a first-world country the kinds of things women across the world are still subjected to. It made me want to do something for others. And *you*, Mr. Hamilton? What gives *you* inspiration?" I return.

"Walking next to you watching you speak."

My breath catches, and I notice that his eyes are shining like beautiful dark satin, and I realize he's flirting with me—and I'm a ball of fireworks on the inside. "So tell me about *C*," he says.

I'm confused. "Culture?"

"Charlotte. Come on."

I laugh as he just smiles his most minuscule smile and I feel my cheeks pinken. "Well, I went to Georgetown, but then you already know that." I shoot him a pointed look. "My par-

ents loved me going to Georgetown. The moment I graduated they said, *you should go into politics now*. But they knew my goal was to work for public service, so that's where I went ..."
I keep on thinking to see what else I could share.

I still can't believe he put my name on the letter *C* ...

"Everybody thinks I'm a good girl. I've never done anything wrong; I just never wanted to embarrass my parents."

I send him a shy look that says *your turn*.

"Law student. As you know." He shoots me a sly look. "I'm the bad boy, but I'm not really that bad. Everything's always exponential when the media picks it up. Growing up, there were actually very few people in my life that I could be certain wouldn't run to the media with the story a night later."

I'm surprised by this, kind of blown away by the realization of how difficult it must be to live your life always under scrutiny. I don't know that I could ever do it. "I was so nervous when we met. For years I had a picture of you on my wall."

"You did, did you?" he croons, chuckling a low, rumbling sound.

I laugh. "My mom let me keep it just because it probably helped keep me away from the boys and, well, I'm an only daughter. I really always tried to be good."

"My dad was a senator before he became president. I grew up an only son, so I know exactly what it feels like to be the apple of your parents' eye."

I smile. "Except you're also an ex-president's son now. Which must be doubly hard because you're the apple of the public eye, too."

"Not really." He frowns as he thinks about that.

"I've been very amused by your fan letters. I enjoy even the crazy ones. Did you know you got several proposals for marriage in the past forty-eight hours?"

He pretends to look surprised and crosses his arms as if super interested. "I hope I declined."

"Of course. Throughout the campaign and presidency, you'll be hopelessly single. Carlisle briefed us all."

He just gives me a glimpse of the merest sexy twitch of his lips and then stares ahead, thoughtful.

"I wouldn't be the first bachelor president, you know," he says as he glances at me again with a casual hike of his shoulder. "James Buchanan already filled that role." His brow creases. "Not a very good president. But a bachelor to the end." His lips quirk.

My curiosity is piqued. "What did he do?" I ask.

"More like didn't do." His frown deepens. "His inability to take a firm stand on slavery and stop the secession led us right into the Civil War."

We keep watching each other with an intensity that nearly curls my toes.

There's a soft breeze and I realize my shirt is plastered to my skin, and his presence has my breasts feeling heavy.

I look down and my eyes widen when I realize my nipples are totally showing—harder than little rubies.

I cross my arms, and Matt smiles. "I made your nipples hard that day at the campaign kickoff too."

"Oh, wow. Well, my nipples weren't the only things getting hard that day, I'd say."

"You don't know the half of it."

I groan and roll my eyes, laughing inwardly but hating how much my nipples have popped now.

I'm so nervous that I trip. He catches me, his reflexes lightning fast as his hand curls around my elbow to keep me on my feet, and suddenly I can't breathe. I'm amazed by how much we have in common, and by the way he reels me back to find my balance and then, somehow, reels me still a little more—a little closer to him.

He lifts his other hand and brushes a tendril of hair behind my forehead, his eyes as dark as ever.

Desire floods me as our bodies connect, my front against his front, and I can feel him. I can feel how big he is, how thick and hard, pulsing against my abdomen.

And in this moment Matt Hamilton, my crush of all ages, the sexiest man alive, the hottest candidate in U.S. history, becomes so real to me. So very real. I can feel the warmth of his body through the wet fabric of our shirts. I can smell him, a scent of soap and rain, and I can see him as a guy, a very hot guy with an extraordinary destiny to fulfill.

I feel something leap up to lick my cheek and I jerk and step back, startled by the dog's kiss.

"Shit," I breathe, laughing.

"Jack!" A harsh curse follows, and I feel Matt straighten me and then put distance between us. "Sorry. You all right?" he asks. He brushes my hair back as if on impulse before we begin walking again, and electricity tingles down my body. I nod quickly. I'm so, so nervous. "Yes. I'm sorry I said *shit*."

"Why?" His lips quirk. "Don't be."

I laugh, not believing I was forgetting who he was, caught up in the moment of his nearness, how much I want him— realizing that, whether he wants to or not, his body responds to me as well.

"I'd better get away before I'm late. I wouldn't want the boss to be mad at me."

"The boss could never be mad at you."

His tone is sober, but his eyes twinkle, and my whole body feels flushed under his regard. "'Bye, Matt," I say, lifting my hand a little awkwardly in a wave before I cut a path through the grass and head to the sidewalk.

That night, my parents invite me to dinner, and I can't stop thinking about Matt and his energetic Jack and the conversations we had about his childhood and mine. Then I think back to the day we met, and the president, and his death.

I ask my dad why he thinks there wasn't any conclusive information on President Hamilton's assassination.

"Killer was never caught." He shrugs. "One theory is it was a terrorist act because of President Hamilton's liberal views; others say it was a conspiracy among the parties."

I frown worriedly.

"You're concerned Matthew will be in danger?" he asks me.

I can't help but look at him with a concerned expression.

He sighs. "He'll be fine as long as he doesn't open that can of worms."

I frown even more. "Matt doesn't strike me as a man who won't open a can of worms, especially if he feels strongly about it."

He shakes his head. "Don't worry about things you can't control. Do your best and keep your head down—that's the only way to get ahead in politics. Otherwise, anybody who's anybody is going to see your head poking up and push it back down."

"But I don't want to be in politics."

He laughs. "You're in it now."

"I'm only there because—"

"You have a soft spot for the Hamiltons, I know. People in the news are surprised you're participating. Good ol' Charlotte, you did charm Matthew that night, didn't you? Even President Hamilton. They have a soft spot for us too." He smiles wistfully, his eyes sad with memories.

"You know what else Matt has a soft spot for? Aside from the country? His dog," I say, remembering this morning as I pick up Doodles from my feet, set her on my lap, and stroke her forehead, hearing her purr happily.

GIFT

Charlotte

The next morning, I take a bath, change quickly, and stop at a pet store on impulse to make a purchase. I don't know why I want to make this particular purchase, but my mother has always been the sort of woman to have sweet little surprises for my dad. I don't know if it's her way of saying thank you for something nice that he did or just the way he made her feel. I want to get something for Matt, but I know that it wouldn't be proper. But when the urge to get Jack a little something hits me, I decide not to even fight it.

Once I get to the campaign headquarters, I step off the elevator and I see Matt in the hall. Immediately my body responds: pulse skipping, nipples tightening, pussy clenching.

He's in dark jeans and a soft-looking taupe cashmere sweater that contrasts strikingly with his dark hair. He's talking to his campaign web manager when he spots me. He pauses mid-sentence, and my heart stutters when he smiles at me.

His eyes look warm and there's something else in his gaze, almost like protectiveness.

He continues talking with the guy—positively oozing that confidence that seems to cling to him like a second skin—and

I head to my chair. I exhale and glance around my desktop, telling myself I have to catch up.

Everyone here is smart, lightning fast, and eager to work, most of them confident. A little more experienced than me, too.

I've seen them effortlessly answer phone call after phone call, letter after letter, email after email. I get sentimental about these things. I've found myself needing a box of Kleenex or to cover my response when I read the letters.

After a whole day back, I still don't know how to answer this little boy's letter.

I've dealt with women in my mom's foundation, but never anyone younger than eighteen. There's something about someone younger having a hard time that gets to me doubly hard.

"Read this letter," I tell Mark, whose desk is a few feet away from mine.

"What about it?"

"I'd like to ask Matt if he could squeeze in a visit—"

"What? No way. He's got four hundred speaking engagement requests this week. He doesn't have time for everything and everyone. We have thousands of letters just like it in these piles. Just answer and go to the next."

I walk to my desk, unhappy about Mark's suggestion.

He leans back in his chair and peers into my cubicle for a moment, and I'm sure he was trying to catch a glimpse of my boobs as I bent to take my chair. "What does it matter asking him? It's just one among thousands," he then asks me, rolling his eyes.

I wave the letter in the air. "It matters to *this* one."

Back to the letters on my desk, I set it aside and duck my head to continue answering in longhand.

Dear Kim,

Matt is very moved by your letter and he would like you to receive his best wishes on your upcoming graduation. Please receive this set of bookmarks with both Matt and his campaign team's most heartfelt congratulations. I'm sure we can expect great things from you in the future.

Kindest regards, Charlotte Wells, campaign aide

A few hours later, Carlisle summons us for a meeting. I grab a yellow notepad and stand to follow my coworkers toward the conference room.

Matt is watching every step I take into the room while we're briefed on the new campaign strategy. When everyone leaves, nerves eat at the walls of my stomach as I go to my desk, get my purchase from this morning, and head to the corner nook of the building where Matt has taken up office.

He's already behind his desk when I step inside.

"I got you a present."

He leans back in his chair and our eyes hold, and the mere way he looks at me makes my stomach grip and my sex clench.

"It's not for you, it's for Jack," I stumble to explain.

He peers into the box, looks at the collar with the metal symbol attached, and lifts it in one hand. "A flea collar." He knocks the flea charm with one finger. "Funny."

I press my lips together to keep from laughing.

"How are you this morning?" He drags the flea charm to the side of his desk, where he has a picture of his father, his mother, and himself.

"I'm absolutely fabulous, Mr. Hamilton," I effuse, pressing the folders to my chest.

"Matt." He enunciates every letter clearly.

"*Matt*," I say.

His grin reaches all the way to his eyes. "Good girl, you get an *A* today."

"You get a bully badge. *Matt*."

I turn away, and when I glance past my shoulder, he's reaching out for a pair of reading glasses and glancing over Carlisle's proposal.

He looks smart and quiet and intellectual as he reads with his glasses on, absently running his fingers over the top of his head. That's when I see him lift his head and eye the charm I bought for his dog, his lips twitching.

Just the tiniest bit.

I've seen Matt at campaign headquarters every day. At first he'd be smiling and looking directly at me, but lately I have seemed invisible to him. He looks past my shoulder when I ask him anything, answering curtly with comments like, "Good, appreciate it."

Yesterday, his gaze fell to a pin I was wearing that was released in commemoration of his father's presidency, a gold circle with an eagle in it and a Latin motto engraved below. I bought it the moment it came out—and the limited edition sold out within hours. The darkening look in his eyes confused me. He looked displeased, or very close to it. He took the folder I handed him and walked away, flipping through it as he headed to his office.

Following that encounter, I go to the restroom. I check my clothes; they're not wrinkled or stained. I run my hands down my slacks and shirt, touching the pin at the collar. Insecurity tugs at me. Maybe he thinks my face is unfortunate? Maybe the ghost of his father stood behind me? Maybe he's unhappy about the bad press I'm getting?

When I walk out, he's talking to Alison—and staring straight into her eyes—and I turn around and use the long way to my cubicle.

Back in my seat, my sleeping computer stares blankly at me.

I've been trying so hard to collaborate and be efficient, and I'm disappointed he's clearly not happy with my job.

"Don't mock me," I say at the screen as I grab a stack of letters and keep on reading.

So many petitions. So many people hoping for change. So many people wanting a piece of Matt Hamilton.

My eyes are tired. I've had about five cups of coffee.

I hear noise, and I spot him in his office.

We're the only ones in the building. Two lights inside. I see him scrape a hand over his face and lift his head, and I lower mine so he doesn't notice I was looking at him.

My stomach twists as I hear footsteps.

Matt's energy begins to envelop me, and I feel my heartbeat start picking up as I hear him grab the chair from Mark's cubicle next to mine and drag it so he can sit beside me.

He sets his coffee next to mine, and a folder, and his reading glasses. "No coffee?" He lifts my empty cup.

"If I have one more I'll never sleep again in my life," I groan, and he laughs, such a pleasant laugh, and takes my cup and goes to refill it.

He sets it down in the exact same spot it occupied before. Next to his.

Then he takes the seat beside me, and I can't concentrate for a moment. I'm hyperaware of him, of nobody else in the building but us.

Matt has a way of occupying more space than his body does. He shifts to prop his elbows on his knees, and my heart trips at his nearness. "Hey. Why are you still here, Charlotte?"

"It's my cubicle."

He smiles sardonically and just eyes me for my sass.

I'm too aware of him sitting there, with the rich outlines of his shoulders pressing into the black, soft-looking fabric of his shirt.

I try not to notice. "I was trying to finish this pile of letters," I finally answer, grabbing the pen as I pretend to get back to work.

I can't.

He's staring at me.

"I'm pretty sure you didn't agree to help me so you could spend all night answering letters," he says.

"Maybe I did. But why did you ask me?" I narrow my eyes.

"When you get a letter from a girl you just met, you know she means business."

"I *perfumed* the stationery—of course I meant business," I say slyly. "Though it seems *you* didn't mean it when you said you didn't want to run when we first met."

"Yeah, well." A chuckle rises up his chest, and he drags a hand over his hair.

"You changed your mind," I say.

"You could say I matured into the idea. Takes time to gather the courage to believe you can do it. Then it takes another to believe you can do it better than anyone else."

He seems calm, as if he's got nothing to hide, his eyes warm and simply … friendly as he leans back and loops his arm behind the chair as he shifts. "I kept thinking if not me, who? If not now, when?" He gazes out the windows at the far end before glancing back at me. "I'd like to change things. Still no equality, still a need of jobs, still too many self-serving ambitions. We're all wild wolves who were fed at the doorstep too long and forgot how to hunt. Where are the workers that built America? On unemployment?"

He sounds so passionate, and he's so close, I'm a little breathless. "I love how proactive you are about jobs."

"Because nothing feels as good as a day well invested in doing something right." His eyes flick down to my lips for a minuscule moment. "Actually, not nothing. But precious few things."

Neither of us is laughing.

In fact the air feels a little charged, a little bit electric.

He means kissing, a part of me whispers.

No, Charlotte, he means sex!

I feel myself flush at that, aware of Matt watching me as if he's enjoying that immensely. I set the pen down and look up at him. "What you said the other day, about never being able to trust someone not running with the story. There are so many stories about your family and you ... Are they all real?"

"Trust me. They're not as interesting as you'd think they are."

"Not true!" I protest. "They're all fascinating."

He smiles. Shifts forward. "*You're* fascinating," he whispers.

I nearly choke on my saliva.

"I find everything about you fascinating. Even the fact that you're sitting here now at this hour."

"So are you," I counter.

"I'm the candidate."

"And you're *my* candidate. So, *I'm* here."

The word *my* sort of feels different when I say it to him. The idea that Matt could be anything of mine is just mind-blowing, to say the least.

But he could be my president.

He was my first crush.

He is my boss, and my candidate.

And right now he is my very breath because nothing has ever felt as exciting to me as this man, this man in this moment, sipping his coffee, leaning back in his chair, watching me with such lazy eyes—as if he has no intention of going anywhere.

As if what happened when we ran/walked together sort of connected with him too.

"It *is* true you had a chimpanzee at the White House? You were gifted it by a foreign ambassador?" I ask.

I admit I'm addicted to talking to him, to learning more about him.

"Baboo. She was six months old when we got her."

"Oh really? Were all your college girlfriends terribly jealous because she got to live with you? I can't even keep up with the list of those girlfriends. Christina Aguilera, Jennifer Lawrence—who was it really?"

Matt sets down his coffee, a smirk on his lips. "Neither. Both are friends. My White House years taught me to guard my every step and after ... let's just say I enjoy being the hunter in the relationship." He eyes me mischievously. "What about you, Charlotte?"

"Oh no." I shake my head, laughing. "My parents have given up on hooking me up with some promising political entity. I've simply not found the right guy."

There's a silence.

Matt seems oddly pleased. He leans forward. So close that his shoulder touches mine, and a part of me wonders if it's on purpose.

"Do you want to?" His voice is deep and a tad quiet. He raises his hand and tucks a strand of hair behind my ear, almost like he did when we were running/walking together, and a white-hot shudder races down my spine.

My heart is flip-flopping in my chest as we stare at each other and Matt lowers his hand, still looking at me with heavy eyelids.

"Of course, everybody wants to find that. I'm a realist, but I dream of finding what my parents have."

"So why not ...?" he prods, his gaze caressing me.

"Most politicians are old, stuffy, or boring."

He laughs—a rich, deep sound.

When he falls sober, his voice drops a decibel. "Good thing I'm a lawyer and a businessman, and not a politician. Because I'm not stuffy, and I'm definitely not boring."

My throat runs dry. Oh, god. He is most definitely nothing like politics has ever seen, even with the Kennedys.

But you're not available, I think to myself, though I somehow feel too tongue-tied to say it.

A silence settles between us. I feel my nipples pop and I fear Matt, with one glance downward, will notice. There's a pool of warmth between my legs and a tight clench in my sex, and I'm desperate to get rid of it.

It takes me a moment and a deep breath to get a grip on the sexual tension crackling between us. I remember why I'm even here, working so late, reworking an itinerary I'd already worked on a couple of days ago. I reach beneath my paperwork to pull out an envelope, glancing questioningly into his eyes.

"Would you read this?"

Before I know it, I'm extending my hand.

He takes an absent sip of his coffee and quickly sets it aside. Then he grabs his glasses, puts them on, and takes the letter. Our thumbs brush as he does, and another clench deep in my tummy happens.

He smiles, as if he definitely did that on purpose.

But his smile fades as Matt scans the letter. I know by memory what it says. It touched me deeply.

Dear Matt Hamilton,

I'm very happy that you're running for president. My mother worries that something can happin to you so I think its very brave. I'm very brave too. I'm seven yrs old and getting a new experiment treatment on my very bad lewkemia called PCL. I asked if it could kill me too. But my dad says someone has to be the innovator and pave new unknown paths like you.

My dream is to go to the white house when you become presi-
dent. I know I will do very well with this treatment because im
hopping to go with every breath. So win Matt! Oh and my
name is Matt too my parents named me after you.
    Matt

"Would you visit this boy?" I ask.

Matt pulls off his glasses and looks at me.

Just looks at me.

So intently and as if he can see everything that I am, have ever been, and ever will be.

I hastily pull out the following week's schedule and my own version of it. "He's a son of one of the women at Women of the World. I recognized her name on the mailing envelope. I think I can fit him in before we leave D.C.—he's being treated at the Children's National on Michigan Northwest."

I put my new version of his schedule out for him to see.

But he doesn't look at the schedule. Only at me. His voice is smooth but deeper than it was before.

"That's why you're here so late; you're trying to fit this in," he says.

It's more a statement than a question.

I bite my lip as a gleam of admiration appears in his eyes.

He slides the schedule over the desk back to me without even looking at it. "I'd be happy to go."

I grin, my chest swelling with happiness.

I launch myself forward and give him a hug and a sweet but chaste kiss on his jaw. "Thank you! So very, very much!"

As my lips touch his jaw, suddenly his scent is surround-ing me in a cloak of elegant cologne and soap. I start easing back, startled by my own impulsive action. I realize his hands fell to my waist, gripping me gently but firmly. He looks down at me with a slight smile on his lips, and I look right back; our mutual shock at my impulsiveness turns into something else.

We share a moment of silent understanding, a more powerful connection than anything I've ever felt.

The loneliness of the building suddenly becomes even more pronounced. The warmth of his body. The specks of black in his eyes, the dark irises, the thickness of his lashes, and most especially, the *look* in his eyes.

I'm aware of the admiration in his gaze when he lifts his hand and brushes my cheek with the pad of his thumb. I hold my breath, aching for closeness, to physically establish this connection that I feel, his breath warm on my skin. He brushes his thumb over my cheek a second time, and then, as if that wasn't enough, his lips follow. The barest touch, a thousand times more powerful than a full-on make-out session with anyone. "You're welcome." His voice is gruff.

As I pry myself free, we both can't seem to stop looking at each other. He's smiling again, his eyes like liquid metal and a little too hot, and I smile shyly in response. And somehow this is the most honest, hottest smile anyone's ever given me and I've ever given anyone back.

I suppose things should feel awkward, but they just feel a little sharper for the next minute. The sound of his breath or rustle of his clothes as he gets his stuff back to his office, the timbre of his voice when he tells me if I'm done, he's done and can give me a ride home, the outline of his body close to mine as he helps me into my jacket.

I ride in the back of the black Lincoln with him, his detail, Wilson, driving us.

Matt's gaze lowers all of a sudden.

Gently he seizes the eagle pin at my collar. He strokes the eagle with the pad of his thumb. Once, that's all.

"You always wear this," he says.

A ridiculously sexy smile curls his lips, but this time, his eyes aren't smiling. He searches my expression with curiosity. And his smile fades. He's still holding the pin. I'm holding my breath, wanting more of these touches, more of him.

But I know how ridiculous thinking about anything with him is.

He's so driven to win, I know the last thing he needs right now is a distraction like me.

"Reminds me of the good old days," I finally reply, trying to push down the thick longing in my veins. "The ones you'll bring back."

"I'm ready."

We smile. The very air between us seems to be on fire.

"Good night, Matt."

I reach for the door, but he leans over me and sets his fingers on mine, clicking it open for me, his warmth enveloping me again, his fingers sliding over mine, caressing like a feather.

"Good night, Charlotte."

He watches in the shadows of the car, his eyes dancing the way they sometimes do when I do something that amuses him, still the crush-worthy guy I met when I was eleven.

Can he see how much he flusters me?

Of course he can.

I get to my apartment and my feet ache, my back aches, my brain aches. I feel too drained to do anything but kick off my shoes, stretch my arms out, and fall flat, facedown on the bed. But I can't sleep. His gorgeous dark-flecked eyes keep looking at me.

And they're looking at me like a man looks at a woman he wants.

Matt is looking at me as if he wants me.

I can't stop thinking about the way I impulsively threw myself at Matt and kissed him. The way he smelled, the way he felt, so warm and male and strong. I'm restless that weekend and call Kayla over to my apartment.

"So how is it going?"

Pushing the thought of having kissed him aside, I think of how great it feels to be campaigning with him. "Incredibly well," I admit.

"Is he as lean and built and tall and dark as he is on TV?"

"TV can't accurately capture his charisma in person. He's … he'd be attractive with his face alone, but combined with his personality and energy it's sort of naughty." I'm starving, eating my dinner in a hurry so I can go to bed early.

"He's running for president. Your childhood mega crush, and mine!" Kayla marches to the TV remote and flicks it on to the first channel. He's on the screen—as attractive as he is in person.

"What are Republicans saying?" I ask her.

"They're shitting in their pants."

"And the Democrats?"

"Shitting in their pants."

She sighs and drops down on my couch. "Never voted for an Independent candidate in my life, but this one is mine. Hamilton for the win!" She glances at me. "We miss you at Women of the World. Are you planning to come back after the campaign?"

"Of course."

"Why leave WoW at all?"

"Because he's what America's been waiting for. We deserve it."

"You hate the spotlight, even though you secretly admire how well your mother takes to it."

"I'm shy." I shrug. "It doesn't come as easy to me as it does to my mother. But I want to be there when he kicks ass."

"What about our trip to Europe this year?" Kayla asks.

I join her on the couch, sighing as I stare at the ceiling. "We can go to Europe anytime, but it's not any day that Matt Hamilton runs for president."

"The perfect baby father and every woman out there knows it. If you can't have him in your bed or fathering your children, at least let him be our chief in command."

"Commander in chief," I correct.

"He can be anything he'd like."

I groan and laugh.

WE FOUND OURSELVES RUNNING THE SAME PATH

Charlotte

I hadn't really realized I was getting into such a high-stress job when I said *yes.* You want to help people, have limited time, and you can't help everyone in the way you want to. It generates some huge pent-up frustrations I'm having trouble venting.

I head up to the park for a quick morning run and he's there. Matt Hamilton is the most easygoing guy I know, one who can keep his cool during adversity. While the world is in a stir over the news, and the TV keeps replaying his announcement, he's stretching his quads.

A cap covers my red hair, which I twisted beneath it. Somehow he still recognizes me, his eyebrows rising just a fraction when our eyes meet. He's not wearing a cap, his hair blows in the wind, and the shirt he wears is pressed against his defined torso.

He's not only running for president, he's running the TCS marathon in New York. Though it's already a huge marathon, the sign-ups have skyrocketed as rumors of his participation leaked. "It's dangerous, Matt," Carlisle warned just this week.

Matt laughed. "I'm not running a campaign on fear—fear has no place when you decide to run a country."

"Reckless!" Carlisle insisted.

Matt rose from behind his desk and slapped his campaign manager's back, shaking his head, frowning down at him. "Relax. It's just a marathon. Besides, running helps me keep my head clear."

I tuck my face under the cap until I run past him with a brief nod of acknowledgment.

I hear his light, agile running steps behind me as he catches up with me, and I'm a little more breathless when I see him in my peripherals.

"Morning, Charlotte."

"Morning," I say under my breath, trying to keep my pace.

We run in silence the rest of the hour.

This has been happening every day, for nearly two weeks. We seem to be … running together. Not on purpose, though. We both simply seem to want to run at *this* time, in *this* park, daily.

"Have any free time this morning at headquarters?" he asks.

"I've got a packed schedule."

"Never too packed for me."

My lips twist wryly.

His lips twist wryly too. "We've got some business to discuss with you."

"What kind of business?" I ask suspiciously. "Yours or mine?"

"Isn't it the same?"

I stop running, curious—more curious than our cats, as my mother says. "What is it?"

He laughs. "Patience, grasshopper. I'll have Carlisle run it by you."

I glance at his huge black dog, promptly sitting protectively at his side. I grin. "He likes his flea collar?"

He eyes the dog as if only now realizing he seems mighty comfortable with it. He smiles, then hooks his finger on the end of the collar. "Come on, Jack." He heads to the car. "Want a ride?"

"I'm fine, thanks."

Looking disappointed, he opens the door and hops in, and they drive away.

I stay, stretching for a little bit, and I can't seem to stop myself from replaying our conversations and grinning. Why do I keep running in this park? Why does *he* keep running in this park? Why is it suddenly important for me to know?

I knew I would be challenged in many ways when I took on the job, but I never imagined I'd become so fascinated not only with the aspects of campaigning, but with the candidate himself. He is a man who could, in less than a year, become our president. Knowledge about our country and a genuine understanding of how it works seeps from his pores.

I'm intensely curious to know more about his views, but it's Matt who makes me most curious of all.

On lunch break, I hear that the news of Matt asking Rhonda to change the schedule to accommodate a request of mine seems to have not sat too well with some of the other female aides.

"You know, he's never paid much attention to any of us." Martha flips her hair, obviously annoyed.

"Matt and Charlotte's families go back," Alison says as I walk in.

"Oh?" She turns wide, questioning eyes my way.

"A little," I hedge.

"Ah, so that's why." She seems relieved.

The energy in the room seems to shift, and all the attention flees from my way over to the door.

My eyes flick over to Matt when he stops by the small cafeteria section to pull out a bottle of water. He cracks it open, thoughtful as he looks at the group of women, then raises his head and sees me.

I smile and pass through the door and when my shoulder brushes his, my skin crackles heatedly.

Absently I brush my hand down my arm as I go back to my desk.

I'm going through my pile of letters when Carlisle stops by my desk.

"Matt wants you to be his new scheduler," Carlisle says.

I start in surprise. "Me?"

"You'll need to be open to traveling; we'll be visiting all fifty states. It's a good idea for there to be only one scheduler or else a ton of mix-ups can arise. Trust me—not fun to have

something in New Hampshire an hour before you have something in San Francisco."

I gape at him.

"Let's run down what's expected of you for the following
months," Carlisle begins.

I'm briefed in a six-by-six room on my duties as political
scheduler.

"As our one and only scheduler, you're to oversee Matt's
agenda for the entire campaign. You'll have political aides and
advance teams to organize, you'll book his gym workouts,
make sure the planes and buses are all stocked with essentials,
organize the rallies and his every social and personal engagement for the rest of the year. We need a good balance among
all his engagements. Do you think you can do that?"

My head is spinning, but I force myself to reply. "I ... if
Matt thinks I can, then I can," I say bravely.

He shoots me a dire look. "Just to be clear, a scheduling
mistake could cost us the whole campaign. Every minute and
second must be accounted for. His father's scheduler remained
at headquarters during his campaign, but Matt wants a more
hands-on approach."

He seems concerned about my ability to do the job, so I
nod more firmly than necessary.

"Rhonda will be on press coordination, but she can help if
you get stuck in any part of the process; she'll fill you in on
any questions you might have."

Matt comes in to see Carlisle, and when my arm brushes
his as I pass through the door, my skin crackles heatedly.

I'm smoothing fingers over the tingling skin of my upper
arm as I head to my table when Carlisle's assistant approaches.

"Charlotte—" She points in the direction of the floor where Matt has his office. "You'll be over here now, outside Matt's office."

I swallow, then start gathering my personal things, more determined than ever to make a difference and prove to myself that I *can*.

WARNING

Charlotte

I t's my first day as his official scheduler when I arrive at campaign headquarters the following Monday, step off the elevator, and immediately get to work.

I'm determined to impress and be as kick-ass as everyone on Team Hamilton is proving to be. Especially now that I'm his scheduler; there's only *one* of me.

I'm trying to get into the meat of Matt's most pressing things-to-do when Rhonda appears.

"How are we doing?" she asks me as she approaches.

"Great!" I grin, then spread out a few pages with scattered itineraries—it takes work to really oversee Matt's schedule, not only because it's his, but because it involves so many people. "I'm a bit concerned I'm losing some valuable time with the times it takes for the team to arrive by bus—I wonder if I shouldn't make use of that time somehow for Matt."

Rhonda drags a chair over and looks at the pages. Matt doesn't want to plaster slogans across every town and city in the continental United States; he's doing aggressive online campaigns with both personal opinions and proposed solutions. But even with the online campaign, his schedule is killer.

It could literally kill a man that wasn't as energetic as this one is.

I can't imagine either President Jacobs or Gordon Thompson, the Republican front-runner, both much older and much less athletic, enduring it.

As the main scheduler and as we embark on the touring of the country, I'll be working in the field now. Rather than being cooped up in headquarters, I will be out *there*, overseeing all the local field campaign aides, ensuring everything runs smoothly on every location and engagement Matt is in.

Rhonda has made it repeatedly clear that my job is to manage both Matt's personal and professional schedules, and not only that, but I'm to manage the advance teams that will arrive at each location before Matt does to make sure everything is as it should be. She tells me that a good flow of scheduling is paramount for the most effective campaigning. That I need to focus on Matt's personal time first and foremost, then shoot for a balance between events aimed at high schools, veterans, industrials, the average working man. I am to include all minorities, and definitely women and young people, who seem to be his most devoted fans. To this list, after talking it over with the managers, I'm adding hospitals and hospices in the mix as well.

"He needs time to run every day. Every single day, be sure to give him an hour's run and at least a half hour to shower and prep for the day. Trust me, he's on the ball and so much sharper when he's started his day with that. Add a night off during the weekends so he can see his friends and family or simply have time on his own," she said when she first explained this to me.

"Just one night off?" I'm appalled to think he's working so much.

"Only one—that came from Matt himself," Rhonda assured me, but she looked as wide-eyed and concerned as I did.

Now we sit here as we jointly create his first active campaigning schedule, one where he'll be traveling extensively.

As Gordon Thompson and Harold Jacobs are throwing themselves full-fledged into their campaigns, so are we. Our first states to visit are states known to be primarily red or blue, which means Texas for primarily Republican and California for primarily Democratic.

"Charlotte, there's been talk."

I lift my head. "Excuse me?"

"Some of the aides." She signals out the door. "They talk about Matt paying more attention to you. Alison has appeased them that you're childhood friends, but I'd still like to give you some friendly advice."

I feel so shocked and uncomfortable at the thought of anyone assuming anything outrageous that I'm mute, unblinking as I meet Rhonda's friendly but concerned gray gaze.

"Don't," she says quietly, holding my stare.

She shakes her head, glancing down at the itinerary, slashing a big red line over one event and adding a big red arrow for us to move it to the next day.

"Matt is unshakable right now where he stands." She looks at me again. "He owns the heart of every American simply because we all watched him lose his father the way he did, keep his mother on her feet, and remain pretty down-to-earth and humble despite him being one of the most famous men in the world. Any dirt the parties want to dig up on him, there's nothing Carlisle hasn't studied and can easily counter-attack."

My eyes widen. "You're not implying …"

"Charlotte, I'm fifty-five, married twice, with three children," she says, smiling a bit like my mother did when Matt and his father, the president, came over for dinner and she told me Matt was handsome. "If you believe in him being the solution we're looking for—"

"I do!" I say vehemently, dragging the schedule over to my side and frowning down at it, trying hard to concentrate on it again.

"Then keep it professional. You'll be spending a lot of time together."

I think of the things I think about when I curl up alone in my apartment and a warmth of guilt creeps up my cheeks, but I stare down at the schedule and try to regain my focus.

Once Rhonda and I finally wrap up the beginning campaign schedule, she claps her hands.

"Guess we're done here. You'll make sure he gets a copy?"

"Of course."

She dons her coat and we say goodbye as she heads to her new office and I head out of mine and toward Matt's.

As I approach, I hear the whispers of Carlisle telling Matt, "We should be unearthing the dirt on Jacobs … He made many mistakes during his administration … and don't get me started on Gordon."

"We're running a clean campaign—and we're playing defense. No attacks unless we're personally attacked—we counterattack. Then and only then."

"Matt, these two are specialists at attacking. That's the way elections are won. You make people afraid, and then you shine the light and don the hat of their savior. Personally, I think Jacobs has let the economy go to shit just so he can come up with a shining plan to save it. As for Gordon—hell, he will throw out everything wrong with you, starting with the fact that you didn't serve in the military."

"Neither did he."

"But he'll be the one to say it."

"And make it easier to point out that I was doing other things that my father, the president, had asked me to. He wanted me to learn to be a leader—hell, Benton, it bugs the shit out of me he didn't let me serve and you know it."

"Gordon will rub it in. Jacobs will keep on the First Lady issue ..."

"Really, if that's what we have to be afraid of ..." Matt lets out a low, self-assured chuckle.

Carlisle sighs. "You have a bit of a sense of humor, which makes you approachable but, god, your stubbornness, Matt."

I knock on the door.

Matt lifts his head, waves me in, and suddenly he is watching every step I take into the room.

I set the folder on his desk and as I slowly leave the room, I hear Carlisle insist, "We need more slogans, Matt. People need to know what you bring to the table."

"I bring me."

Carlisle sighs.

"Carlisle. For years the public has come to believe every promise made by every candidate has been pure bullshit. Nobody believes in them anymore. Politics have been totally tainted by propaganda. It wasn't like this in the beginning,

Carlisle. There weren't slogan campaigns; hell, until Andrew Jackson, not even slandering campaigns. I serve my country."

"Speaking of. Our opponents are barely underway with primaries and they're already attacking the streets with propaganda."

Matt listens attentively, then says, "We're in modern times, Carlisle. The internet works. Hamilton is tree-friendly." He angles his head. "Charlotte." Matt raises his voice as he calls my name when I step outside.

I peer back in.

"You can save more trees as the president," Carlisle mumbles as Matt waves me forward. I'm tempted to tell Carlisle that I do like Matt's different approaches.

Political figures are loved and hated across the world. They've come to be seen as necessary evils. But it wasn't that way with Washington. He's the only president who received every single vote—he was a champion, a leader, not a "necessary evil." There was no propaganda, no marketing campaign, no bullshit slogans. Matt is not a politician, and I think it makes a difference. He gives no practiced speeches. He doesn't even look 100 percent polished. He prefers sweaters and slacks and button-down shirts when he goes out in public. He looks steady, which is what the country wants, a little bit rebellious, which is what the country needs, and different, the embodiment of the change we crave.

But I keep my thoughts to myself.

Carlisle exits and Matt steeples his fingers, nodding in the direction of the now empty doorway. "What do you think?"

"I … about what Carlisle says?"

He nods, that infuriatingly adorable dancing sparkle appearing in his eyes.

I smile privately. "I do think you're stubborn," I admit, scrunching my nose playfully at him.

"Is that all?"

I shrug mysteriously.

But no, that's not all at all!

He has good judgment, drive, and discipline.

When the character debates come up later in the game, Gordon has had four wives, President Jacobs lets his wife rule the country for him, and Matt, on the other hand, is a very balanced man. He listens to opinions of people he respects and whose intelligence matches his own, but ultimately he makes his own choice.

We've raised hundreds of millions of dollars for his campaign, most of the funds coming from small donations from average Americans ready for a change. The technological infrastructure we've set up at headquarters in order to reach the three-hundred-plus million Americans through the net is unprecedented until this election. But people's interests have never been harder to pique than in the days that we live in now.

"I think going heavy on the internet can get you a lot of traction with the young voters," I finally say, "and if you can figure out a way to get them interested in your most exciting plans with each alphabet letter, it could really stick."

He rubs his chin with the tips of his two index fingers, makes a *hmm* sound, and frowns thoughtfully. "*C* is for Charlotte."

"*J* is for junk food in cafeterias, which must be stopped at once."

He laughs.

I signal at his schedule. "Here's the schedule for the months of April, and May. Since things get very heavy in late April, I thought I might include a free weekend for you to re-charge."

"That's thoughtful of you." He slips on his glasses and scans it.

"Yeah, well, I'm a thoughtful gal," I say.

I turn away and glance out the window, because something about the times he slips on his glasses always gets to me.

"A thoughtful gal who somehow manages to make me think of her a lot." I turn my attention back to him in surprise as he looks up at me over the rims.

My heart thuds.

He sets the schedule down and pries the glasses off, folding them and setting them over the schedule, his eyes fixed on me.

A silence settles in the room, making me aware of how disquieted I am on the inside.

"Why did you want me to be your new scheduler?" I ask quietly.

He leans back with a sardonic smile that quickly turns admiring. "Because I believe you have a good head on your shoulders, you're dedicated and smart, and anyway"—he grins even wider—"I thought you were a tad too soft to keep answering those phone calls and letters."

"I am so not soft!"

"*P* is for pudding."

"So not pudding, Matt!" I narrow my eyes and lean one hand on his desk. "You wanted me to keep an eye out for letters like that one little Matt sent."

"And I know you still are."

I scowl. "How do you know me so well? Hmm?"

He spreads out his arms and crosses them behind his head. "Some say I'm a perceptive man."

"I disagree. You failed to see how stone-hearted I am, able to read your letters, day after day. How hard I can be. *H* is for heart of stone."

He laughs. It's so nice to hear him laugh. "No, Charlotte, it's optimally just one word per letter, so that'd make you just all heart."

I shake my head, frowning. "I can show you my hardheartedness in your next schedule I draft."

"Be my guest—I thrive under pressure."

"Good for you, 'cause I'm bringing it."

"You always do."

His gaze slides past my shoulder at the sound of a soft knock. Alison is at the door, watching us, narrowed-eyed. "Matt, the pictures you asked for."

She walks in as I excuse myself and leave, but soon Alison catches up with me. "Were you just flirting with Matt?"

"What? No! We were having a discussion."

"You were *discussing* with Matt?"

"I ... no!" I flush and head to my desk, sit down, and lift my head to glance past his office window, where he's wearing those sexy glasses of his, reading, a hand over his mouth as if to cover his smile.

EYES

Charlotte

I called Children's National and told Carlisle about Matt's visit so he could alert the press coordinator and everyone who needed to be involved.

"You're coming with me," Matt says before he leaves.

"Me?"

"It was your idea."

I groan inwardly. Spending more time with Matt is the last thing I need right now. But I do love seeing him in action, so I hurry to slip into my sweater and follow him outside. When we reach the hospital, there's a small crowd, waving placards and chanting.

"*Matt!*" one of the younger female crowd members breathlessly gasps out his name.

"*Matt Hamilton!*" her friend calls, louder, cupping her hands around her mouth so that her voice carries over.

He thanks them, then waits for me to go in along with Wilson. Little Matt is wearing a Redskins T-shirt, a matching cap, and an IV.

The way his eyes light up when his hero enters the room makes my chest tighten. I turn away and try to regroup when I hear Matt's voice.

"Heard there was a tiger in the building. I had to come see."

"Where?!" the boy asks excitedly.

"I'm looking right at him."

When I turn back around, Matt is chucking the boy's cap, smiling down at him.

The boy grins. "Wow. You came."

Matt pulls up a chair to sit next to him in bed. "Charlotte—the lady you see by the door—seems to be as big a fan of yours as you are of me."

"Wow," he says.

Soon they get a crowd. Little Matt tells Matt he wants to be a football player when he grows up. The parents approach me and begin telling me how grateful they are as Matt and little Matt chat.

"If you win you'll invite me to the White House—" tiny Matt says.

"Not IF, WHEN … you're coming to the White House," Matt promises.

He plays chess with the bedridden boy. The nurses start to line up out in the hall, grinning and ogling.

It's not the fact that he's doing this, it's the fact that you can tell he's genuinely having fun that touches me. I believed in him: Hamilton and all that the name represents. But right now if I'd never seen him and had a stupid little crush on him, if he'd never been raised under the spotlight and with the fame of his name, it's today that Matt—for all the flaws the media tries to exaggerate—wins my vote.

When we leave, Wilson picks us up at the curb.

Matt is quiet.

I am too.

"Thank you." His voice is low and sounds achingly honest.

"Makes me sad." My own voice cracks, so I stop talking.

I glance out the window and try to regroup. He seems to realize he's out of his element with a nearly weeping female in the car. "Let's go get you some food."

"No."

He frowns, then his eyes gleam in confusion and amusement. "You're too warm for politics, Charlotte. We need to toughen you up."

"Take me sword fighting, but not eating. I'm not hungry right now." I sigh and shoot him a sidelong glance. "It's your fault."

"Pardon?"

"I wouldn't be in politics if you hadn't run."

"Says the lady who offered to help me when she was what? Seven."

I arch my brows. "Eleven." I thrust my chin out. "I can still vote for Gordon."

"God, no. No," he says emphatically. He laughs and runs his hand in frustration over his hair.

"Well, someone needs to knock you down a peg. Gordon Thompson has my vote," I declare.

"You wound me, Charlotte," he says.

"Oh you look so wounded, haha."

He looks deathly sober except for his eyes, laughing at me. "My wounds run deep."

"How deep? This deep?" I hold my fingers a hair's breadth apart. He frowns, then takes them to readjust them to a centimeter. "This deep."

I should laugh.

It was funny up until he touched me.

Now it's warm and gooey and he's looking at me with a frozen smile and intent eyes.

I see a flash of yearning in his eyes—yearning as deep as I feel, truly deep, not measured in tiny fractions.

I laugh, finally, as I try to stifle the sensations shooting through me. "Wow." I look at the centimeter. "A centimeter. That's deep."

I refer to the space between his fingers, but I don't know what we're talking about anymore.

"I told you." He smirks. He lowers his hands, and I can't help but notice how strong and long-fingered they are as he drops them to his side.

Every living woman in America has probably had fantasies about Matt.

And I have him close enough that my senses swirl.

I remain affected throughout our ride.

My mind rushes, wondering … simply wondering.

Matt checks some emails, his thigh touching mine.

He doesn't move it away.

I wonder if I want to move it away.

No. I'm out of air and burning inside. And I don't want to.

I have to remind myself that what I'm doing here is so much more valuable than a silly little crush. What I'm doing here transcends beyond me … beyond even Matt.

Not only has campaigning been exciting, but hearing about Matt's views and ideas keeps renewing my hope.

I hadn't fully realized how much we missed a strong leader, an inspiring leader, until every time I stare at the one I want.

He could make such a difference. A man like him could make *such* a difference.

So we ride like this, in silent tension, my mind full of Matt and my body empty.

His eyes meet mine, burning with importance. "I want you to be my eyes and my heart, to keep me in touch with the real people out there, the ones my whole life I've never gotten to meet."

"Okay, Matt," I say.

And then he leans over, and I catch my breath and close my eyes when his lips brush my cheek—and he kisses me there. It's as brief a kiss as the one he gave me when I was eleven, but I'm a woman now, and he is all man, and suddenly, unexpectedly, his arm starts coming around my waist and he's reeling me toward him, pressing me against his side.

Next thing, I feel his head dip down slowly toward me, his nose grazing my cheek. My breath catches in my throat, and I feel myself fighting the urge to turn my head just a fraction of an inch and kiss him flat on the mouth.

He smells like mint and a little bit of coffee mixed with his cologne. I inhale shakily and feel his lips touch the spot on my cheek where his nose had just been. His lips are warm, soft, yet firm.

His hand grips my hip, holding me close to him, as he tilts his head and places a kiss on my neck. I let my head fall back, and he chuckles darkly, rubbing his nose lightly against my neck, nuzzling me.

He uses his hand to turn my head to face him, and as I look into his eyes, I feel my world tilt on its axis and spin in all directions.

Everything else is drowned out as all of the thoughts in my head center around only him, and me.

All I'm thinking is what I'm feeling. How hard my heart is beating. How my breath is coming in faster intervals. How my skin is warm and tingling; how my whole body seems to be holding its breath in sweet anticipation for Matthew to move again, to touch me again, to kiss another part of me.

I whisper his name and he groans, "You feel incredible."

He leans in and kisses my collarbone, running his nose along my neck and inhaling me.

"God, and you smell so good ..." he brokenly whispers. His deep voice burning through me, consuming everything in its path and leaving only this deep, almost primal need to be as close to this man as possible.

When I feel his tongue between his lips tentatively touch the skin on my neck, I hear myself moan.

He holds me closer to him, until I'm almost sitting on his lap, his head buried in my neck, kissing and nuzzling, licking and tasting.

I start to get worried, wondering where we are and when we will get to the campaign headquarters. I know no one can see us, since his car has black-tinted windows and a partition separating us from his driver, but still, something about this feels dark and forbidden.

"I—"

"Shhh ... just let me do this, Charlotte. Please," he says as he lifts his head from my neck and holds my head between his hands, his eyes gazing into mine and then lowering to my lips, and then traveling back up to my eyes.

I feel him inch closer to me, and I slowly start to realize that he wants to kiss me. Right now. In this car.

Matthew Hamilton, possible future President of the United States and my first crush, wants to kiss me.

I reach out and hold his face in my hand too, and his eyes flare.

I don't know whether I should do this or not, but right now all I hear my body say is that I need to touch this man.

I kiss his cheek, my lips lingering.

I feel him relax, but his grip on me tightens.

What are we doing?

"Sir, we're here," Matt's detail's mumbled voice sounds through the partition.

I think I hear Matt curse under his breath. I inch myself off his lap to sit back in my own seat, and inhale a shaky breath as Matt opens his own door and comes around the car to open mine.

The look we exchange when we lock eyes as I come out of the car I cannot possibly describe. It's charged with need, lust, longing, curiosity, and something else …

I force myself to look away and walk toward the building, the feel of his lips still on my skin.

GETS LONELY
AT THE TOP

Matt

That was me being a whole lot reckless and foolish.

I've been thinking of red hair, blue eyes, soft lips, and how much I wanted to dip in my tongue and taste her. I wanted to open her mouth and kiss her, slow and savoring, then fast and wild. At this point, only both can satiate me.

I thought that following that one impulse after the hospital would be enough to calm the fire burning me …

It's not.

She's been in my head for the past eighteen hours.

I'm running on no sleep. I need a good workout or my focus scatters, but my schedule couldn't allow one today. My grandfather flew in from Virginia after the resounding success of our first two months of campaigning, and my mother—who'd opted to quietly ignore the fact that I'm running—had no other choice but to welcome us for breakfast this morning.

I'm aware of early campaign troubles. Among them, my grandfather.

My grandfather was the tireless political engine that drove my father to the army, to the Senate, and later, to the White House. He pulled strings left and right and put my dad on

George Washington's white horse, but it was my dad who rode the horse like he owned it. The one who'd won the reelection by the biggest margin in history, keeping almost 70 percent of the country happy when polled about his first term. My grand-dad got him there, but my dad stayed there.

I don't want my grandfather's political engine to back me now—it would require sacrificing merit for favors during the appointment of my cabinet. That's a sure way to keep the country from growing and blazing brighter than ever, and that's what has been keeping us from irrefutably being the most powerful force in the world.

Habits need to be put aside, new ideas proposed, new blood brought in to freshen up the antiquated outlook on how to run America.

The world is changing, and we need to be on the forefront of that change.

My grandfather has made it no secret that he wants me on the forefront … but of one of the parties. Who like to keep the status quo.

I'm the last to arrive at my mother's brownstone.

My mother sits in a high chair, regal in pearls and a white designer skirt and jacket. She's a modern Jackie Kennedy, sweet and composed, morally as strong as titanium. There are strong resemblances between our families, the Kennedys and Hamiltons. To the point where the media has speculated, after Father's murder, on whether the Hamiltons also have a curse on their heads that won't let them carry out their bright desti-nies.

Mother sits as far away from my grandfather as possible, her hair still the same near-black shade as mine, her poise re-markable.

Big, brusque, and no-nonsense, Patrick Hamilton's relationship with my father was a close one. Until my father was gone, my grandfather meddled and insisted I get into politics. The last thing my mother wanted was to see me do that.

"Get a life, Matt. Go and study anything you want, be anything you want." *Except a politician.* She didn't say it, but she didn't have to. In her mind, she wouldn't be a widow, but instead a happy wife had my father not been president. In her mind, she'd have lived a happy life. She led one of duty instead, and she did it formidably, but no makeup and hairstyle can hide the shadows in her eyes regarding my father's unresolved murder.

I kiss her forehead in greeting. "I'm sorry this is making you worry. Don't," I command.

She smiles lightly at me and pats my jaw. "Matt."

Only one word, but combined with the look in her eyes, I'm quietly reminded that my father was one of five sitting presidents to be killed—all by gunshots. Lincoln, Garfield, McKinley, JFK, and Hamilton.

I take a seat in the living room and she signals for Maria, her live-in cook, to bring us coffee.

"I had lunch with the Democrats," Grandfather says as he sips his coffee. "They want you joining the primaries; they're sure you'll win the ticket."

"I've already told them, I'm running independently."

"Matt, your father—"

"I'm not my father. Though I do plan to continue his legacy." I glance at my mother, who seems to be battling a mixture of pride and worry.

"Why won't you at least consider the Democrats?" Grandfather insists.

"Because"—I lean forward, looking him dead in the eye—"they failed to protect him. As far as I'm concerned, I'm better off alone." I stare him out. He's not an easy man—but I can be as difficult as he is. "My father told me never trust your own shadow. I've kept people at bay, but now I'm choosing who I let in. And out. Out is my competition. I'm letting in my country. They deserve better than what they've gotten lately. I'm going to pave the path for that better."

"Fuck, Matt, really!" Grandfather rants.

His temper is formidable, and my mother quickly steps in with her usual soothing charm.

"Patrick, I appreciate you voicing your opinions to Matt, but I'm not happy with him even running. Matt"—she turns and looks at me beseechingly—"we gave this country all we had; we gave them your father. We don't owe anyone anything anymore."

"Not all we had. There's still Matt," Grandfather says. "This is what Lawrence wanted."

I keep my attention on my mother. I know this is her worst nightmare. She doesn't want me to run. "I'm finishing what Father started—this is our legacy. All right?" I nod firmly, quietly asking for her understanding.

She's not over what happened to my father.

She shakes her head with her signature stubbornness. "You're still so young, Matt—you're only thirty-five."

"Yeah, well, *my* thirty-five years count as double." I smile wryly and lean back in my seat, glancing at my grandfather. "I was closer to my dad than the vice president for a term and a half. I'm doing this, and when I get to the top, my cabinet will be appointed on merit, not political favors we owe."

"Goddamnit, boy, you have a will of your own, but you need to look at the big picture here. The parties' resources *cannot* be denied."

"I'm not denying them. I simply trust that I have resources of my own to combat them."

Grandfather sighs. He stands and buttons his jacket, then kisses my mother on the cheek. "Thanks, Eleanor." He looks at me as I come to full height too. "You're making powerful enemies, Matt."

"I'll be an even more powerful one."

He laughs and shakes his head in disbelief, then pats my back and says, "I'll support you then." Grudging and grumpy, he leaves, and my mother sighs.

I stare after him. His words hit a bull's-eye, though not the target my grandfather had aimed for.

All of this effort, the dream I'm pursuing ... I've been determined to do it alone. I saw what my father's neglect did to my mother. I experienced firsthand what it did to me. I wouldn't want to wish it on someone I cared for.

But a redheaded, blue-eyed scheduler with a gentle heart and true love for her country keeps hammering in my head. For the first time, I wonder what it would be like to reach the heights I aspire to with someone by my side.

"Matt." My mother presses her lips together as she wages an inner battle, the mother's battle between supporting her son and protecting him. "You want to use the White House to change the world, and I'll support you." She walks over to me and pulls me into her arms to speak in my ear. "But it changes *you* before you can change a centimeter of *it*," she says sadly, kissing my cheek.

I drag my hand over my face in frustration as I watch her head upstairs. She's a strong woman, but even strength breaks. When Father won, she went from private citizen to public and handled it with grace and style.

The country never saw her quiet suffering as she slowly lost my father to his job—and then to two bullets, one to his stomach and the other to his heart.

Yeah, the White House changed us all.

But what happens in the White House is reflected across the entire nation, and I'm determined to change things for the better.

I still have a busy day ahead when I step outside and climb aboard the black Lincoln that Wilson has parked by the front door.

I ride in silence toward my first speaking engagement of the day. In my mind, Charlotte is gasping as I slide my lips across her cheek and toward hers. She's holding her breath as I press softly, testing her, nearly losing control when I realize she wants it.

She wants it as much as *me.*

I push the thought aside as the car stops, and I step out into the crowd.

"Matt!" I hear my name surround me, and I start shaking hands on both sides of the people flanking me, as many as possible on my path to the main building, thanking them for coming.

COFFEE

Charlotte

'm nervous the next day after what happened in the car between Matt and me. I'm at the kitchenette, sort of wondering if I should go and take him coffee. Maybe because I want to talk about it, to know why he kissed me. Or maybe because I want to see him.

Before I can think better of it, I pour two cups—remembering the time he brought coffee to my desk the night we both stayed in late. I set mine on my desk on the same spot he did, then head to his office and peer past the opening.

"Can I come in?"

Matt was looking over some paperwork and when he lifts his eyes to look at me above the rims of his glasses, my heart trips a little. He nods permission, and I start when I spot Jack getting to his feet from where he was lying by Matt's desk.

"Hi, Jack," I say awkwardly. "I brought you coffee," I then tell Matt as he comes to his feet.

As I hand him the warm cup, the dog races toward Matt and jumps up, desperately trying to lick the coffee mug, accidentally spilling its entire contents over Matt's shirt.

"Jack, down!" The dog immediately sits, but the coffee is already soaking into the shirt. "Coffee's his weakness."

"That's definitely something *you* can't relate to. How does it feel to live a life without vices?" I ask.

He winks at me as he crosses the room to shut the door. As he passes, he gives me a heated once-over, and says, close to my ear, "I wouldn't be so sure about that."

My stomach feels like he just lit it on fire with the combination of his words and the look in his eyes as he raises his hands and starts unbuttoning his shirt.

Suddenly I'm staring at an expanse of bare chest.

He's so hot I can barely breathe.

Though it's a well-published fact that Matt Hamilton looks amazing in clothes, *amazing* cannot even capture the complete athletic perfection of his shape and form and muscles. Every single muscle of his chest is defined and flexed hard. He's also got silky dark hairs on his chest—and I find this so hot that liquid heat seems to flood between my legs.

Something warm and female starts flickering in my tummy as I stare helplessly at him.

"Hand me that campaign T-shirt?" he asks.

I glance at the shelves behind me. I reach over for a white T-shirt with a purple Hamilton '16 logo. It's like a sports jersey.

I hand it over, trying hard not to notice how his slacks accentuate his lean hips, how his broad shoulders taper down inverted-pyramid style to a narrow waist, and how those freaking abs make me want to trace each square with my fingertips. And those incredible arms, the bulging biceps as he lifts the shirt over his head.

"I like it." I point nervously at the T-shirt.

"I wanted someone to test it out. Guess I found him."

He pulls it over his head, and I swallow. *Oh god.*

I can't stop flushing.

He tosses the stained shirt aside and runs his fingers through his hair. Jack has stealthily gotten up from his ass and is licking the coffee at my feet.

"Oh no, Jack." I kneel and try to stop him. Matt comes to grab him by the collar and leads him away.

"Well, I don't think he'll be getting any sleep," I say, by way of apology.

"That makes two of us."

I watch him smile down at his dog and run his hand over his head even as he frowns at him for being mischievous. "You never sleep, do you?" I blurt out.

He lifts his gaze. "Got a lot on my mind. I'm lucky if I grab a few straight hours." I watch him grab his sodden shirt and drape it over the back of his chair.

"I could wash that for you, Matt," I say. It just sort of slipped out, but I'm mortified a second after I hear myself say it.

Matt glances at the shirt.

"I mean ... unless you have ... you probably have someone to do your laundry."

"Yeah. My dry cleaners." He laughs. I feel stupid as he leans over with the napkin I had brought to sop up the coffee, then balls it up and tosses it into the trash can. "But that's the most titillating proposition I've ever received from a woman."

"Really. It turns you on to get your clothes washed."

"I'm as surprised as you are."

I laugh, then I bite my lip and reach out for the shirt hanging on the back of his chair. His eyes are super hot. I steal out of the room with his shirt folded in my arm.

I don't sleep more than four hours either that night.

I can't stop thinking about him, and the fact that we were flirting and his eyes were hot and he is so very hot, and I'm not sure I like it.

I toss and turn, then leap out of bed early in the morning. I'm in the office before almost anyone. I set his clean shirt, perfectly folded, on his desk when he arrives—I know it's perfect because I tried folding it a bazillion times.

"Good morning, Matt."

I walk by, and he catches my fingers for a second as I pass. "Good morning, Charlotte."

THE TIDAL BASIN

Charlotte

That day after lunch, Matt stops by my cubicle, where Alison is showing me some pictures of him at an event that are making my toes curl.

"How's my month looking?" He looks at me, and somehow it feels as if "month" means a whole other thing, his gaze is *that* searing.

I swallow at the sight of him in a crisp business shirt and plain black pants. "Busy," I hasten to say.

I don't know how that tiny tilt of his lips can cause such a *big* tilt in my chest cavity. "Just the way I like it." He smiles at me, nods at Alison, and Alison quickly tucks the pictures against her chest and leaves.

Matt stays by the entrance for a moment. The area feels a tad smaller as he comes over, walks around my desk, and leans over my shoulder to look at my draft. "When am I free tonight?" he asks.

A shiver runs down my spine, hearing his voice so close.

I try to stop the skip of my heart as I skim down the page and tap my finger to show him.

"Perfect." He leans over a fraction more, to my ear. "I'll pick you up at six."

I don't ask him where we're going or why, I simply nod as he walks out.

I'm quaking with nervousness as I head home to change. I don't even know what to wear but opt for a skirt and a silky top. For some reason I keep changing shoes from ballerina flats to pumps, and the instinctive female urge to look feminine and a little sexy wins out. I suppose I'm not proud of this, but there you go. High-heeled peep-toe pumps it is.

At 6 p.m., Matt is downstairs waiting inside a black Lincoln Town Car, his detail, Wilson, opening the door for me. I'm a nervous wreck. The memory of his whisper keeps tingling down my spine, warm and exciting.

I climb into the back of the car, surprised to notice Matt is wearing black sweatpants and a black T-shirt. And running shoes.

His hair is perfect. He looks like some athletic centerfold for Nike.

As Wilson pulls us into traffic, I study my own attire—skirt and a blouse and heels—and finally ask, "We're running?"

Matt is staring at my shoes with a tilt to his lips, his eyes rising to mine. "More like some light hiking."

"I ..." Helplessly, I look at my three-inch heels. "These are going to be a problem," I say.

He just smiles at me, but he doesn't look especially heartbroken. "They are."

We ride in the back of the town car in silence, and I frown at him, wondering why he doesn't even seem concerned. Matt has never struck me as selfish.

"Wilson, stop to get Miss Wells a pair of running shoes."

"Wait. Matt!" I protest.

He grabs a white Nike cap from the back of the car and slips on a pair of Ray-Bans. "Two minutes, we're in and out," he tells Wilson as he climbs out and peers back inside. One eyebrow goes up in question. "You coming?"

Two minutes inside the shopping center end up being twenty.

I try on a pair of white-and-pink Nikes that I'd always salivated over, and when they fit just right, Matt glances at Wilson, and Wilson takes the box and goes to pay while Matt and I wait outside the store. People are glancing in his direction as if speculating but unsure, and Matt keeps his eye on his phone to avoid getting their attention.

When we're back in the car and he jerks off the cap and the sunglasses and sets them aside, I say, "I guess Hamiltons never get any privacy."

He smiles at me, but with a haunted look in his eyes. "Never."

We ride on.

He admits, "I've almost forgotten what it was like when it was simpler."

Simpler.

Like … taking a hike with me, I realize. *People are going to see.*

I'm anxious now.

"Turn the car around."

He swings his head, shocked. "Excuse me?"

"Turn the car around now, Matt."

He chuckles and drags a hand over his face, as if I exasperate him.

"Really. This ... can look a way that it's not. Tell him to turn around." I drag my eyes to Wilson, then look back at Matt.

"I can't." He shakes his head in bemusement.

"Why can't you?" I'm getting testy, and so is he.

"It's the only slot on my schedule open and my only chance to be alone with you for a while." He looks up at Wilson through the rearview mirror when the car stops and tells him, "See you at Jefferson Memorial in a couple of hours."

He opens the door for me, and I grab my notepad to keep it professional. His lips quirk when he sees that, but he says nothing as we start heading down the trail, which treks around a large body of blue water surrounded by a path that runs all around the basin's circumference. From here you can see the Washington Monument, the tall columns and majestic white dome of the Jefferson Memorial, and right up ahead, the spot where the first cherry blossom trees were planted.

It's spring, and the trees are fully bloomed, their long, slim limbs dotted with cherry blossoms.

It's a chilly day, but the sun warms my face as we walk toward the nearest memorial, which is only a few years old.

"I've never taken this walk before," I admit. I take in the huge marble carving of Martin Luther King Jr. "I've only been to this area once, really, when my father brought me to the paddle boats."

"Robert in the paddle boats? That I'd like to have seen." He seems amused at the thought as I absorb the thirty-foot-tall monument of a man whose favorite quote of mine is, "Darkness cannot drive out darkness; only light can do that. Hate cannot drive out hate; only love can do that."

I realize Matt is watching me, as if he knows the site by memory—but not the sight of me. My cheeks warm as I start walking down the trail by his side.

He glances at our feet, stops walking, and drops to his haunches to lace up my running shoes.

I'm breathless as he stands to his full intimidating height and jerks his head toward the white dome across the water. "See that?"

I look around, thinking he spotted some reporters. Call it paranoia.

"I don't see." I'm trying to figure out if anyone is recognizing him—a six-feet-plus, gorgeous-looking man, who's not looking? I quickly open my notepad and pretend to scribble something.

He laughs and turns my head to shift me around to face the water. The touch sends a frisson down my spine and I can't see straight. "Seriously? You think that little notebook makes a difference? People will see what they want to see. This is no different than our morning runs. Now look."

"At what?"

He laughs softly. "Stop talking and look."

Matt turns my face an inch higher over the water, and I *see*. How the monuments reflect in the water, the water doubling the effect of their beauty.

I stare at the white classical building across the water. "Oh."

And he's looking at me, at his finger on my chin.

"Take me," I say, then clear my throat when I see the male laughter in his eyes as I point at the Jefferson Memorial. "I mean, take me there. I've never been inside."

"That's the plan." He grins, obviously still just a guy with a guy's mind underneath the famous name.

We start forward, my body acutely aware of his moving beside mine.

We pass a Japanese stone pagoda and other memorials, until we reach the Jefferson Memorial.

We take the steps, walk past the tall white columns, and walk into the cavernous building until we're standing under a huge domed ceiling. Inscriptions cover the marble walls. Front and center, standing atop a large block of marble, is a massive nineteen-foot-tall monument to Jefferson, third president of the United States, one of our founding fathers.

We take a bench near one of the panels, one that quotes the Declaration of Independence.

I glance around the place. It's one of those memorials that's a little more difficult to access because there's no parking space outside. It feels as if it stands on its own island ... away from it all, but so close to the heart of the city at the same time.

"Do you always find far-off places to get away and think?" I ask Matt.

"I usually come alone."

The dark flecks in his eyes look a little blacker as he takes me under the warm yellow lights above us. There's a bright flame there, in his eyes.

"Except I find myself craving some alone time with you." His lips tilt in mischief.

His smile soon fades and shadows enter his eyes.

"It would be easier had I not run. During my father's terms at the White House, I used to dream about freedom. A thousand times, my father said I would be president. He told his friends, his friends' friends, and he often told me. I'd laugh and shake it off."

"He even told *me*," I say good-naturedly, and the warmth of his smile sends shivers through me.

He makes no effort to hide the fact that he's looking at me tenderly. "He did, didn't he?"

His eyes.

They just eat me up.

"I lost my father the day he decided that being president would be his legacy." His eyes are leveled on mine beneath his drawn eyebrows. "He tried juggling it all, but he couldn't do it. We kept thinking when it was over, he'd be ours again. He kept promising when it was over, he'd have time for us again."

I swallow a lump of emotion in my throat. I know what comes next.

"Never happened." The cold glint in his eyes sends a chill through me.

"It's been thousands of days since. Too many years spent living in the past. Too many years wondering why. Too many nights wanting things to be right in our country."

We're silent.

There's a tension emanating from him, pulsing around me, tempting me to draw my arms around him and simply crush him against me if that were even possible.

Matt glances at the statue and drags a hand across his jaw.

"Charlotte, I have enormous respect for you and your family. In so many ways, I feel responsible for you."

"Matt, you're not, you're not responsible for me—"

"I'm not supposed to want you," he says, cutting me off.

"What?" My eyes widen in disbelief.

What can I say when he looks at me in that way?

He's looking at me as if he's frustrated that he wants me.

Silence settles between us.

"I think of you. I think of you *too* often, if you ask me," he says.

I nervously tuck a loose strand of hair behind my ear and stare at my lap. "I think of you too."

My comment seems to come as no surprise. "So what are we going to do about it?" he asks softly.

"Nothing," I say.

He laughs, and drags a hand over his face and *tsk*s, shaking his head. "*Nothing*'s just not in my vocabulary. Is it risky? Yes. Is it selfish on my part? Maybe. But I'm not just going to do nothing."

I swallow. "Matt." I glance around nervously, trying to steer away from the path this conversation has taken. "Have you realized people could talk if anyone recognized us? Why did you bring me here?"

"Isn't it obvious? I knew you'd love it here."

I laugh. "I really do, you wicked man." I try to push at his chest teasingly, but he catches my wrist and pulls me closer, his eyes darker.

"I'm so wicked you have no idea."

He's looking at my mouth not as if he wants to kiss it.

Matt is staring at my mouth as if he means to devour it.

"You know you can't kiss me," I croak even as we now look at each other's lips.

He brushes his thumb over my lips. "I can kiss you. I definitely want to kiss you. I think we both know I mean to kiss you. Long and hard. I want my tongue rolling around yours, Charlotte, and I want your delicate little moans, too."

God help me. I'm pretty sure nothing could stop this man from getting anything he wants—nothing. Except maybe me.

Because Rhonda is right.

What we're doing together transcends me, transcends even him.

And even though I'm twenty-two, I know that getting Matt back into the White House will be the biggest thing I ever did.

"Except ... *C* is for campaigning. We can't do something foolish," I say, trying to brainwash myself that I don't want this just as much.

He smiles tenderly. "If you'd ask me right now, *C* is for Charlotte coming in my arms."

Shocked and breathless by his bluntness, I turn to stare blindly at the inscription of freedom on the wall across from me—of all of us having freedom. And yet I have never been more aware of not having the freedom to fall in love with this man.

"There won't be any of that," I say.

Matt slides his hand to stroke the top of mine, pausing and leaving it over mine when a group of teenagers shuffles into the cavern, and he tightens his jaw and remains silent as, fortunately, they don't glance our way.

I shift on the bench—an inch away from his touch—then turn back to Matt and narrow my eyes in exaggerated suspicion, wondering how many women have caught his interest. And how long it lasts. "Why aren't you married yet, anyway?"

"I'm waiting for her to grow up."

He's leaning forward now to recover the space I just put between us, his eyes dancing in a way that makes my heart thud a million miles an hour.

"Well," I fumble for a reply, "I suppose that's why you're a playboy—you've been practicing all this time, so your child bride can eventually enjoy your expertise ..."

"She will definitely enjoy it." He nods in mock somberness.

"Okay," I say flippantly. As if my stomach isn't flipping and I'm not clenching my thighs together in my seat.

Matt's eyebrow quirks. "You don't believe me?"

"Oh, I don't want a sample. Thank you. Besides. You can't take a woman like me."

"Woman?" he scoffs. "You're what? Eighteen years old?" He leans back and stretches his arm out behind me, eyeing me.

"Eighteen to your fifty!" I shoot back.

He's leaning forward again, his shoulder touching mine, and the teasing in his eyes has become more dangerous and exciting, a little more challenging.

"One day I'll do all the things I need to. And she'll be mine. Mark my words."

"Does she know this yet?" I ask, quietly.

"I just told her," he says.

His voice is thick and low, but his eyes are still alight with mischief.

"Maybe ... maybe she's already yours."

"Is she?"

"Just a little bit," I say, lifting my thumb and index finger to draw a centimeter.

He glances at my fingers, then at me.

"I'm not a man that is satisfied with just a little bit." He smiles.

"That's all she's got."

He shakes his head. "She can do better. Much better."

The teenagers shuffle out of the memorial, and Matt and I are left alone again.

He slides his hand to cup the back of my neck in a proprietary gesture, then he gazes into my eyes with such a possessive look that a million butterflies flutter in my stomach. A smile begins to tug at the corners of his mouth. "Come here, Charlotte," he softly commands.

I sort of freeze.

He said he doesn't mean to do nothing, and now I can see in his eyes he's got a whole lot of something in mind.

Matt's smile fades, and he grabs the back of my neck and pulls me closer, then he leans his forehead on mine, his eyes holding me spellbound. "They'll try to find dirt on me. Anything they can find. I don't want you to be on that list. You're better than three minutes on the evening news meant to attack my character."

"I might not be concerned about me if it didn't affect *you*," I breathe.

"I can handle their attacks. I don't want them laying them on you," he angrily lashes.

He scrapes his thumb across my lower lip.

Impulsively, I lick the pad of his finger.

For one heartbeat, his eyes streak with need. Then he gingerly tips up my face as he lowers his to bring our eyes to the same level. First he nuzzles my nose and strokes his thumb again across my lower lip. He presses gently down on my lip to open my mouth. My eyes drift shut. Every thought in my head scatters to nothing when he swoops down and takes my mouth with his.

Everything falls away.

He kisses me gently the first second, and then without apology, deeply, like the revving of a rocket engine, followed by the launch into space, and then I'm in a galaxy of pure bright stars and endless night, lost and weightless, warmed by a sun I cannot see, his mouth a hungry vortex, a delicious black hole, sucking me in.

He holds my face in one hand, doing the most wicked things to my tongue until he tears his lips away, glancing at my mouth.

He looks at my kissed lips as he slips his hand beneath my skirt, touching the bare skin on the inside of my thigh. His fingertip touches me over my underwear—trailing a feather-like path across my wet sex.

It's a ghost touch—barely there, but it causes a shudder to run through me.

I moan, and his forehead hovers above mine as we both pant and brush our lips across the other's. Matt licks my bottom lip, then inside my mouth before he retreats.

He sets his face on mine and smells my neck. He groans again and kisses me, tongue plunging heatedly inside. Pulling back seconds later.

"Are you torturing me?" I gasp, so aroused my whole body is shaking.

He's breathing hard, his chest expanding with each breath. "If I'm torturing you, then what I'm doing to myself has no name."

"You're unobtainable, Matt." I look at his *GQ*-cover face. "Matt Hamilton. You're so unobtainable you're like a poster, something I can look at but not touch."

A dark look settles in his gaze as he leans forward again.

I'm thoughtless, mindless as he presses his lips to mine. A kiss with just one flick of his tongue. So perfect and so right, I forget that it's wrong. I inhale, and he inhales me through his mouth.

I groan his name this time.

"Matt."

It cannot work. It won't work. The scandal it would cause, the way it would ruin everything that he—that we—are so methodically working for.

"I'll find a way to get you alone with me. I want to spend time with you. I want to feel more of you," he rasps, kissing my earlobe, his breath hot and haggard on my skin as he lets his fingers trail up and down my thigh, beneath my skirt.

His fingers sweep across my panties again—eliciting another mewl from my lips.

"I'd like that," I moan when he rubs my nub a little.

He looks down at me with primal possessiveness, watching me catch my breath and moan as he rubs harder, when a new group of people walk into the monument.

He clenches his jaw, then smoothly pulls his hand away. I breathe, "Is this a mistake?"

"It won't be." His voice is firm. Eyes flashing and determined as he lifts his head to scan the crowd. "Let's go," he says gently, taking my elbow and guiding me.

We head back to the car in silence—his hand on the small of my back as he guides me into the backseat. His touch searing—reminding me of where else his fingers have just been.

Matt

I usher Charlotte into the car, and Wilson shoots me a look through the rearview mirror when we settle in. I shoot one back that tells him to save it.

I close the partition between us, and my gaze lands on Charlotte.

She sits quietly in the back of the car, and I can't fucking shake off the taste of her in my mouth. My heart is kicking into my rib cage, my body wound up with desire. The feel of the damp spot I caressed between her legs is seared on my fingertips.

I might excel at being in control and I may feel protective of her, but I'm a man. I have instincts; I have needs. And those needs have been building up, every day looking at her, every night thinking of her, and right now I just damn well need her. I want to taste her mouth again. I want to taste every inch of her until we both drown in pleasure and then, I want to do it all over again.

I study her lovely profile and god, she's so beautiful.

"Should we forget what happened?" she asks, bringing her eyes to mine.

I smile, shaking my head no.

"No," I tell her, my voice thick.

I reach out and gently seize the back of her neck, pulling her to me, unable to resist crushing her lips beneath mine.

As I feel her sag, I rub my tongue along hers, coaxing her to let go as I use my other hand to run it up her side, around her waist and to her back, pulling her flush so her breasts are crushed against my chest and the only thing between me and feeling those lush little nipples is our clothes.

She's soft all over and god, she smells as good as she feels.

I groan at the thought of having her beneath me, wanton and wild. As things get heated and I've got her breast in one hand, her nipple puckered under my circling thumb, our panting breaths become audible in the back of the car and I kiss her lips, then go to town with the skin on her neck and jaw. I trail a path to the back of her ear, where she quivers and seems to go even crazier with desire.

We're both out of control, an urgency to our kisses, our movements, our need.

I slip my hand under her skirt and ease her panties aside, easing my middle finger through her opening. She jerks and her fingers sink into my shoulders, her breaths blasting out of her lips and into my mouth.

"I want you," I tell her, dipping my tongue into her mouth as I pull out my finger and insert it back in, feeling her shudder from the pleasure. "I mean to have you writhing in pleasure like this," I promise.

I ease back and look down at her, and Charlotte inhales sharply as I stroke my finger along the outside of her folds, now slick and wanting me.

I smile and rub the pad of my thumb of my other hand along her lower lip, pulling it apart from the top.

I groan when her breath catches, getting one last taste of her and one last feel of her sex clenching around my finger as I drive it inside.

I'm playing with fire and I don't care.

This girl does things to me, from the way her hair smells to the way she moves right now as I move my finger. I've never wanted to take a woman the way I want her.

When the car stops, I hold her small face between my hands, ease back, and lower my forehead to hers, my gaze hovering before hers as I look into her glazed, lust-filled eyes. "I'll find the right time for us. Let's keep our head in the game. For now," I rasp.

A quivering smile appears on her lips, then she gets out of the car and into her apartment building. I press the mic button.

"Wait until she's safely inside," I tell Wilson. "And don't even *say* it."

"I didn't say shit," Wilson says.

I laugh to myself, my eyes falling on her retreating back. My blood is boiling in my veins as I watch her disappear. I stick my finger into my mouth, suck her sweet and acid taste, and shut my eyes. I let my head drop back and stare at the roof of the car, exhaling heavily as I lower my hand.

Keep our head in the game, I said. Though she and I both know, it's a whole other game we're now playing.

When I get to my apartment, my best friend from college, Beckett, is at the door, clad in jeans and a turtleneck, with his usual preppy sweater draped around his neck.

"Well, hello, Romeo," he snickers.

I frown at the comment, open the door, and let him inside, tossing my keys and my wallet on the coffee table.

"Moody. I take it it's the redhead," Beckett says.

"What?" I turn round to face him, and Beckett seems taken aback by how fast he was able to bait me when usually ... I never take the bait.

"It's all over the news. You took her shoe shopping. How suave," Beckett explains, snickering on the last word.

What the ...

Charging across my living room, I turn on the television and spot the headline.

"Matt Hamilton shopping with mysterious redhead ..."

"Jesus." I throw the remote aside, punch my hand into a pillow, then I grab a beer and toss one to Beckett as I drop down on the couch. "This girl has me losing my mind." I drag my hand over my face, my molars gritted hard enough to break a lesser man's jaw.

"What's going on?"

"She's in my campaign. Senator Wells's daughter."

He sighs. "Matt, shit, man, you need to be careful."

"Hell, I know that. You think I don't?" I scrape my hand across my jaw, trying to loosen it, then I take a swig of my beer, drop my head back on the couch, and exhale. "I'm so wrapped up in this girl. With the tension of the election, and the fact that I see her every day, I'm going insane." I shake my head.

It was reckless—and it didn't matter. Nothing mattered but feeding this wild thirst. Getting rid of that fucking feeling of having my hands tied. Quenching the hunger to touch her, fully knowing that she wanted it, craved it like me.

I not only want this girl, I enjoy being with her.

Growing up the way I did, it feels like a thousand and one expectations are piled on me, one after the other. It can be isolating when people put you up on a pedestal.

It wears on you, having to be the bigger man all the time, to always live up to the Hamilton name.

Everybody has always wanted me to be something bigger than I am. To guard and follow the legacy of my father and the family name.

Even as it feels as if it is my one driving desire to do just that, with her, it feels like she wants me to be nothing more than I am, and nothing less. The few moments together that we've had, I was able to let loose with her. Be real with her. She's the only woman I've ever been truly confident won't leave my bed and take our story to the press. The only girl I'm myself with, no mistrust there, no other agenda—not from me, and not from her.

But I also know that I may have a dose of pixie dust with the public. They've been forgiving with me, with my every transgression, rumored or real. But I can't say they would be as forgiving with her if this got out.

"Yeah. I need to be more careful." I glance at Beckett, a ton of frustration weighing on me.

Wilson's familiar three knocks resound in the room, and he opens the door. I know what he's about to say. The press is probably outside. And they want a statement.

"Are they all outside?" He knows very well who *they* are.

"Yep."

I get to my feet. "Let's go, Beckett—let's give them a diversion to keep them away from her door."

"How can you stand having to give a statement for every time you take a shit, man?" Beckett growls.

"You get used to it."

RUMORS

Charlotte

B y the next morning, everyone is talking about an affair. Last night on the eleven o'clock news, the first spot featuring Matt and me appeared on a local channel. *"Security camera footage of Matt and a mysterious redhead thought to be a campaign aide 'secretly' trying to buy shoes …"*

I hate seeing it, I hate it with every fiber of my being, but the moments we shared … the lingering feeling of his hands on me at the Tisal Basin … it almost makes the scandalous rumors of shoe-shopping worth it.

I go downstairs to check my mailbox, only to find two reporters at my building door. I know Matt must be fielding so many more, but to me, two reporters is two too many.

"Miss Wells—"

"No comment, thank you." I struggle to open the door once more.

"Are you and Matt Hamilton on the tape?"

I slide into the building and see my message machine blinking madly with fifty-two—*fifty-two*—messages. I disconnect it.

I get an email from my parents. *SCANDAL,* the subject line reads.

I don't open it.

Kayla texts me.

I text back:

I'm fine, thanks for worrying. I AM NOT ROMAN-TICALLY INVOLVED WITH MATT HAMILTON!

Sent. *Not involved,* I tell myself.

Women voters are going crazy, though, and by that evening, Matt is on the news.

"It is not true that I'm in a relationship with Miss Wells. We took a hike around the Basin as we reviewed my upcoming campaign schedule, so let's keep the focus on that."

I turn off the TV with a heavy feeling in my stomach. I eat and think about the situation over my grilled chicken and salad, then change into my running gear. That night, I plunge myself into a run, and run like I'm running a marathon when I head to my parents' house to say goodbye before the campaign tour.

They're expecting me in the living room—and I know they were discussing the news. The somber looks on their faces say it all. My father only hugs me and tells me in his gruff way to take care of myself, then heads upstairs.

My mother hands me a glass of lemonade and eyes me worriedly as we sit on opposite couches in the living room. "We saw the news."

I groan. "Not you too, Mom."

She nods. "Definitely me, Charlotte. For decades, your father and I have avoided any sort of scandal. Scandal is a career killer in politics."

"Mom, I know—it was completely innocent."

"Just remember you're a lady, Charlotte. Ladies are always ladies first, women second. Understand?"

"Yes, I understand. Don't worry—I wouldn't cause any scandal for us."

"It's not that Matt isn't … Goodness, he's a breath of fresh air for this country and he's running independently. Charlotte, the parties will be out to destroy him—you don't want to fuel that fire. He belongs to America now. He always has."

"I know, Mom, I know," I say.

"Don't fall in love with him."

I duck my head, laughing mirthlessly. "Why would you say that?"

Her eyes shine with sympathy and understanding. "Because any woman would. But you're not any woman. You're your father's and my daughter."

I placate her for the next half hour, and I know I should be concerned; I *am* concerned. But nothing can stop me from hitting my bed and reliving Matt's kisses a thousand times.

TRAVELING

Charlotte

We're traveling on a twin-engine plane for the campaign. Our first stop is Dallas, and I'm the only woman flying among a group of four men and a dog. Matt's junior campaign manager, Hessler, his intimidating grandfather Patrick, Carlisle, Jack, and his *hot* owner, Matt

Heavenly Kisser

Hamilton.

I'm nervous about the news. Those kisses we shared were *so* dangerous. I had no idea that I could be so reckless and impulsive until that night.

Matt smiles at me ruefully when he greets me—and I swear every single existing butterfly in my stomach takes flight because he looks genuinely happy to see me. Like he regrets almost getting caught, but he doesn't regret the kisses one bit.

God. His kisses.

I try not to remember the launch of heat they caused inside me as I greet the men by the plane steps. Carlisle, judging by the tension in his shoulders when he looks at me, seems pretty unhappy about the news.

And the first clue I get that implies I shouldn't even be traveling with Matt comes from his grandfather. He sees me and asks, "Who is she?"

"My scheduler. She's Senator Wells's daughter and an old family friend." Matt introduces us. "Charlotte, Patrick Hamilton, my grandfather."

"I know who she is—why is she here?" his grandfather huffs, turning around and boarding the plane.

Wow.

The man hates me.

Matt shoots me an *ignore him* look and puts his hand protectively on the back of my neck as he urges me up the plane steps. A frisson shoots down my spine and though the touch lasted only a second, the feel of his touch lasts for much longer. Matt settles his big body on the chair facing the cockpit. I take the seat behind his.

I have never before been more grateful that Matt brought Jack. He lets him out of his crate after takeoff and Jack immediately comes over to sniff me and lick my hands. He's keeping his eyes on Matt while I plug in my earbuds to give the men some privacy while they talk.

Still, I overhear them discussing various subjects—the stabilization of the economy, Matt running as an Independent.

"You're a Harvard graduate, like your father ... You've lived abroad; you know what's out there," his grandfather passionately argues. "Your father was too young the first time he wanted to run and was told to wait and he *did*. You take the cake of it all, Matthew, really you do."

"People are loyal to him, Patrick," Carlisle appeases. "No one sniped about Lawrence after his death. There were no unauthorized leaks of information regarding his presidency. The people are insanely loyal to the Hamiltons."

"But they're loyal to their parties, too," Patrick counters with a meaningful look in Carlisle's direction.

"What did you want me to be, a senator?" Matt asks in a steely voice that silences everyone.

Even his grandfather finally seems to shut up.

I'm aware of his grandfather constantly glancing in my direction during the flight. He doesn't even try to lower his voice when he says, "You keep your hands off her. You belong to the country now."

Dead silence falls.

Jack's ears perk up as if he senses something. And though the air is thick with tension, Matt leans back in a lounging pose as he eyes his grandfather. "Yeah, Granddad. I appreciate you being here ... but I know what I'm doing."

Leaping off the seat next to me, Jack bounds up the aisle and sits at Matt's feet, nudging Matt's thigh with his nose.

Matt keeps his intimidating stare on his grandfather as he absently strokes a hand atop Jack's head and glances at me. He's got the sleeves of his shirt rolled to his elbows and he's so muscular that veins pop out on his arms.

I remember our conversation and my mother's words, not completely dissimilar to his grandfather's, and I quickly break gazes—too sucked in by the dark, proprietary flash in his eyes—and get myself busy once again, going over all the names of the local aides we will be meeting and greeting at the Dallas headquarters today.

We check into the hotel and head to our local office, and for the next week, the marathon of media and crowds begins all over the Southern states.

Wherever we land, there's always a receiving committee of people waving placards and chanting.

"HAMILTON FOR THE COUNTRY."

"BORN FOR THIS!"

I'm so proud of stupid wonderful Matt and how he's impacting people.

His easy charisma simply wins over the people instantly. For years he protected his privacy, while giving off the air of a handsome, cultured rake with unlimited money and unquenched appetites. He looks like the bad boy of politics at the same time as he looks like the man you want to entrust yourself and your children to.

He already has international respect. His father has a whole library in his name, as many ex-presidents do, and a history of preserving relics, and now it seems like the media has been waiting decades to lie down before the powerful Hamilton legacy again.

He knows just how to greet the reporters; he even knows the names of most. Bulbs flash as we land in Miami and step out of the jet toward a silver SUV.

"How do you do that?" I glance at Matt, who's dressed in jeans and a white button-down shirt, emitting more heat than the Florida sun up above.

He shoots me a questioning sideways glance. "What?" he asks with a grin, the wind playing with his hair. *Damn wind.* My fingers are jealous.

"Know exactly how to treat them," I add.

He shrugs, as if getting along with the press is simply second nature to him.

"The thing with the press is," he says, "you need to keep them fed so they don't steal into your home and have a picnic at your expense. Keep them sated with just the right amount of info so they're not hungry enough to try to rummage through the entire contents of your kitchen."

I smile. "You're cunning."

"Cautious," he easily contradicts.

"Calculating."

He continues to smile, silent, then he looks at my lips for a second—long enough to make my stomach clutch with wanting—and he quietly admits, "No contest."

I laugh and try to shake off his effect on me as we climb into the SUV.

I'm nervous.

Tummy-clenching, butterflies-fluttering nervous.

Not because of traveling. But you know the flutters that are there even when your mind is somewhere else? I have them. I've had them for the past week. I can't get rid of them.

My breath keeps catching when Matt's and my gazes meet. I keep feeling my sex grip when he looks at my mouth, or asks me for something and seems to purposely drag his fingertip over my thumb when I hand it over.

We're in the car now.

I'm sandwiched between him and his grandfather, and yet the car is all about Matt. Matt's smell, the space Matt's body takes.

This is the first guy I've ever fantasized about, and the young version of him was only an inkling of the man he is now.

The whole ride to our hotel, I'm aware of a low, dull hum in the pit of my stomach and the things his hands are doing as he fiddles with his phone and takes a call from someone named Beckett, who I've learned is one of his Harvard friends and who it seems will be catching up with us later.

Quietly I stare out the window at the scenery, and then I opt to review the week's itinerary. When Matt ends his call, he leans over my shoulder. His jaw is about an inch from touching my shoulder.

And is it strange that my shoulder feels hot simply by that nearness of him?

Stomach clutching harder than before, I lift the schedule so Matt can look at it.

His beautiful lips curve, and he shakes his head, that adorable smile still on his lips. "Don't show it to me. Difficulty reading small type. Remember?" he chides, but then he reaches for his reading glasses, slips them on, takes my copy—dragging his thumb over the back of mine as he does—and skims it.

My lungs feel like rocks; I can't really say I'm breathing right.

But I don't want to pass out here, in front of him and his grandpa!

I study the hard planes of his face as he reads, which soften as his hair falls on his forehead. He shuts the agenda and removes his glasses. "I'm going to be busy," he says.

"I know you like busy. And at this point, you kind of don't have any other choice."

He frowns as if offended I even implied this. "I don't want one." Then a gleam of admiration settles in his eyes. He lowers his voice so that only I can hear him. "You're doing a great job, Charlotte. You're one of the most hardworking people I've ever met. I can tell you really believe in what you're doing."

His voice so close shoots a million and one sparks along my body. I keep my gaze on his.

I keep my voice low too. "I was born here. And I'm going to die here. And I want my children to live here. And my grandchildren. And I want it to be as wonderful as it was for me—even more wonderful than it is now."

He looks intently into my eyes, and for a mere second, a smile appears. "Well, I'm not planning on children or grandchildren, but I'd like to make sure yours have it as wonderful as you'd want it to be."

I didn't expect that.

Hearing Matt—young, virile, every woman's fantasy—say that confuses me.

"Why?"

There's a silence.

"Why don't you plan to have children?" I ask, this time being more specific. My voice still low.

I sound a little stunned and maybe a little regretful, but that's because I think Matt would be a great father.

Matt Hamilton would be the hottest baby daddy in the continent.

In the world.

A smile tugs at one of the corners of his lips, and amusement lights up his eyes over my brazenness. "I don't like doing things half-ass."

As I register what he's said, I glance down at my lap. Out of the corner of my eye, I'm aware of Matt's grandfather staring at me with a scowl.

And then it hits me. His plan to be president will take precedence over everything else, even his personal plans.

I don't even know what to say.

It hurts to know this, but beyond that …

I just didn't think it was possible to admire him more than I already did.

"Charlotte!" Alison says beside me as we mingle with the crowd, her camera always at the ready for her to snap the next shot. We're at a fundraiser consisting of mostly businessmen and women, and the room is packed to capacity, almost a thousand people here at the exclusive event, all craving to meet their candidate.

"You two are looking lovely tonight," Mark says as he joins us to mingle.

We're in Miami, and because the event fell on the weekend, Mark surprised us by joining us unexpectedly.

"Couldn't miss the fun, Mark?" Alison teases.

There's a silence between them and Alison giggles, and all the time, I keep stealing covert looks at Matt. One second, his eyes flick up from the crowd and in my direction as if he has an extra sense. I turn away and laugh with Mark.

"Uh, what's so funny?"

"I'm sorry, I ..." I shake my head and smile.

While Alison goes to take a good shot of Matt, Mark and I compare life stories, mine a bit sheltered, I suppose, and I learn that he married his childhood sweetheart and divorced at only thirty.

"Sounds hard," I tell him.

"It is. Adult love is different, more ... sacrificing than we thought. It sort of opened our eyes. We grew apart. But enough tear-jerking. I want to know about *you*."

"Mark."

He turns to one of our co-workers, a middle-aged man who's in charge of web advertising. "When I come back," Mark then finishes. He winks and leaves just as Alison returns.

"He's nice and he's into you, FYI," she says.

"He's nice and he's *not* into me."

I watch him leave and search myself for a tiny spark and nope, there is no spark. Alison starts circling the room, taking shots of other significant figures in attendance. I look at where Matt was and feel a kick of disappointment that he's no longer there.

"He was thirsty."

I swing around when I hear his voice behind me, and he shows me a glass of wine.

I frown. "I was looking for Mark," I lie.

"Hmm." His eyes twinkle, and he takes a sip. We stand side by side, his shoulder touching mine.

I glance at Carlisle across the room, whose expression is more than ecstatic—obviously the fundraising is going well, and the turnout was greater than we'd all anticipated. "You seem to have an innate ability to draw crowds," I compliment.

Matt glances around the ballroom, and then back at me. With that mercurial face, he'd make any other president sweat during negotiations.

"You're not drinking anything," he finally says.

"I'm too lazy to go to the bar and I'd rather the waiters take care of the guests, but Mark offered."

"Mark's with Carlisle." He waves at one of the waiters, who immediately comes forward. "The lady would like … what would you like, Charlotte?"

"Any white wine is fine." Butterflies rush down my arms when he plucks a flute from the tray and hands it over.

He's looking at me, watching me sip, when he's approached by a group of newcomers, and I reluctantly duck away and start blending with the crowd again.

"Charlotte, ah, yes."

Turning in surprise at the voice, I spot a young, tall African American. His face is vaguely familiar, but I can't seem to place it. "Do I know you?"

He nods in the direction of our candidate. "I'm friends with Hamilton."

"Ahhh."

"College days," he explains.

"Ahhhh!" I point at him cheekily. "I bet you know quite a few things." I steal a look at Matt, but he's in such a large group that I can't spot him.

He lifts his fingers and invisibly zips up his lips. "Definitely won't be telling."

"Oh, come on." I now realize why he seemed familiar. Clad in jeans and a preppy sweater, I realize Beckett is Matt's best friend. He's got a shaved head, pristine-smooth complexion, warm eyes and full lips, and teeth that flash white against his smile.

He grins and signals for me to take a seat at one of the nearby tables, joining me. "We used to try to lose the Secret Service—they tagged along everywhere he went. It annoyed Matt. He tried to lose them for life. And look at him now."

I laugh. Somehow I can tell that he is protective of Matt.

We then talk about Matt's dad and the golden era, and what got him killed.

We fall silent when we see Matt approach us.

"Beckett was telling me some stories …" I tell him.

He eyes his friend dubiously as if suddenly, he just doesn't trust him.

"He said you'd do anything to get rid of your detail. That you learned to fly the Marine One helicopter as your eighteenth birthday present from your dad, and that your first dog in the White House was named Lucky but your mother called him Loki because he loved to tear up the tulip beds."

"Did he tell you all that?" He lowers one brow a little farther than the other and gives him a *you didn't* look, and Beckett laughs.

"I couldn't resist."

He slaps his back and as Beckett stands up to cede his seat next to me I swear he tells him, "I don't blame you."

Butterflies pop in my stomach, swift and violent. It's not just the words but the tender tone that surprise me. I tear my eyes away and stare at the glass in my hand, suddenly very preoccupied with how much liquid is in there and the exact situation of the wine.

Matt simply says something to Beckett that I can't hear, his hand resting on the back of the chair Beckett just vacated.

I sit here, struggling with all my emotions.

"If these are the crowds you draw as a candidate, I won't want to know what kind of power you'll hold as president," I say as I glance around.

Matt watches me all this time. His sharp espresso eyes narrow a little. "What else did Beckett tell you?" he asks suspiciously.

I shrug mysteriously, and his lips quirk over my stubbornness when Carlisle comes and asks Matt to give a speech.

As Matt stands and crosses the room, the crowd breaks out in applause, and I get hit with a THIS IS WHO YOU ARE moment. THIS IS WHAT YOU'RE DOING.

I can't stop smiling.

He's quiet as he goes up on a small podium. Matt Hamilton. I want the warmth of the light that Matt Hamilton represents.

Matt waits for everyone to settle down and then everyone waits in silence, all eyes on him.

"I'd like to thank you all for coming tonight—nice to see so many familiar faces and so many new ones as well." He nods at everyone. "I'm sure you've noticed we lack slogans in tonight's decorations ... I'd like to thank my team for their efforts—the truth of the matter is, nobody pays attention to slogans anymore."

"They need to know what you bring to the table!" a very boisterous elderly man yells.

"I bring me."

Silence.

He spreads his palms on the podium and leans forward. "For years the public has come to believe every promise made by every candidate has been a lie. Nobody believes in them anymore. Politics have been totally tainted by propaganda. I want it to be clear we're running a very easy slogan campaign, and a no-slandering campaign. I serve my country. When asked how I plan to serve, my *team*," he looks pointedly at me, "and I have to come to this." He nods behind him to where Carlisle has turned on a visual. "We're calling it the alphabet campaign. We're fixing, reworking, and improving everything from A to Z in this country. It's an ambitious goal and one I will work tirelessly to achieve. There are so many things right about this country, and so many things that can be better than right. We want to go back to the times—we want to even surpass the times—when they've been phenomenal." He starts naming them. "Arts. Bureaucracy. Culture. Debt. Education. Foreign relations policies …"

There are titters of excitement rushing across the room.

I stand there, awed like the rest of the room, feeling a connection to him.

A kind of connection I've never in my life felt before.

ONE TOUCH

Charlotte

The crowds are surging.

For the past month, we've had over 500,000 people in each state.

Strange. But I somehow feel like I know these people. Sometimes it's the look in their eyes. Like Matt is their only hope in the world.

He speaks to them about everything, not just the present, but how we mold the future within our present. How the decisions we make now affect those who haven't lived yet.

Our best engagements come with kids. But guess what?

They cannot vote!

And still, they're my favorites.

There's something about Matt when he's with children that tugs at me on so many levels.

Today we're leaving a children's hospital, and I've been handing out treats to the kids when Matt walks up to me and tells me it's time to leave.

That's when one of them yells, "Kiss her, Matt, kiss her!"

Carlisle instantly mutters in Matt's direction, "Yeah, that's probably the opposition wanting to hang you for it later."

"He's a kid," Matt tells Carlisle, laughing.

He shoots him an amused look, then me—our eyes meeting, something mischievous lurking in his gaze as he lifts my hand and passes his warm, velvet lips across my knuckles.

There's a dark sparkle in his gaze, reminding me that we both know a secret that nobody but him and I know.

It's over too soon; and I drop my hand as if he burned me and try to focus on the delighted kids, all giggling because of what Matt did.

The touch stays with me. It stays with me as we head out to the car, where savvy reporters who'd been peering through the hospital windows mill about.

"Matt, do it again—we missed it!" a reporter yells.

"Good." He grins as he helps me into the car and shuts the door. We all head off.

I'm silent, the hand he kissed sort of balled protectively over my lap. I'm aware of our shoulders inches apart. Our thighs touching, his scent in my lungs.

And his kiss remains. His touch remains. *He* remains.

I shift and put some distance between us as I pretend to peer out the window. My thoughts race to the pounding of my heart. I feel him glance at my profile, his stare like a weight, tangible on me. *He'll know how you feel, Charlotte.*

He'll know that a part of you is right now only thinking— kiss me. Kiss me when we're alone. Kiss me because you want to, like you did in D.C.

I fight the feeling all night in my hotel room, telling myself that it's better we haven't picked up after that night at the Tidal Basin. It's risky, and the country's future matters more than a week or a month of delicious sexual activity.

Matt was just indulging the child at the hospital, I remind myself. But no matter how much I analyze it, the flutters won't stop; this want for him builds and builds inside of me with nowhere to go.

I head to bed early, with images of watching him work out that morning at the hotel gym dancing through my head.

He loves working out. He's been giving this campaign all he's got. I wonder if he's as arduous in loving as he is in the rest of the things he does. I picture him in the highest office in the land, his bed always warmed by someone capable of relieving the stresses a president must endure. I feel a pang of jealousy, then press my lips together in disgust at myself and push the thoughts out of my mind—opting to pick up some of my work files because I already know I won't be able to sleep yet.

I grab my pens and start making notes when there's a knock on the door.

MEETING

Charlotte

It's midnight.

So why is there a knock on the door?

Matt.

The name sort of blooms in my mind and suddenly, deep in my stomach and in my chest cavity, hope is kicking and leaping and screaming as I pull a robe over me, tie the sash, and hurry to open the door.

Be Matt.

Be Matt.

Wilson stands on the other side. "He wants to see you." He scans my room over my shoulder. "Alone."

Oh. *God.*

Ten.

It's been ten days since he said he wanted me.

I wondered when the day would come. I'd even started to believe it might not ever happen.

But now Wilson is at my door. Saying Matt wants to see me.

I don't even know what to expect of this meeting. He could very well want nothing but to brainstorm—or to maybe tell me it's a bad idea, now that he's had time to reflect on it.

He'd be right. So right.

So I try to calm down my reckless desire for Matt Heavenly Kisser Hamilton and I prepare for a professional meeting —notebook in hand, ready to record any ideas or changes. Even though Wilson said he wanted to see me alone, I refuse to get my hopes up … or have them drowned.

I have trouble swallowing as I nod and say, "I'll meet you at the elevator bank in two minutes."

I shut the door and then lean on it, trying to catch a big breath.

Fuck.

Matt is going to be the end of me.

Maybe the end of my career, too.

And I should probably take that into serious consideration before I do something reckless.

I don't.

I kick into action and rush to my small closet. I change into a skirt and blouse, gather my things, grab my room key, and shut my door, following Wilson to the elevators, then down the back exit to the hotel's underground parking lot.

The door opens from within the car as I approach.

"Charlotte," a deliciously wicked voice murmurs from the shadows of the backseat.

"Matt."

I swallow the lump of excitement and desire that gathers in my throat. I'm wet already. Nipples pressing into the fabric of my bra and blouse. He scoots over and I slip inside, shutting the door behind me.

He's dressed in black.

Smells expensive.

And he looks hotter than sin.

He also moves fast as sin as he reaches out to take my chin between his thumb and finger and forces me to look into his beautiful dark eyes. "I hope I didn't disturb your sleep."

His voice is husky, and so is mine.

"Actually, you did. But you didn't have to send Wilson to knock on my door to do that."

He smiles and gazes at me, sliding his other hand over the seat until it covers mine. I catch my breath at the touch. He squeezes my fingers, forcing me to meet his gaze.

Wilson drives down the darkened streets while Matt lifts my hand with both of his, turns it over, and drops a kiss on the inside of my palm.

I catch my breath, the warm and silky tip of his tongue flicking out. Circling the sensitive skin at the center of my palm.

I groan, inching closer to his body. Emanating heat.

Matt grips me by the hips and pulls me the rest of the way to him. He brushes my hair behind my forehead. "I asked Wilson to help me secure some privacy for us." He studies my features.

"I'm glad," I admit, thickly.

I reach up to his shadowed face.

God, is this happening?

Really?

I'm stroking my fingers lightly over his taut flesh. Loving the feel of the shadow of beard across his jaw beneath my fingertips. The way his jaw clenches as he lets me touch him, his eyes absolutely feasting on my face.

"If you don't stop looking at me like that, we won't make it to the elevators," he warns.

"How am I looking at you?"

"The same way you looked at me when I kissed your knuckles at the hospital."

"Oh no! I looked at you a certain way? That can't be too good! People could see."

His lips tug at the corners. "They're used to girls flirting with me. It's my own reactions I need to watch." He smiles, then leans over and pecks my lips.

I lick my lips, tasting him on them. "You're very good at controlling your reactions."

"I wouldn't be so sure. My grandfather's on to me."

"He hates me, doesn't he?"

"He hates the idea of anything standing between me and what he wants for me."

I exhale.

"You looked great with the kids out there today. At the hospital," he says. Voice low and appreciative.

"*Me?* It's *you* they love."

He chuckles, slowly shaking his head. "If that's true, then you've won them over just as much; otherwise why would they ask me to kiss a girl if it's not someone they'd want to see me with?" He smiles and leans back, eyeing me. "See, kids aren't affected by norms and rules. They just see what is and know exactly how they'd like it to be."

"It made me laugh that you indulged the kids but not the nosy reporters."

"They threw it as bait, I'm not giving them that. At least, not willingly." He looks at me then, and the understanding of the risks weighs down the silence between us.

Wilson pulls into a smaller hotel just a few blocks away from ours.

It's more low-key, not exactly one-star but not five, either. A place where Matt wouldn't be expected to stay.

"I'm right behind you. Power off your phone," Matt instructs.

I'm so nervous that I'm chewing on my lower lip as I take the room key Matt gives me before I open the car door.

"Don't play too hard with that lip—that's for me to do later."

I pause.

Release my lip.

Watch his lips curve into a slow, satisfied smile.

And I smile back.

Then I quickly turn off my phone, exhale, tuck the key into my side pocket, and head to the elevators.

This is so reckless. So reckless, but the prospect of his touch is too thrilling.

A woman in a red sweater boards the elevator with me.

My heart starts thrumming in my chest.

I keep my head down, busily staring at my Mary Janes. My pulse throbs with adrenaline, anticipation, and fear. Down the hall, I slide the key into the slot and enter the room.

Spacious, simple, modern, and elegant.

I hurry to the bathroom, shake my hair loose, pinch my cheeks, and then head outside, pacing.

I wait for minutes, until …

The door opens.

His tall form fills the doorway. Still dressed in black—except for a cap on his head.

The only guy I've ever wanted.

He steps in and shuts the door with one elbow.

I exhale. "Did anyone see you?" I ask.

He takes off the New York cap. "No."

"I was sure to keep my head down, I—"

Large and agile and gorgeous, he crosses the room, takes my hand, lifts it to his mouth, and skims a kiss over the back of my fingers.

I watch, transfixed, when he starts to suck the tips ever so exquisitely in his warm mouth. His gaze is like a missile of heat aiming straight for the hot spot between my legs as he licks me. Watching me with heated eyes as he nibbles and sucks carefully on each one. I groan softly.

He releases my hand, his warm fingers curving around my hip. I feel his nose at the top of my head, against my scalp.

The stroke of one hand on my hair, from the top of my head to my back.

Under my shirt, his arm now sliding around my waist, pulling us flush.

I'm so undone, a shudder wracks me. Making him tighten his hold more.

I know I shouldn't want these things.

He won't be the kind of man to kiss me goodnight every night. He might have so much that it'd even be understandable if he forgot your birthday. He's not the guy you can have your happy life with; he's the guy women throw themselves at, he's the guy who wants more than what you can give and he will always restlessly pursue it.

I know all this, but I cannot stop from moving closer and feeling his heartbeat through the cotton of his shirt.

We've been working tirelessly for months.

He feels too good right now.

And it feels too good to feel his eyes quietly caress me as his hands slowly stroke my hair and he tells me, "Have you thought about this?"

I nod.

He grabs the back of my neck and holds me still and kisses me.

The next few minutes, I'm trembling under his kisses and caresses. His hand running from the top of my head down to my feet as he removes my shoes. I feel protected, cherished ...

What we're doing is risky, but how can it be wrong when it feels so right?

Matt eases back and cups my face, and he looks so hot right now, I could be staring at the sun. He's staring at me as if I dazzle him too, and the smile on his lips softens a little as his eyes start pulsing like a living, breathing thing. We're both high from the adrenaline, the forbiddenness of finally, finally giving in to this attraction between us.

He scoops me up by the hips and lifts me in the air, just a few inches, so that my lips are exactly where he wants them.

And he takes them. Hard.

His lips forcing mine apart, his tongue plunging, his head angled for the best, most instant access.

The longing that's been building inside of me bubbles up and I wrap my arms around his shoulders.

It feels as if every day since I joined his campaign, I've been waiting for this. To feel Matt's hands around me, holding me to his hard chest. Engulfing me in his strong embrace.

All my resistance vanishes as his tongue strokes mine, and I suck and lick and rub his tongue back in a whirl of heat and passion and recklessness. I tighten my arms around his neck, and he makes a low sound from deep in his chest, as if he approves of my wild kiss.

He's breathing fast, but I'm breathing faster. He sets me on my feet, and his hand covers my cheek and his fingers stroke along my temples. "I've been trying to do the right thing. I fucking can't," he says.

"Don't."

I turn my lips to nip at the heel of his palm. He releases a sound I'd never heard him make before, like a growl that contains one word inside it: *Charlotte*.

His lips smash down on mine.

We kiss madly for about thirty seconds, then pull free to study each other.

I look into his face, and he stares down at me, still the guy I craved when I was younger, but now so much hotter, and more unattainable than ever.

Nothing matters, it doesn't matter.

All I know is I want him. My body is so on fire I could splinter any second.

I take his hand and put it on my shirt and drag it lower, lower, beneath the fabric of my blouse, then upward, pressing it to my breast—over my bra.

Matt rewards me with a slow, languorous, sensual smile as he cups me fully in his warm grasp.

He leans in and kisses me slowly this time, stroking his thumb over my nipple. I let his hand remain on my breast, thrilled when he flicks open a button with his free hand and steals it under my shirt. Now both my breasts are getting fondled.

Teased.

Kneaded.

Swallowing back a groan, I grip his shoulders and fist the fabric of his shirt in my hands, arching up against him.

"I want to strip you down and run my tongue over every inch of you," he rasps. His body vibrates with his desire, and I can see that he likes how I'm rubbing up against him like a cat.

He peels my blouse away and exposes me in my lace bra.

"God, you're so beautiful I need to see all of you." He takes me in with his eyes, then our mouths are fusing back together. He kisses me with relish, as if he plans to enjoy me all night. *Yes!*

Things are getting heated when there are noises out in the hotel hall.

Matt peels his lips away.

He lifts his head and turns to watch the door, and I wait, holding my breath. His nostrils flare as the noises fade.

Doubts try to trickle in, but they don't stand a chance against this—against him.

He glances back at me, his chest heaving, his lips tipping a little. He looks at me and licks his lips. "Charlotte, Charlotte. You have no idea the kinds of things I want to do to you, baby."

Show me! Do it!

For long seconds, he looks down at my lace bra and slowly lowers his head and captures one nipple. He flicks it with his tongue. It's already hard, but when he sucks over the thin fabric, it hardens more.

His growl excites me.

I groan and rub my hands over his back when he eases his hands between our bodies, under the waistband of my skirt. His fingers slip into my panties, brushing over my folds.

"Give me this, beautiful," he part growls, part croons as he finds my nub, my folds, and teases his finger along my wetness. "God, give me everything."

"Please." I tilt my hips as he pushes his finger inside me.

I clench around him, my whole body tightening as a low mewl bubbles up my throat.

"That's right, baby, do you like it when I do this?" he asks thickly as he inserts a second finger.

He's easing my bra down and circling the tip of his tongue across my bared nipple, murmuring, "God, you're so gorgeous like this," when there's a knock on the door.

Matt peels his lips away and curses under his breath, extracting his finger and licking it clean.

That has to be the sexiest thing I've ever seen, god help me.

Smirking, he heads to the door. He looks through the peephole and then waits until I straighten my clothes before he opens it.

Wilson steps inside swiftly and shuts the door. "Someone must have recognized you and tipped off the press. We need to leave, Matt." He's frowning and seems to be avoiding looking at me.

"Jesus," Matt growls.

He rakes five fingers through his hair, obviously pissed. Then Matt glances at me in apology. He shoots a glance at Wilson next. "Give us a minute."

Wilson steps out, and I can't move fast enough.

I can tell Matt can see I'm mortified as he crosses the room while I scramble to straighten my clothes.

He grabs my face and looks at me closely, our eyes only inches apart. "Hey, stay calm, baby. We're adults. We're not hurting anyone."

"I know; I just don't want to mess anything up. It's just that, since that night ..."

I shake my head. I could just hit myself for being so weak around him, for having such little self-control when it comes to him.

"I couldn't forget you—no years were enough. I watched you everywhere you went. I wasn't even sure if I should take the job. When Carlisle came to offer me the job, I thought that if I still felt the spark I did at the mere thought of you, I'd stay away. I *should* be staying away—"

"Tell me about the spark," he says, his eyes sparkling now.

I purse my lips, frowning, suddenly mad at him for looking at me with those laughing eyes right now. "It's not a spark."

"No?"

I grit my teeth, shooting fire at him with my gaze. "It's ... *sparks*, plural." I shake my head. "It's a torch. The Olympic torch."

"Ahhhh," he says.

I swear this man can chuckle silently with his eyes.

I don't know how he does that!

I shove his hard chest a bit and keep scowling. "Why can't I dislike you like I do your opponents?"

"Because you want to sleep with me."

I laugh despite myself, then turn away to the window.

Sober now.

He steps behind me, inhales my hair slowly. My heart flips in my chest because he's brushing his nose lightly into my scalp. His voice is close to my ear. "Sleep with me when we get to D.C. this weekend."

"Matt ..." I begin.

Yes!

No. No. NO.

I'm torn as I slowly face him.

He's *People*'s Sexiest Man Alive, despite years working to be taken seriously. Fooling around with a young intern isn't the image he's worked to achieve.

"We've started something here. I'm not about to let it go," he says, cutting me off.

Wow. He's really stubborn.

I exhale.

He catches my chin and smiles down at me. He repeats, "Sleep with me in D.C."

I ease an inch back, away from his touch. "I'm just realizing that I don't know if I can do this."

"Why?"

"Because I'm not sure that I don't want more."

My admission is sobering to myself. And to him.

"More," he repeats.

He drops his hold. Then rakes a hand over his hair while a restless little muscle starts working in the back of his jaw.

"My biggest fear is my kids will experience things in life and I won't know about it. That I'll be the last to wish them a happy birthday. That my wife will be alone every night because I'm too busy to even kiss her goodnight. I couldn't do that to you, Charlotte. I watched my mother suffer greatly next to my father when he took office."

He shoves his fisted hands into his pockets, looking down at me intently.

"I want you, Charlotte. I want us. This. But if I win …"

Shadows fall across his eyes and reality floods my heart at the unspoken words that hang heavily in the air—winning doesn't come with *more*. It's a sacrifice he's willing to make to become this country's leader, and one I admire him for.

"You *will* win," I tell him.

I'm fighting to keep the regret from my voice.

Matt just stares at me, my lips, my face, lifting his fingers as his lips curl. "All this conviction," he croons, rubbing the pad of his thumb over my lips.

My heart is tripping all over itself.

I can't help staring at his full, sensuous lips. I might not get more, but I can't deny myself another kiss from this man.

I lean up on my toes, slipping my arms around his neck. Around this stubborn, confident, kind, sexy, larger-than-life, rebellious man's neck.

And my lips meet his.

We're kissing heatedly, and there's a light tap on the door, and the stolen moments are gone—and as he chucks my chin, smiles, and heads out the door, reality starts to sink in.

FLIRTING WITH DANGER

Charlotte

I exhale and pull the zipper of my black sweatshirt up to my neck. I slip on a baseball cap, guiding my ponytail through the small hole in the back, and place glasses over my eyes even though the sun is already setting.

I'm in my D.C. apartment and it's Saturday afternoon.

Ever since our "meeting" in that hotel room, and almost getting caught, I can't shake this overwhelming feeling of dread. My stomach twists and turns in knots thinking of what I'm about to do.

I know that this is risky, *beyond* risky, going to his house on his one night off, but I need to talk to him. In private.

If I don't do this one risky thing, we'll keep doing a million risky things right up until Election Day.

I need to stop this before we get in too deep … to the point of no return. A part of me fears that we already have, and a part of my soul tells me that no attempt on either of our parts can really stop the avalanche of emotions now surging between us, present in every look, touch, smile, and kiss.

I need him to know that we can't continue this dangerous thing we have started, because I would never forgive myself if

I cost him his presidency. Presidential elections, and especially presidential campaigns, are very delicate things.

One wrong move, one wrong comment, one slipup can mean game over. And for Matt, an Independent candidate already having to fight against two long-standing parties with history, loyalty, dirty tricks, and a lot of money on their sides … he can't afford a slipup.

I ask my parents if I can borrow their car for the night and say that I'm going out for drinks with my friends.

However, I drive toward Matt Hamilton's house. I didn't want to take a cab because I didn't want anyone else knowing of my little trip.

When I roll up to his house, I feel my stomach turn and twist into a million knots. I force myself to open my car door and walk up the steps to ring his bell.

A couple of shaky breaths later, and a couple more thoughts of chickening out, Matt Hamilton stands in his doorway. Barefoot, hair rumpled, in black jeans and a dark blue T-shirt.

He inhales a sharp breath when he sees me, and rakes his eyes over my body before asking me in a gruff voice, "Why are you here, Charlotte?"

I smile, but I know it doesn't quite reach my eyes.

"Can I come in?"

He doesn't respond, merely eyes me with curiosity and steps aside to let me walk past him. He moves just enough to let me go by, but not enough for me to do so without touching him.

My shoulder grazes his chest, and his scent envelops me.

He leads me to his living room, where I see the TV is on with the volume low. On his desk is a mess of papers and folders.

He sits across me and clasps his hands behind his head, his eyes never leaving mine. He sits in silence, piercing gaze on me, and I just take him in. Every fiber of my being telling me to go crawl into his lap and let his warmth soothe away any doubt or fear in my head, but I can't move.

"I can't do this, Matt. What happened in your hotel room …"

I meet his gaze, his eyes like hot coals, his jaw clenched tightly.

I gulp and continue. "We almost got caught. I can't be the reason for you losing this presidency."

"You will not be the reason for me losing. If anything, you'll be the reason for me winning."

I shake my head. "You know that we're playing with fire. This is the Oval Office. The White House. I can't let you throw it away for me."

"I'm not throwing anything away, Charlotte." He eyes me steadily. "Why are you so worried?" he prods.

"Why do you think? The whole nation has their eyes on you, Matt! The last thing you need is a scandal."

"There will not be a scandal. I won't allow it. You need to trust me." He leans forward, his eyes scanning my features, his voice unwavering, hard and deadly serious. "I would never let anything happen to you. And even if something broke out in the news, I would protect you."

"If anything happened, you know you would need to throw me under the bus. It would be the only way to salvage your image with the people and keep your campaign going."

My heart breaks at my words, because as much as it hurts, it's the truth. He would have to place the blame on me, control the narrative in such a way that made me seem like a power-hungry girl looking to sleep her way to the White House, and make Matt seem like the victim. That's just politics.

He stands up and starts pacing, and lets out a sarcastic laugh. "You really think I would do that to you?"

I stay silent, unable to speak.

"Jesus, I would rather lose the presidency than hurt you," he growls, in a voice so low I wasn't sure I heard him.

"That is exactly why we need to stop!" I plead.

He digs his hand into his hair in an exasperated motion.

"I don't want to stop," he says, looking at me with such conviction and desire in his eyes, it almost scares me.

"Neither do I," I whisper, "but we have to."

"Fuck, Charlotte—just let me have you! Let me have this!" His eyes pin me to my seat, his raw, unrestrained frustration burning bright. "I may be the next President of the United States! I'll be damned if I don't have what I want," he growls, "and I want *you*. I not only want you, I need you. No matter what I'm doing, I'm thinking of you. No matter who I'm with, I would rather they be you …"

He stands there, his chest rising and falling with his every breath, his fists clenching at his sides, the muscle in his jaw ticking.

I sit there in shock at his outburst … at his words.

My heart is practically bursting in my chest at the adoration I feel for this man—and I let myself go. I let myself go to him. Because I want to.

I rise from my seat and his pupils dilate as I walk toward him, his fists still clenched at his sides. I see him fighting the urge to reach out to me.

I walk right up to him, our chests almost touching. Matt tips his head down to look at me, since he towers over me, and the turmoil in his eyes sets me on fire.

I wrap my arms around his neck and plaster myself against his body, and I start to kiss him with everything I've got.

I don't care about more. I don't care that there is no future for us if he wins. I won't deny us both this moment. He said he needs me. And *I* need *him.*

I kiss him and in my kisses, I unleash all the desire, all the passion, all the need I had been so desperately trying to fight; and he does the same.

Immediately his arms wrap around my waist and I feel him lift me up. Instinctively, I wrap my legs around his waist. His hands grip my ass, holding me against him, and he keeps returning my kisses with equal intensity.

He kisses the shit out of me. All memories of anything existing in the universe other than this man, this moment, completely disappear.

He growls against my lips and I feel him start to walk while kissing me.

He breaks the kiss for a moment to take me up the stairs, but I can't keep my mouth off him—his jaw … down his neck … nibbling and sucking on his delicious skin.

He kicks the door open, and I think he just broke the hinges but I don't care.

The room is dark except for one lamp next to his bed.

He sets me down on his dresser, the first thing he finds, and stands between my legs, his mouth back on mine—taking my breath away.

His kiss is drugging, his lips warm and soft yet firm. His tongue is warm too and every time he puts it inside my mouth, I feel tingles all over. It feels intimate and incredible. I sigh against him, but my sigh quickly turns into a moan as his hand travels down and unzips my sweatshirt. He pushes it halfway off my shoulders, the straps of my top following. He doesn't even take my bra off, just yanks down one of the cups and takes my nipple in his mouth. I gasp and wrap my legs tighter around him, letting my head fall back because of how exquisite it feels.

"Matt ..."

He sucks harder, twirling his tongue against my nipple, making me wetter and wetter by the second.

"I could do this all day," he groans as he pulls down my other cup and takes my other nipple in his mouth.

Just as I get used to the warmth of his mouth on me, he pulls back, gaining a moan from me in protest.

He looks at me and reaches up to cup my face, giving me a slow, tender kiss before reaching between us and unbuttoning my jeans.

I feel my heartbeat get faster as I realize what he wants to do.

I quickly jump off the dresser and take off my jeans, my sweatshirt, and my top, leaving on just my panties and bra.

Matt yanks his T-shirt off, revealing miles of hard, strong male-ripped chest muscles.

He takes me in, standing in just my bra and panties, his eyes filled with admiration and lust.

I look back at him, silently begging him to take me to his bed already.

And he does.

He picks me up and lays me down on the bed, following close behind. He lies on top of me, kissing me senseless, his hands traveling town my torso and gripping my ass.

He sucks on my neck, licking and biting.

I rake my nails down his back and moan, rocking my hips against his hardness.

"Please ..." I beg.

He chuckles against my neck, and then lifts his head to look me in the eye when he places his hand over my panties.

"What do you want? My lovely, beautiful, sexy Charlotte." He continues kissing my neck and rubbing his fingers against my soaked panties.

Before I can answer, he pulls my panties to the side and slips his finger inside me, and I gasp in response.

My breath is coming fast and hard, and I'm out of control with want as I pull his head up so that he'll kiss me again.

He doesn't need to be asked. His lips fasten to mine without apology or restraint, then he swipes his tongue down my neck, kissing and nibbling my skin.

I'm high, absolutely high on him, on this moment. Matt drags his fingers along my stomach.

I stroke his pecs and kiss his nipple too. A groan of pure hunger and approval rumbles up his chest.

He leans over me again.

Matthew unhooks my bra and exposes my breasts.

He touches me.

My nipples harden under the feathery touch and I suck in a breath. I wait, my body tense, wanting. He strokes the pad of his thumb over the tip of my breast, sending a shiver down my spine.

"So responsive," he says as he leans over and kisses the inside of my thigh. I squirm a little, and his laugh caresses my skin. "So sweet." He moves his lips over my sex. *Oh god.* He trails his hand up my hip, to my breasts. My muscles contract deeply and a low groan leaves me.

He tugs my panties off and tosses them to the floor. His thumb circles my clit and passes over my wet slit, over my folds, then penetrates me. I clench my muscles, even my belly muscles. "Ohhh."

He pulls on my breast with one hand.

He breathes in my skin and licks and laps my nipple. His warm tongue moves languidly over my skin, and my body beneath it is on fire.

He swipes his tongue over my belly and lower, to my sex again.

He's so hungry. *I'm* so hungry.

I want to touch him. I reach out and run my fingers over his chest, his muscles visible in the city lights streaming through the window.

He kisses the inside of my other thigh. I squirm and thrust my hips up in a silent plea.

His tongue dips into my sex, tasting me.

I'm about to come. It feels so good. I'm so hot for him it's not even funny.

"I can't get over how good you taste. How gorgeous you are."

His eyes look tender and wild as he kisses my sex for another minute, watching my reaction, and it's an intoxicating combination.

I pull him up and kiss him. He kisses me back, tasting like me. Our tongues move, our hands searching, his exploring, mine kneading.

He grabs my hips and leans in to lick his tongue across my nipple. I gasp and thrust my chest upward, and his laugh again brushes over my skin.

"Don't laugh at me—this is serious," I groan.

"It's very serious."

He kisses my sex lips with a languorous, wet tongue. I buck, but he stills me with one hand on my hip bone. He eases his thumb over my clit and starts rubbing in circles as his tongue dips languidly inside me.

My clit is getting rolled in delicious little circles by the pad of his thumb, and I'm biting down on my lower lip to keep from moaning too loud.

My breath comes in a fast, choppy rhythm as Matt shifts back and strips his jeans with fast, powerful jerks of his hands —I see all of him, golden skin and muscles, and I salivate in silence.

He's well delineated, athletically built and perfectly proportioned, and I want every inch of the guy. He rolls on a condom. He's so big and thick, I lick my lips, screaming silently in anticipation.

"This is what you want, Charlotte."

And then he pushes in.

He's so thick and he moves fast, taking me by surprise with the delicious stretching sensation in my sex.

I go off.

"Oh god, Matt!"

My orgasm gains intensity, a curling, twisting, tightening rope, stretching from the tips of my toes to the tips of my fingers.

I groan one second, and the next, I'm experiencing the most intense, breathtaking, body-shaking, soul-shattering orgasm I've ever had in my life, caused by Matt's thick cock inside me. I'm bucking beneath him, the pleasure almost agonizing, clutching onto his shoulders for dear life.

He grabs me by the hips and moves inside me, faster, deeper, and shouts as he releases.

He holds me against him as he comes, really hard, his cock jerking several times inside me, bringing me to a second orgasm.

Cursing under his breath, he continues rocking his hips as he brushes my hair back behind my face, prolonging the pleasure, gazing down at me until the convulsions in my body turn to tremors and then to lingering little shivers. Then he rolls to his back and brings me with him, brushing one stubborn wet tendril of red hair back again.

I'm panting against his neck. I'm sweaty; we both are.

I shut my eyes, not certain that just happened and not certain that I don't desperately want it to happen again—even if it *shouldn't*.

My body throbs from the way he just fucked me. My nipples feel sensitive.

I stroke my finger up his chest.

I'm curled against his side. My mouth is probably red. I love that his mouth is red from my kisses too, his hair is rumpled, and even in this state, he looks like he could take on the world.

And then I'm reminded that soon, he will.

I glance at the clock on the nightstand, wanting time to stand still. Wishing we could stay in this moment. For our lives to be different. Him just a guy. Me just a girl. The two of us just here, with no expectations from anyone but each other. No campaign. No media scrutiny. No guilt for knowing our actions affect not only us but those around us—the team. My parents. His mom ... *the country.*

"Your mother isn't thrilled that you're running, is she?" I ask, stroking my finger up his chest as the tips of his fingers feather my back.

Matt peers into my face, looking puzzled and amused that I chose to ask him something about the campaign rather than what just happened. "How do you know?"

"She has avoided every event and isn't speaking about it."

He drags his hand over his face, then curls his arm behind him as he slides his hand under his pillow. "She worries."

He tightens his other arm around me and I curl closer, craving his warmth.

Matt is staring at the ceiling, thoughtful. I know they're close, he and his mother. And I really feel for his mother. Her husband was brutally killed. Matt is all she has; of course she's concerned. But I can see Matt wouldn't be a man to back down for anything. "Matt? When you told me about your biggest fear?" I pause for a moment. "Mine is to disappoint my parents. To fail to be whatever it is they wanted me to be, somebody great, responsible, respectable. Look at me now." I groan.

He peers into my face, thoughtful. Just a bit concerned. "We're quite a pair, aren't we?" He runs his fingertip down my nose. "America's playboy and America's sweetheart."

I grin up at him, still breathless. "They may have thought you were just a gorgeous face, but they take you seriously now."

"I take *them* seriously. And I take *you* seriously." He strokes his hand down my face, his gaze so very warm and endearing. "I don't want you hurt. This shouldn't even be happening. I shouldn't have my hands on you." He strokes a path down my body with those hands, the most delicious hands. Then, he ducks his head and adds, "I definitely shouldn't do this." He cups my sex in his hand and grazes a kiss along my cheek.

I grab his jaw and pull him to my mouth, whispering, "Yes, you should."

He shifts above me, all stealth and muscles. "I can't get enough of you, beautiful. I just can't get enough."

He's so hard he immediately rolls on a new condom.

I wrap my arms around his shoulders as he drives slowly in, as if I'm precious. Or as if he knows I'm a little sore.

He moves inside me. I groan and relish it, clawing my nails down his back.

I move beneath him. I know that it's crazy, dangerous, terrible for both of us. And I know that it's also exciting, inevitable, and nothing I could even contemplate denying myself.

I cannot deny myself him. If I want to stop crushing on him, even after eleven years, he will be the only antidote.

Linking my hands behind his thick neck, I raise my head and set my lips on him. I'm hungry, moaning as Matt grabs my face to hold me still and tongues me.

SHIFTS

Charlotte

When I arrive at campaign headquarters early Monday morning, I'm not entirely certain if I should be feeling dread,

anxiety,

uncertainty,

fear,

arousal,

bliss,

or plain just happiness.

All I know is that I can still feel him between my legs.

Visions of Saturday flutter in my mind throughout the day and serve as beautiful, fleeting reminders of a night I will never forget.

There is a visible shift, invisible to anyone other than Matt and me. Every time we lock gazes there's a silent understanding that we now share something special.

Every time I hear the sound of his voice direct his staff or make campaign-related decisions, I remember it whispering dirty things in my ear, moaning my name, groaning in release. Multiple times.

Things have changed. I've been with him in the most intimate ways anyone can be with another, and it feels absolutely blissful. When I look at him, I get giddy and my heart starts to beat faster and faster. If anyone spoke to me at that moment, I wouldn't hear whoever it was over the sound of my heartbeat, going crazy over this man.

There is a change in him too.

It's as if his masculinity has been multiplied by a thousand. His smile holds more mischief. His walk is now more a confident strut, and god, his voice ... He could be talking about state taxes and by the tone in his voice, you would think he's describing sex positions.

The looks are killing me. Sometimes they come with a sexy, private smile. Sometimes with no smile at all, his expression almost like a thoughtful frown. Sometimes they come with a look of surprise, as if he's surprised to catch himself staring at me.

I try not to be caught staring too, but there's always that one second when I'm staring at his profile, and the next when he somehow feels it and turns and I quickly look away. It's just one second, but it's enough. It makes me try harder not to look and harder to be fully professional. Because I *know*, when he looks back, that he's thinking of that night too.

That Thursday, we're on one of the biggest college campuses in Colorado and Matt is speaking to a besotted crowd of tens of thousands. He was pretty excited about this visit.

"Our future rests in our college students and our kids. Hell, I can't stress enough how important it is to inspire them to get actively involved, make a contribution." He told me this during the flight, and it made me doubly determined to make sure everything went smoothly all across the board.

Even the weather seems to have been in on the plan (and the weather is almost a scheduler's worst nightmare). The sky is clear, and the crowd is larger than we expected.

Matt's powerful speech leaves no doubt of his ability for leadership.

As Matt stands behind the podium, there's a voice from the crowd. "Go, Hamilton!"

Another shout from the crowd. "Where have you been, Hamilton?"

"Sorry to have kept you waiting," he says, his lips shaping into one of his most killer grins.

My stomach shudders with excitement.

The crowd keeps interrupting, shouting, "Matt! You're our candidate, Matt!"

Sometimes Matt laughs, or salutes them, as if they're old friends. But when he turns sober, so do the people. His hands on the podium, he stands erect and confident as he speaks of us being the best, of how in order to be great you need to work harder than the rest.

How the same old doors won't open to new opportunities.

How easily being at the top has tempted us to drop the ball and relax on our own glory ... a glory that we need to light up, as a nation, together. "No one man will bring you what you seek. No one will drop your fulfilled dreams right on your doorstep. So what is it that you want? And more importantly, what are you doing to get it?"

"Hamilton, Hamilton, *Hamilton!*" the people shout.

A ripple of happiness runs through my body as the chorus ripples across the stands.

God! They love him, they adore and worship him, and by the way he smiles and laughs at the praises they throw his way, he adores them right back.

No other candidate in the history of the U.S. has won the presidency at this age, but the crowds are coming to see him. His wealth and name would have gained a few followers, but it's his charisma, that earthiness, that relatability that he has that makes you feel as if he gets you, your problems, as if *he* knows what you need, even if *you* don't.

And it's not only that, but compared to his competitors, the Republican front-runner and the Democratic president (fossils, the both of them), he looks so young and strong, surrounded by a team with fresh, new ideas. The odds are against him, but the points are in his favor. America wants a change. America wants to grow. America wants to be young and powerful again.

"How do you think it went?" Matt asks me as we head to the hotel.

I shake my head and try to look disappointed, but when that smile of his appears, I can't keep up the façade any longer. "Standing ovation," I say, lifting my brows. "People connected. That was insane!"

Matt grins and stares out the car window, stroking his chin thoughtfully, his smile still there as he softly admits, "That *was* insane."

I hurry to bathe and make it on time for a staff dinner. I'm heading downstairs to meet Carlisle and other members of the team at one of the hotel restaurants. When the elevator doors open, only Matt is inside.

My heart skips, and we share a smile as I step in.

He smells so good, like cologne and soap, and the warmth of his body next to mine sort of intoxicates me.

"What are you wearing under there?"

"You'll never know," I say, tongue in cheek.

"Hmm. More like I'll know by midnight." He lifts one brow, warning me, and sort of kissing my lips with his gaze.

The mere thought of being in a room alone with Matt tonight does nothing to calm my body right now.

We step off the elevator, walking side by side with a good distance between us. He pulls out my chair when we arrive at our table, but Matt is typically courteous, so fortunately nobody seems to pay extra attention to that.

Except he grazes his thumb along the back of my neck as I take my seat—it's a subtle touch.

Completely stolen.

And it takes all my effort to keep my whole body from openly trembling in response.

We sit through dinner as the team discusses and discusses and discusses, and I can't quite calm the buzzing inside me. He's watching me from across the table. I watch him take a sip of his water before he slips on his glasses to read the polling numbers Hessler brought.

I'm suddenly thirsty and take a quick sip as well, trying to read the folder in front of me.

When we leave and shuffle up in groups to the elevators, Matt steps into the same one I do.

He's standing to my left the whole ride upstairs. His nearness affects me so much that I almost can't wait to get away.

My heart is whacking madly in my chest.

My shoulder burns where it grazes his hard one. I'm aware of how tall he is next to me, at least a head taller.

I'm aware of his every breath, slower than mine.

My floor comes up, and as I step out, I turn to say goodbye to the group. I look at Matt last.

He's gazing at me piercingly beneath slanted eyebrows, looking a little thoughtful and a lot hungry, as if we didn't just have dinner.

I go back to my room and wait for him to text me that the coast is clear. Ten minutes later, my secure campaign phone pings.

Ten minutes more, warm hands are sliding up my skirt to reveal my underwear. Pulling it down. Revealing every single wet fold beneath.

I'm in his room, and the next thing I know, Matt's wet tongue is in *me*.

TOWEL

Charlotte

We're in D.C. again.

Matt finished our last tour early and he request-
ed a new expedited schedule, which I've worked on
the whole night.

He said he'd meet me at his suite at The Jefferson, which
he used tonight when two members of his detail informed us
that his home was too swarmed with paparazzi.

Late in the morning, I knock on his suite door.

I primp my hair and then chide myself.

Stop primping, Charlotte!

I expect to find Carlisle here, but when Wilson opens the
door and allows me in, I find only silence.

I wander past the living room with my printout in hand.

I freeze as Matt steps into my line of vision, his large
body appearing in the open double bedroom doors.

He's wearing nothing but a white hotel towel draped
around his hips, his skin gold and smooth.

God help me.

The towel is hanging so dangerously low I can see the V
at his hips. He's got long legs with muscled thighs and calves,
hair-dusted and tan. He's also barefoot.

His hair is wet from a shower and slicked back, revealing his strong forehead and perfect features to their best advantage. Though he looks amazing in clothes, "amazing" cannot even begin to capture the complete athletic perfection of his shape and form and muscles. Every single muscle is defined and flexed hard.

And those incredible arms ... the bulging biceps as he lifts the small towel he has in his fist and runs it over his hair to dry it.

He tosses the towel aside and runs his fingers through his hair as he turns his attention to me. "Did you get it done already?"

Oh.

Yeah.

THAT.

"Charlotte." Chocolaty eyes begin twinkling, and my entire body flushes as I realize he clearly notices me gaping, his hair looking haphazard and even sexier as he props those glasses on his nose and reads.

I've tried to shift the next engagements so that our field team has time to arrive on the bus, but I can't help that flying always gets us in earlier—even though Matt hates wasting time waiting.

"This pushes us back a day," he says.

He groans in displeasure, and inside me, I feel a deep, instinctive, visceral tightening of my belly muscles at the sound. Not just my belly. My sex grips too. Even my chest seems to constrict. All of that in reaction to that very male, very sexy sound.

Reminding me too much of sex. Between Matt Hamilton and me.

"I'm sorry, Matt, I'm just ... I can't figure out how to get the rest of the team there on time to fit in another big speaking engagement. Maybe something small—"

"Hey. It's all right." He slaps the folder shut and eyes me. Can he tell I hardly slept? His gaze softens. "I should take you somewhere. Treat you to breakfast and coffee."

I bite my lip.

Matt's eyes darken.

I release it.

"I wouldn't say no to a big vanilla coffee."

"Let's do it."

I feel myself flush because—it sounds too much like a *date.*

"We can't!" I laugh. "I can't even stay here for more than a few minutes for fear of them watching us even more."

He sits, and his thick thighs are revealed by the towel. "I'm sorry. I can't really blame them for being obsessed with you," I add.

He looks at me.

All I can think of are his hands on me. My hands creeping under the towel. Fingers touching his chest. And that big, heavy cock of his.

Wow. Did I just think that?

What is happening to me?

"Come kiss me."

Matt seems to read my mind.

Startled by the command, I laugh and bite my lower lip. "What?"

"I said, come kiss me. I'm the one who should be nibbling on that lip."

I take one step forward, Matt's eyes darkening as he watches me.

There's a knock on the door. Followed by the sound of a room key. I quickly take back the one step forward I took.

Carlisle and Hessler join us.

Carlisle dives straight into business after a brief, "How's our American prince today?" and a wink in my direction. Matt heads into the bedroom, to change I suppose.

"I should go."

Matt steps out in slacks, buttoning up a blue shirt. "No. I'll take you home."

"No, it's okay. I'm meeting a friend actually for a croissant and a catch-up—it's three blocks away. And her birthday is coming up; I promised to make it. I'll be home later. Call if you need me."

I hurry outside, then check the time and head to my favorite coffee bar near Women of the World. I wait there for my friend Larissa. She arrives ten minutes late, and all that time, I'm sort of mad at myself for physically responding to Matt as hard as I do.

I've tried so hard to be focused on work and my career. Why do I need to be falling for the man I work for?

I exhale when I spot Larissa hurrying across the restaurant, trying to push America's Prince off my mind.

We end up doing coffee, then shopping, and then drinks.

"So what's it like working for that god?" she asks me, lowering her voice as we sit at the bar of one of our favorite cafés. "No. Really. Tell me—I'm dying to know."

"It's exhausting," I say.

Please, god, don't let my expression give anything away.

That I want him.

That, miraculously, he wants me.

That we've slept together.

That I still don't want it to end and I'm pretty sure because of the proprietary way he looked at me at his hotel room, neither does he.

As I sit there lying through my damn teeth, I realize that for the first time in my life, I'm doing something that I shouldn't.

I realize how uncomfortable it is to have a secret. To want to scream something to the world but at the same time, want nothing more than to protect it. Have the world never, ever touch any part of this precious secret of yours.

For nobody to ever know your weakness has a name, and a heartbeat, and a very famous face.

"I would kill for just one day in that campaign, Charlotte. I mean, *Matt Hammy*! Is he as gorgeous in person as they say he is?"

"More so," I groan, rolling my eyes.

I divert the attention to her new boyfriend, and thankfully, that's the end of my Matt Hamilton conversation.

If only it were that easy to steer him out of my every thought.

By the time I reach my apartment that night, I've had too many coffees mixed with alcohol. The exhaustion is weighing on me and there's a pain in my temples when I step off the elevator to my floor. A figure sits by my door, a large figure. In a blue cap.

Matt.

Scrumptious.

Hamilton.

"I needed to get away. Mind if I crash here for the night?" A devilish light glimmers in his eyes, and his lips tug at the corners when he notices the shock on my face.

Inside, I'm babbling and stumbling.

How did he shake off the press?

I'm pretty sure Wilson must have kept the coast clear for him to escape unnoted, but … oh my god, Matt is at my apartment door.

My mother would die that he's at my "shitty" little apartment.

I open my door with shaking hands, letting him inside, worrying she might be right. He's looking around with a frown, and suddenly my worries multiply, and I grab his hand and try to distract him.

"I have a big bed. Come on," I whisper.

"You really shouldn't live here all alone," he says, frowning deeply at me.

I smile and tug him toward my room—swaying my hips until that catches his attention.

He follows quietly, his eyes taking me in now, instead of my apartment.

I kick off my shoes and lie down on my bed, wondering why he's not at The Jefferson Hotel with a do not disturb sign on the door. Why he's here. I catch him glance around my bedroom and at my window, a look of protectiveness in his eyes, but when his eyes return to me and he sees me here—lying in my bed, sort of panting, waiting—his gaze shifts. It becomes partly tender, partly hot, and that alone gives me a hint of why he's here.

Plus knowing his staff never really lets him rest, I suspect the moments with me are his only rest times—the only times he truly disconnects.

"Was your place really swarmed tonight again?" I ask.

"Yeah, but it always is."

He speaks casually.

He kicks off his shoes, tosses his cap aside, and stretches out on the bed next to me, both of us on our sides, up on one elbow, facing each other. He smiles and reaches out to run his index finger down my cheek. "Couldn't stay away. Wanted to see if you got safely home."

"Or just wanted to see me," I whisper.

"Yes."

Suddenly, he shifts over me, and I'm on my back, with Matt's big body on top of mine.

He's stroking his hand up my arm, his thumb caressing my skin, his weight the best feeling in the world next to ... sex with him.

"Do you really want to spend the night here?" I ask, breathless, rubbing my toes along the sides of his bare feet. "I'm sure your bed is so much more comfortable. Or the one at the hotel. I'm babbling, aren't I? I just ..."

He's nodding slowly, looking at me.

"It's surprising to see you here," I finally admit.

"A good surprise?"

It takes me a while to admit it, but I do. Nodding. "A good surprise."

"Are you done?" he asks, curling his hand beneath my hair to lift my head up a few inches. His eyes are impossibly dark as I continue to nod.

I swallow, then smile and raise my head a little higher. I don't have to lift it too far. Matt closes the distance between his lips and mine, and I'm being kissed for the first time on my own bed. Little as it is.

"We should get you a safer neighborhood, and a better apartment," he says, nibbling my jaw.

"No," I say, canting my head back to give him access.

"Why?" He eases back.

"Because there's no *we* here. I'm not your kept woman."

He pulls back and his eyebrows pull together. "You work for me."

"I'm underneath you right now, Matthew."

He smiles, shakes his head chidingly, then eases back to eye me as he smooths a hand to brush my hair back.

"I like how real you are, Charlotte. The way you stand up for yourself, and the way you stand up for others. I like how honest and hardworking you are. How sweet you are." He captures my lips between his, brushing his hand along my forehead again, looking into my eyes.

"Can you blame me for wanting to protect you? I never thought I'd meet a woman like you. That pushed all of my buttons like you do. I want you against any hard surface available and I want to shield you from everything at the same time. I never expected you. And I didn't expect you now."

It takes a few seconds to find my voice. "Did you really believe you'd never meet anyone who would be herself with you?"

"Most worry too much about putting up a front they believe matches mine."

"I don't."

"I know. Which makes you rarer than anything to me. So precious." His voice thickens as he expresses his appreciation.

I grab his jaw and kiss him, and Matt grabs my hands and pins them over my head, kissing me, softly but with an underlying urgency and force. And then I'm getting disrobed and taken, in a bed I've always slept on alone, by the only man I've ever really wanted and the only one I can't really ever have. Not if he wins this.

But I take what I can get, moaning softly beneath his kiss as his roaming hands move over me.

THE LAST PRIMARY

Charlotte

The next weekend, Matt visits his grandfather in Virginia. I'm sort of glad for the distance. We're sinking too deep. Though a part of me wants to get in deeper, deep enough to drown, I know that's not the best for him, for me, for anyone.

Matt is a stallion in bed. We spent all night touching, coming, and talking at my place. Neither of us slept, and neither of us seemed to want to sleep. I didn't want him to go.

I am addicted to the times we spend together.

I keep wanting *more*.

But at this stage in the campaign, we're not playing with fire. Our secret, scandalous affair is a nuclear bomb, and any slipup in keeping it hidden will be the match that sets it off.

My parents have me over for dinner one evening and grill me on the campaign. I know, ever since growing up in their household, that in politics, discretion is a must. The last of the primaries are tomorrow, and Dad says he heard Matt had been courted by both parties but had declined.

"You're doing a good job combating decades and decades of power shifts between the two parties, but is it going to be enough, Charlotte? What's Matt plan if they attack, find some scandal in his past?"

"Dad, I'm not his shadow and I'm not a mind reader, either—I'm busy helping organize his schedule and that's that."

"Will we be invited to the fundraiser for literacy he'll be holding near campaign close?" Mom asks.

"You're on the list. Everyone's on the list, even the whole of Hollywood and Nashville; Matt loves music and he loves, *loves* scientists and tech geeks. The campaign has had endorsements so far from nearly six dozen public figures. Even Mayweather posted on his social media with an image of piles and piles of money and a note that read 'Floyd Money Mayweather doesn't do two-hundred-dollar checks, I do cash, and it adds up to a couple more zeroes.'"

I realize how fantastical it all sounds once I hear myself talk about it. How does Matt sleep at all?

How does anyone carry the expectations of a whole country on his shoulders, and carry it well?

"We're not sure we can attend the gala, though," Dad warns me quietly. "You do realize my appearance at such an event would be an endorsement too?"

I meet his gaze and nod quietly, wanting to ask him to please, please endorse Matt, but I respect him too much to ask what he's waiting for. I simply know he's afraid that no matter the people, the parties will make sure the one who ends on top won't be Matt Hamilton.

Later that same night, I check in with my friends at the same bar where I celebrated my birthday months ago. "Hamilton for the win," Kayla says over dinner. "He has my vote. And I know he has yours!"

I laugh, saying, "Of course."

She frowns. "Wait. What? Does he have more than your vote?"

I laugh it off, but, oh god, it's not at all funny.

How could I let this happen? I'd been afraid it would, and I admit to myself that was primarily the reason I was hesitant to join his campaign.

But ... you can't control who you crush on.

Except a part of me believes that you can, that it was wrong of me to fall the way I've been falling, that I know it can go nowhere. But still I want him. And I think of him. And despite wondering if I've let things go too far, if maybe I should quit before they get worse, I've stayed.

Craving to make a difference. Craving ... to be with him.

I look at Kayla, and she has a good guy; she's the one being taken home tonight, who has a job she loves and parents who didn't care if she was a teacher or a guitar player (she's actually both).

I have a job that's temporary, a man I can never truly have, and if my mother realizes that I'm dangerously attracted to Matt, she'll worry. They wanted me in the arms of a promising politician, true, but not the candidate for the presidency, who every woman in the country believes belongs to *her*.

I swore I'd never be a politician's girl—they either cheat on you with another woman or with their jobs, or the truly sleazy ones cheat the voters who put them on their thrones.

But no matter how distasteful I find it all, I live in D.C. I live and breathe politics. Politics has fed me my whole life, put me through a career. Politics is now my job.

Politics is in every pore and cell of the man consuming my dreams.

The fact that he's driven and the most uncorrupted person in the political world as of now only adds to his appeal, to my admiration, to my respect. My desire to remain at his side until the end is too great, no matter how much it hurts the girl inside me who just wanted a guy to love and for him to love her back.

That night I climb into my bed in my little apartment, realizing how lonely I really am when all around me is quiet. Campaigning is exhausting. It's also invigorating and enlightening.

We've met with hundreds of thousands of people. You get to see all the varieties, all the ethnicities that now make up Americans. You get to see courage, suffering, hope, politeness, rudeness, anger, despair—all of that is America.

Sadness is when you don't listen to those in pain until they're crying. You don't listen to those suffering because sometimes they're the ones most silent.

The next day, we're all gathered at the bunker preparing to watch the primary results. And I miss him.

I miss his energy and the passion I feel when I'm around him. I miss traveling with him, him asking me for favors, like getting him coffee, and I miss the focused looks he wears when he puts on his glasses and reads the schedules I bring or the files he asks me to print out.

Tonight, nearly a hundred members of our team are here, watching the flat-screen TV in one of the media rooms as we watch the last primary. The two men in the lead for the parties are the Democrat President Jacobs, and the Republican Gordon Thompson.

President Jacobs. The only good thing he's done for our country he has *yet* to do, which is step out of office and let someone more competitive with better ideas step in.

Gordon Thompson. He wants to increase the military budget while cutting spending on social programs. He seems really pro-war.

And clearly interested in the ratings Thompson seems to garner, the media has been nonstop replaying what he's been blogging, Facebooking, and spouting on TV—when Matt arrives.

He meets my gaze. Our eyes seem to lock for an eternity.

Matt stops staring only when everyone begins to greet him. He greets them back amicably and then sits to my right.

The lights are lowered—and then they're out.

The TV flashes and everyone is silent, watching and listening to the speculations about who the Democratic and Republican nominees will be.

And I'm trying to keep up, except that I'm hyperaware of Matt sitting exactly two inches away. I am aware of the warmth of his body. And amazed at the crackling trail of fire in my veins because he's so close. His clean, manly scent makes my lungs ache. An overpowering urge to get closer won't leave me. I lean back a little instead. I breathe, and then realize he just turned to look at me.

He's staring at my face as if he's branding it to memory, and it seems to frustrate him because he runs a restless hand over the back of his neck.

He stands and goes to get himself coffee, then he stands a few paces to my right, staring at the TV, frowning very hard.

He looks so good.

We've been in a blur of campaigning in reception halls, high school and college gyms, sprinting towards Election Day. Things will get even more intense after today—I'm sure we'll spend another few months away from D.C.

And suddenly I don't know if I can do this. If I can live with this relentless little ache while I travel with him, watch him kiss those babies and genuinely, truly hold them because he wants to, not because it's good press.

As the news continues, *he* flashes on screen. Full head of tousled sable hair with highlights. The entitlement reflected in his informal dress only makes him stand out more. "Matthew Hamilton's good judgment, drive, and discipline are going to be strong weapons against the Republican and Democratic nominees," the newscaster is saying before they head back to tallying the results.

So here we are, watching the early returns as the presumptive nominees of the opposing parties are named.

No surprises there—Jacobs and Thompson. Though Hessler is still surprised, it seems.

"What the ever-loving crap. One is about as old-fashioned as a goddamn priest. And don't get me started on the other. There aren't enough bullpens in the country to hold all the bullshit he spouts," Hessler groans of the opponents.

We all seem to glance at Matt for his opinion.

Matt runs his hands over his neck, frowning thoughtfully. "Our government will keep whoever wins in check. That's the beauty of our system."

Hessler huffs. "As long as they don't cozy up to the idea of issuing a ton of executive orders."

Matt smirks at that, then stares thoughtfully at the TV, obviously weighing his opponents' virtues and flaws.

I stand up and head to the kitchenette outside the viewing room and have to pass by Matt. He doesn't move to let me go by. His gaze darkens as I approach, and he reaches out impulsively to my neck.

Gently he seizes the eagle pin at my collar. He strokes the eagle with the pad of his thumb. Once, that's all, his eyes shining with pride as he does.

I hold my breath. He searches my expression with curiosity. And his smile fades. He's still holding the pin. I'm afraid that he can see I'm almost panting—damn my body! There's a little hurricane of butterflies in my stomach and I'm afraid this guy—so damn perceptive all the time—can see it too.

I'm nervously inching back, and the move makes him drop his hand. He finally moves to let me pass, and Mark suddenly follows me for a refreshment.

"Something going on with you two?" he asks.

"Yes," I say, annoyed at how nosy he is. "Nothing."

"Good. Phew! I was worried for a moment."

I press my lips together and extract a water bottle from the small fridge.

"It's all everyone talks about here—all those phone calls from girls claiming they're Charlotte and they want to talk to Matt."

"Maybe their names are Charlotte." I close the fridge and crack the bottle open.

"All three dozen of them? No way." He shakes his head and wiggles his eyebrows. "There's only one Charlotte as far as I'm concerned ... and unfortunately, there's also only one Charlotte as far as *Matt* is concerned. He can't stop looking at you."

"Mark ... nothing's going on."

He grins then, and he leans an elbow on the doorknob.

"Good. Do you want to go out with me this weekend?"

"Excuse me?"

"A date." He grins.

I hesitate, then realize Matt is still a few steps behind him. He'd been in a conversation with Carlisle, but is now looking in my direction.

If I'm determined to get him out of my system and nix any rumors about us, too, a date is a way to go. Other fishes in the sea, no need to go for the Great White Shark. But all I can say is, "Not until we win."

Then I quietly step out and go back to the viewing room, sipping my water.

The crowd soon disperses, and I find myself battling the urge to linger behind and ask Matt about his weekend. I head to the elevators with the crowd, doing my best to force myself to go home.

Matt frowns when I pass him dismissively. He moves abruptly to stop me, taking me by the elbow. "Hey."

I look up and glance around, concerned that anyone could have seen. But they've all shuffled into the elevators.

We stare at one another, and there are a thousand messages in his stare that I can't decipher but somehow feel, in my belly, like a tangle of crackling wire.

Lips tipping upward in an adorable way I try not to notice, Matt waves me forward. I cautiously walk with him. He has so much power he's not just a person, but a presence.

He's wearing a smile, a wicked little twinkle in his eyes as if he knows … everything.

He frowns down at me and jerks the knob of his office door open. "After you, Miss Wells."

He smiles like a gentleman, but his stare is that of a naughty caveman as I go inside and he shuts the door behind him.

I inhale for courage, but there's one thing about his office here in headquarters. The upper half is glass, and anyone who returns to the building could see us.

My heart is thudding madly as I hear him approach from behind. He slides one hand around my waist and pulls me back against the wall of his chest. "Hmm. Your hair smells good."

I exhale.

"Always different," he adds as an afterthought.

"We're always hotel-hopping; I'm at the mercy of what's offered in my room."

"This is real, though. This is yours," he murmurs.

He seizes my shoulders. His tanned, long-fingered hands giving me a delicious little squeeze.

I try to suppress my reactions as I turn around in his hold and lift my eyes to his face. He's staring down at me quietly, as if trying to figure me out.

"So, Mark," he says, his eyes scanning me.

"What Mark?"

He lifts his brows pointedly.

"Oh, you mean *Mark*."

"Mark Conelly." His eyes flick to the door, then to me. "What does he want with you?"

"Nothing. He's just a friend."

"You sure?"

There's an odd little hum in my body when I see the roiling swirls of darkness in his eyes.

Is Matthew Hamilton, the man who has everything, the world at his feet, jealous?

The angle of his jaw looks about as sharp as ever. "I'm sure. Nothing's going on yet."

"Yet?"

"He wants a date, but I want to concentrate on the campaign first. I didn't decline him outright because he was … speculating about us."

"I see."

I want to know what he's thinking, but he shutters his gaze and simply looks at me.

"He's too old for you," he finally states.

"He's one year younger than *you*," I counter.

"He's divorced. Completely ineligible for you."

I shrug. "I have other options. My friend Alan has been trying to make things serious for years."

His eyes widen. "There's no winning this one with you?" He laughs and rakes his fingers through his hair, frowning in a mixture of amusement and puzzlement.

Although Matt looks calm, I fear there's some sort of tempest lurking in his gaze. Something being held tightly under control.

I remain silent while I struggle with a thousand things I want to do or say. I missed him. I missed his face and the way he smells and the way the office buzzes when he's here. I missed waking up with tangles in my stomach simply because I know I'll see him. I also don't like these feelings, but it's hard to push them away when they're simply ... there. Stronger than ever when he's near.

"Why are you even considering going out with him?"

"Because." I glance away, and then whisper, "It could help dissipate any rumors between us. And because ... you're under my skin, Matt."

There's a silence.

I stay in place even when all my instincts tell me to walk away and not look back.

"Don't go out with him." He waits a moment, then adds, "With any of them."

He draws me to his chest, shaking his head chidingly down at me.

I hesitate, then I lean forward and set my cheek there. He turns his head into my scalp and inhales. Then he nuzzles my nose and strokes his thumb across my lips. He presses gently down on my bottom lip to open my mouth and rubs his thumb over my tongue.

My eyes drift shut. I suck his thumb and then take his hand and turn it and kiss his palm. His hold tightens, and he drags his face lower, his jaw slightly stubbled as he presses his lips to mine.

We groan as our tongues flick over each other, again and again.

My hand fists his shirt. He slides his hand to cup my buttock and drags me a little closer as he parts me with his mouth and kisses me again.

I groan his name.

"Matt."

He snaps his lips back and looks at me, breathing hard. Reality comes to me slowly. We're at headquarters, with glass surrounding us. I'm kissing the Prince of America.

President Jacobs. Thompson. They would leap all over this.

Matt seems to know what I'm thinking.

"The guy you campaign for, I don't know how not to be him. That's who everyone expects me to be." He touches his fingers to my cheek. "But with you it's different."

I exhale as his words sink in. What he means is that in the dark of night, he doesn't want to be president, or Matthew Hamilton.

He wants to be just a man able to lose control without having a story the next day in the media.

I want to hold him to me, and I want to tell him that I love the way he loses control, and that I love the fact that he wears all of the expectations the world has placed on him because he just happened to be named Hamilton really well.

Instead I simply ask him for a ride home, wondering if a man as isolated as Matt has ever really let down his guard with anyone before.

"Lose the tails. I want to drop Charlotte off," Matt tells Wilson after we get in the car, and Wilson makes a few movements—slipping into several underground parking lots to lose the tails before he pulls over in front of my apartment.

Matt follows me inside my building.

His face is set, and he looks thoughtful.

"If you're still thinking about the Mark thing, now you *know* how I feel watching a thousand and one gorgeous women throw themselves at you."

He laughs, then drags his hand over his face. "I'm jealous. I'm man enough to admit it. I'm jealous of any guy who can take you out, walk down the street with you in his arms."

My eyes widen at the confession.

Matt Hamilton jealous of any normal guy?

I feel like I can't compare anything to the delicious electrical current the words send through me.

I'm melting down my thighs, to my toes, as I walk to my apartment.

One of my female neighbors appears.

"Charlotte, I—"

Matt turns.

My neighbor stutters. "Oh, wow."

"Nice to meet you." Matt smiles easily, and my neighbor's eyes can't flare any wider.

Matt sends me a questioning look, and I briskly announce, "Matt, my neighbor Tracy."

"A pleasure, Matt!" my neighbor calls.

Matt greets her and then I lead him into my apartment. "The paperwork is right here, Mr. Hamilton," I say as I usher him inside, making sure Tracy hears and praying that will keep her appeased. Once we're inside I tell him pointedly, "My point. About the girls either throwing themselves at you or dropping to the floor for you."

It's so dark in my apartment, I flick on a lamp and it still feels like the shadows are engulfing us. I enter the kitchen and pull out a loaf of bread just to try to keep my hands busy—not going to his shirt, his jaw, his hair. "I'm going to make myself something to eat. Sometimes I get dizzy when I haven't had any food for a while ... Want some?"

He drops down on a stool and drags out the other one with his toe so he can prop his foot on the footrest and lean forward. "Look at you," he says.

"What?"

"Quite the little homemaker," he croons appreciatively.

I prepare a sandwich, laughing. I can't think with Matt in my kitchen.

"I know some recipes," I boast. "Jessa would teach me when I was young. The day you and your dad came over, I was shocked the president's food would be tasted before he could eat." I glance at him. "It was the highlight of my life. I felt like I'd been selected for something special, which is why I bought the pin. I was even inspired to join Women of the World because of that. I kept you very present in my mind." I laugh.

He just looks at me, and I realize he seems a bit thoughtful.

"Please. Don't be so charming. Don't try to impress me. I would probably vote for you anyway." I laugh, and he doesn't laugh. He stands as I bite into my sandwich, and as I chew, I lift the sandwich in offering. He watches me finish chewing, and when I set down my half-eaten sandwich and wipe a napkin across my lips, he silently tucks my hair behind my ear, leaning forward as if he wants to be close.

I say, nervous now, "Really, I'm smitten with every part of you already."

I freeze when I realize what I said, and my eyes widen, and his eyes darken and narrow as he lifts his hand and drags his thumb across my lips—a mix of rough and tender, lustful and loving.

"If you're so smitten, why are you giving Mark even a second's thought?" he husks out.

I'm panting. "You haven't dropped that? That's totally an only-son syndrome. Not sharing his toys?" I *tsk*.

He looks as if he wants me up against the wall, and I want to run my tongue and fingers all over him.

"I can give a second to Mark," I add. "More than that after the election. You can't have it all, Matt."

"But I want it all, and you want me to want it, you want me to want *you*—is that what this is about? With Mark and now this other guy?"

"No."

"Don't go out with Mark. Don't go out with Whatshisname. He's not right for you." He shakes his head and strokes my lips with his knuckles now. "Don't give these lips to just anyone. They're too pretty. And too rare. And they're mine."

I groan and put my hands to my face, hating that I'm still that eleven-year-old with a crush, except now the crush is crushing me in his embrace. "Matt ..." I lift my gaze. "My neighbor saw you. You have to go."

"Are you worried she'll be daydreaming about me?" Cockiness flits in his words and across his lips.

"No," I deny, but maybe *I am*!

"It's the rumors, then," he says, his gaze darkening.

I nod. "But I'll say I seduced you. That I had evil designs on the White House."

A smile plays on his beautiful lips as a new texture laces his voice, making it sound rougher. "Charlotte, there's nothing remotely evil about you."

"There is. Because I shouldn't even be here, wanting what I want from you, knowing what's at risk. I'm evil personified. In fact, I've never sunk so low."

He takes a lock of my wild red hair, curling it around his index finger. His frown is puzzled, but his eyes seem nothing but fascinated. "Why do you insist on claiming you're stone-hearted and evil—is that a secret fantasy of yours?" He tugs the hair a little forward, which draws my entire head a bit forward as he adds, "Because I happen to like you as you are."

My voice turns smoky. "I simply like to point out I am multifaceted …" He tugs the strand closer and my brain starts scattering. "There are many parts of me you don't know. Like"—he releases the strand and uses his finger to trace my earlobe—"the fact that I have the courage to … I have the courage to seduce you."

"Really?" There he goes, laughing at me with his eyes again and causing wild little flips in my stomach.

I step back and tug on my top, my heart beating faster and faster as Matt continues looking at me, his smile starting to fade.

"You don't believe me?" I prod.

He just looks at me, his stare wolfish and intense.

I grit my teeth together in determination and slowly undo all the buttons, then part my top and shove the material over one shoulder.

The trace of laughter in his eyes becomes shadowed with heat as his gaze falls on my bare shoulder.

Suddenly there's nothing but silence in the room.

Nothing but silence and his eyes tracing my shoulder, up my neck, to my lips, then looking straight into my eyes.

I've lost all power to breathe.

He always towers over me when he's close and right now he looks all male, dark, and there's a little bit too much testosterone in the air.

Matt has never looked sexier than he does now, standing there battling a battle I don't want him to win.

I lick my lips and gather my courage as I shrug off the next shoulder and draw up my arms to cover my front. I watch his face, afraid of his rejection, afraid of my own recklessness.

I should probably stop right now.

No. *Matt* should probably stop me right now.

I should get out of his personal space, or more likely *he* should get out of mine, and yet I let the shirt drop, and Matt remains before me, his eyes fixed on my face—dark like twilight.

More silence.

Matt is so focused, so passionate; I've never seen such passion in a man's eyes before when he talks about the United States of America. I love it, but I also love the way he looks at me with the same passion now. *Me.* Just me.

He can have any woman he wants—and yet he chooses nobody. He's chosen his country for now, and I know I should respect that. *What are you doing, Charlotte?!*

The seconds pulse, and I stand before him in my skirt and bra.

I can't think of anything when he lifts his hand to touch me and slowly drags his knuckles, up from my belly button, between my breasts, up my neck, then back down.

A caress, soft as a feather, the bump of his knuckles barely grazing my skin—his gaze grazing mine with that gentleness, and a tormented frustration I'd never seen there before. It's etched in every line of his handsome, perfect face—in the line of his jaw, the set of his lips, as if they're pressed together to keep from pressing against mine.

I have no words for the things—the want—that I'm feeling.

I've never wanted anything the way I want—need—for Matt to kiss me right now.

I can barely speak. "Do you believe me now?" I swallow. "Aren't you going to stop me from … from taking off the rest?"

He runs his knuckles up my torso again, this time up my throat, where he spreads his fingers open under my jawline, his open hand encompassing my face as the heel of his hand cradles my chin.

"Quiet now. I'm going to look at you for a long, long time." His hot eyes turn my bones to cinders.

I swallow, dazed with desire under his gaze.

He brushes a kiss across my cheek, his breath warm. "I'm going to make these cheeks flush bright red with the ways I'm going to let my fingers play with you," he says, then he leaves his nose there and inhales against my skin.

He caresses up my sides, his nose grazing my ear now.

"You're so passionate … You've got more love for your country than anyone I've ever seen. And it drives me crazy when all that fire comes alive for me. I won't mind watching that fire burn right now."

My voice is thick with lust and longing. "Our country is wonderful," I say, only responding to the first comment. *And you're wonderful in bed,* I think to myself, but I'm not feeding his ego anymore. The world does that in excess already.

"You know what would be wonderful?" he says, twitching his lips thoughtfully to the side.

He cups my ass in his hands.

"What would be exquisite?" he continues.

He squeezes the mounds and in one jerk, pins me flat against his chest.

"You."

He dips his head.

And Matt is kissing me. Hard. Almost as if punishing me for the Mark thing, for tempting him, for *I don't even know what*.

His tongue thrusts, that first thrust wet and hard and oh so good. His grip tightens on my neck, possessive. He deepens the kiss, if that's even possible. "I thought of this mouth all weekend. And these gorgeous breasts ..."

He curls one hand around my breast, the other on the back of my neck.

His hand is warm and gentle on my nape and as he fondles my breast. The touch is so wanted, all I can do is absorb the feel of that large hand teasing my nipple, breaking me apart. While the other is cupping the back of my neck as if it alone holds my spine together, keeps my body from falling, my cells locked together.

He looks down at me and pinches my nipple and pulls me closer a little roughly, and I hold my breath—a breath that is scented with him.

His lips curl a little, and heat charges down my body.

I inhale sharply when he lifts his hand and runs it up my curves, looking into my eyes as he traces the contours. Flesh and blood.

But he looks at me as if he thinks I'm made of something else.

His fingers edge into my waistband and then into my panties as he starts gently kissing me again.

I open my mouth and breathe, "Matt."

He inhales me, then starts kissing my lips again. Hot. Firm. Urgent.

I groan and wrap my arm around his neck.

"Matt—I didn't think. You need to go," I groan, pushing my tongue into his mouth, grabbing fistfuls of his silky hair. "I know that this is ... we can't ... are you going to stop or am I going to have to stop you? Please don't make me stop you. I don't know if I can ..." I groan.

I not only worry that my neighbor will hear us, that a scandal will erupt, but I also don't know how much more of him I can take before I hit the point of no return.

Or maybe I've already reached that point.

There won't ever—ever—be a man who excites me like this one.

He's all I breathe, all I see, all I *want* as he lifts me up to the kitchen counter, and I gasp in surprise but hang onto his shoulders for support.

He reaches under my skirt to pull down my panties. His eyes meet mine and hold them in his penetrating gaze as he takes my mouth with his and starts rubbing my folds between his fingers.

I don't know how to feel, how to react—my world is fragmenting, piece by piece; there is no reality, nothing but my arms around his neck, clenching, and his hot mouth, and his expert fingers, giving me what I need.

"Matt."

He holds me on the kitchen counter and my knees are weak as he opens up my thighs to make more room for his fingers.

Need burns fiery bright as he slides two inside me. Cupping my breast in his hand, caressing. Pulling his mouth free of mine to roam down my neck, to suck on a nipple. I break apart in his arms, beneath his touch and his kiss.

Only after I come, with him saying *shh, I got you* against my lips, do I seem to return to earth.

I stand on shaky legs, and he grabs my hips and rests his forehead on mine. His eyes are lit up with heat and devilish mischief, melting me a little more—if that's even possible.

My voice comes out breathy. "Wow." I lift my hand and set it on his jaw, stroking him with a tenderness I'm not sure I've ever shown him. "It never feels like enough. I keep craving more of you."

He turns his head, placing a soft kiss on the inside of my palm. Voice thicker and more textured than ever, he says, "We're not done yet."

He gingerly kisses the inside of my wrist as he draws my hand to curl it around the back of his beck.

As he brings me flush, he ducks his head and kisses me goodnight. The kiss slow and languorous, an underlying hunger in every thrust of his tongue. I'm trembling, weak from my orgasm, as he's whispering, "I'll see you tomorrow, beautiful," and he pecks my lips, slowly, almost as if in gratitude, and he's gone, telling me before he exits, "Lock up."

The next morning, I'm flushed as I dress for work, anticipating the moment when I see him.

When the hectic pace of our campaign catches up with me and Matt spends all morning running, I almost think I made it up, it didn't happen, all the things he said, all the ways we keep sinking deeper, but my mouth feels that last lick of his lips on mine.

And when Matt finally gets into headquarters and looks at me, the look in his beautiful dark eyes keeps reminding me that it *definitely* happened, and that he means for it to happen again.

NEVER ENOUGH OF YOU

Matt

I can't seem to get enough of her. I've been biting, nibbling, kissing her, *sucking* her ...

We're in the shower and I've got her stripped to a camisole and flimsy white underwear.

I shift the showerhead and aim it toward Charlotte, then watch the water slide down her curves.

I take in the pink, hard little peaks of her nipples against her top. The cotton clinging to her wet body. My eyes trail downward, to the lace of her panties and her pussy visible through the wet cloth. My eyes rise, slowly, to her face, and her tongue darts out, her eyes wide with concern. There's more than concern there. There's yearning, and a little recklessness.

"Matt?"

My throat feels thick as I reach up to touch her cheek with my thumb, trailing it down her jaw as I lean toward her ear. "Yeah?" I say, looking into her eyes, then at her sweet mouth.

The mouth I want beneath mine again. Here, there's no reason for me not to take it, devour its softness until she gasps. I inch down and slide my arms around her waist, pulling her closer, then I brush her wet mouth with my lips.

I'm using her. I can't use her like this. But I can't stop myself.

My alarm wakes me.

I jerk my arm out and shut it off, then pull back the covers and head to the shower stall. Ten minutes under the cold water and I still can't cool down, counting the hours until I can get her alone again.

"I want to see Charlotte tonight. I need your assistance again."

Wilson glances at me as we have coffee in my suite at The Jefferson, waiting for the rest of my team to get their asses over here.

Wilson eyes me in silence, then drags his hand over his bald head. "What are you doing, Matt? I thought you worked this shit out of your system in college, man."

I shake my head. "It's not what you think—it's different with her." I meet his gaze. "I want you to treat her differently. I want you to protect her as if she were me. If this shit gets out, I don't want Hessler or Carlisle throwing her under the bus."

"It won't get out. Not on my watch," Wilson states.

I clench my jaw and stare into my coffee and just see her. Only her.

"I can't not pursue her. I can't give her up yet." I laugh sardonically. "You probably think it's an obsession … but it's more than that. She means more than that."

She grounds me.

She obsesses me.

She fuels me.

This woman not only makes me want to be a great man, she makes me want to be the best goddamn president that ever lived.

She's what I never knew I wanted and have discovered that I need.

I know full well I'm going to have to give her up soon—but I can't bring myself to give her up yet.

Wilson nods. "I got your back."

INTENSE

Charlotte

Before we left D.C., Matt booked us a suite at a small five-star hotel, where he had one of D.C.'s best restaurants deliver an amazing dinner. It felt like a very secret, very wonderful *date* with the man the country swoons over and the one that I am slowly and secretly falling for, and now each time our eyes have met afterward, it seems like we're both remembering that evening and the night of hot sex we shared.

Unfortunately, the last time for a while.

Over the past two weeks, we've been intensely campaigning. The race feels so real now. We're in Matt's suite at the Wynn Hotel in Las Vegas. The work has been so consuming, we haven't had the opportunity to enjoy any more private moments save for one—all the others have been stolen seconds that almost always happen with a room full of people.

A kiss here.

A brush of his fingers there.

Hessler, a man with even less sense of humor than Carlisle, seems to have cracked his first smile in all the months that I've known him as he skims the most recent poll results. "Polls are giving you the lead."

"No time to sit back and sing a victory song just yet," Matt says, his Starbucks in hand.

I've already finished my coffee.

When coffee fails to do the trick to keep you awake, it's really time to switch to Red Bull.

I'm barely awake right now.

I'm sitting on the couch, and my head is leaning on my hand as I try to keep my eyes open. I don't want to miss a single word from the anchors on TV, and at the same time, hearing the men's conversation swirling around me lulls me to sleep. Since we've started, it's been so many months of extensive traveling and nights like this.

Brainstorming, planning, thinking, and, for me, wanting. Wanting *him* ... so much.

I thought that with time, it would get easier. His proximity.

And instead it's grown harder.

We still have a few months of campaigning left. Odd how I yearn for it to be over so I can get over *him*, and at the same time, I'm so alive—I feel like I'm participating in something historical, something that will define our collective futures—I just don't want it to end.

"Charlotte, go get some sleep," Matt says.

I try to shake myself awake when I hear the command nearby.

God. I was snoozing on the couch?

I crack my eyes open and Matt is leaning over me, his shadow covering my whole body.

His eyes are a swirl of bronze, and I wonder if they see right through me. His hand is a brand of its own kind, one that penetrates my skin. Like the touch of a live wire, his grip on my shoulder shoots sparks through my body. How I can possibly sit here and remain still while all this happens inside me is a mystery.

"I'll sleep when I'm dead," I say, smiling halfheartedly.

A brief smile touches his lips.

It's his amused smile, the one that makes his eyes a shade lighter.

I sit upright, glad that the campaign managers are busy taking notes. Matt hands me a cup of coffee, and I know it's his because I was the one who brought them and marked each with a felt-tip pen. His has the word *Matt* inscribed in my own handwriting.

I lift his cup, and it's still warm. He takes a seat beside me and my tiredness fades a bit.

It's hard not to feel the things I do for this man when we've traveled together for months. When I've seen him holding babies, dancing with old ladies; when I've seen him stir the crowds into a roar; and especially when I've seen him with his hair rumpled and a pair of reading glasses on as he skims the morning newspapers, tactically gauging the effects of the campaign we're waging against the Republicans and the Democrats.

Jack bounds up onto the couch between us so part of his head is on Matt and his body is fully on me.

It's amazing how much I've grown to love his dog, considering the way we met was less than stellar. Now I crave his fuzzy warmth, the lick of his warm, wet tongue on my cheeks. As I sip my coffee, Matt reaches down to pet him at the same time I do.

Matt's thumb traces the back of one of his dog's ears, stroking slow and long, as I stroke the other, both of us looking down at Jack as we pet him.

I steal a look at Matt's profile and he looks thoughtful, a muscle working in the back of his jaw.

I'm remembering our last time alone, a fifteen-minute tryst where he followed me to the women's bathroom, locked us in, and kissed me like crazy as he eased his fingers into my panties. He licked his fingers afterward, and I spent all day swooning whenever he met my gaze, brought the tip of his finger to his lips, and then brought out his tongue to lick it.

His smile after he licked it?

His smile was sexiest of all.

I'm thinking of all this, when his thumb moves from the back of his dog's ear to brush over mine.

I lift my eyes, and he smiles at me, a smile I feel everywhere, and I smile back, petting Jack more vigorously, electrified every time Matt purposely passes his hand over mine as he does the same.

"You're a good dog, aren't you? Very sporty with your flea necklace," I tell Jack, and I look up at Matt.

The smile on his face is amused. Tender. I start flushing, and his smile starts to fade, and his gaze becomes a little dark and a whole lot intimate.

Of course he knows his effect on me. He knows his effect on every woman, and though I know he dislikes his physical beauty to detract from the issues he wants to discuss, it doesn't seem to bother him one bit that it has this effect on *me*.

Worst of all, it's not just his beauty. It's his mind, his passion, his dedication, and the way he makes me feel alive, ambitious, hopeful, vital.

I duck and focus back on Jack.

Soon, the team starts shuffling out. I keep playing with Jack, loath to leave until I hear the last of the team head out the door and Matt speaks to Wilson, who's just outside, standing guard.

"Wilson, will you come in for a moment?"

I stand to leave as Matt leads Wilson inside.

"Stay, Charlotte."

I turn to him, and Matt cups my face as he looks into my eyes. "It's been two weeks. I need to see you. I need to touch you."

"We're exhausted."

He smiles, nodding.

Wilson shuts the door behind him, and Matt raises his head. "Wilson, think you can get us out of here? I'd like to take Charlotte somewhere private. Not a hotel."

"I'm on it. Any idea where?"

"My dad's place."

Wilson lifts his brows, then nods and leaves.

"We can't stay here—the staff can walk in at any time," Matt tells me.

"Where are we going?"

"My father had a secret getaway and we never sold it." He heads over to grab his room key and his phones, and fifteen minutes later, we're each leaving through a different hotel exit.

It turns out President Law Hamilton's getaway is in Laguna Beach. We board an aircraft that flies us from Vegas to Los Angeles, and the pilot is an old friend of Matt's and sworn to secrecy. Matt and I fly alone in the cabin while Wilson rides with the pilot. The rest of Matt's detail was told he needed no covering for the evening as he would be staying in. The pilot seems happy to see Matt with me. He smiles as he greets us and says farewell with a "you go, man!" expression.

Once we land, there's a black BMW SUV waiting at the hangar, and Matt leads me to the passenger door, then climbs behind the wheel, telling Wilson, "Take the night off. Meet us there early morning."

"You got it."

Wilson shakes Matt's extended hand, then he peers inside and smiles at me. "You take good care of him, all right?"

"I will," I say, laughing.

Wilson grins and shuts the door once Matt is settled behind the wheel.

We drive for thirty-five miles to the beach, taking in the scenery, Matt reaching out to take my hand and bringing it to his mouth so he can brush his lips across the back of my palm. "It's almost worth having waited to get you alone again."

"I almost feel odd that we're completely alone."

He chuckles, then squeezes my hands and continues driving with this soft, satisfied smile on his lips, frequently bringing my hand up to kiss the back of it or lick the tips of my fingertips.

He pulls into the garage of a beautiful modern home sitting right at the beach.

"I thought the Hamiltons had a home in Carmel, not Laguna."

"We do. This one's my dad's secret place. He used to come here to get away from it all, hear himself think. Now it's mine." He winks as he opens the car door to hop out.

He leads me inside through the garage door and with a command, "Lights," gets the lights to immediately turn on in the living room and kitchen.

As I follow him inside, I'm struck by how unpresidential the home is. How normal. Modern and simple, it's also very homey, with filled bookshelves to one side, family pictures dotting the shelves, and instead of artworks, maps from around the world decorate the walls.

His father loved the world, like Matt does.

"I come here sometimes. Reminds me so much of him. I come here to be close, and to get away and think."

Moved by his words, I follow him past what seems like the library and wander into the living room, breathlessly taking in the view.

"This is like another monument you come to think at."

He laughs, then heads into the adjoining kitchen and opens some cabinets. "Nothing fresh here, but would you like some ... canned beans? Spam?"

"God, what is this?" I laugh, then I watch him pull out a bottle of wine.

"Wine is good. I'm not hungry, though."

"You tired?" He pours two glasses, sets them aside, and opens his arms. I walk inside those arms and press my cheek to his chest. I exhale, letting loose.

"How do you do it?" I ask him.

"Sometimes, I don't know." I'm charmed by the honesty in his voice, but he also sounds confident, as if he does know, as if he has no doubt about being able to do it every day. He settles us into one of the couches, his arm still around me.

"I sometimes think I'm going to just collapse."

He shifts to get us comfortable—and closer—stroking a hand down my hair. "Feel free to collapse here. You're safe, I've got you."

"I can hear the ocean. And I can hear your heartbeat." *And I can hear you breathe.* I find myself inhaling too, inhaling the warm, expensive smell of him. "You should hit the bed. You have a busy day tomorrow," I warn.

"If you'd take it easier with my schedule, I might even know what it means to sleep on an actual bed."

I laugh.

He shifts forward. "I don't want to sleep. I don't want to miss a second of this."

"You will get more moments like this if you keep suavely organizing our escapes."

"I've spent so much time planning our escapes, it's embarrassing." He smiles. "To be honest, you're the only woman I've ever spent this much thought on."

"Wow, Mr. Suave Presidential Candidate. You successfully managed to make me sound like a chore."

"The chore is not you. It's not having you like I want. It's not having you all."

He leans back, stroking his hand absently down my arm. "So many people accidentally fall into what would become their most renowned accomplishments. Steve Jobs, his friendship with Wozniak. Even Escobar didn't wake up one morning deciding he'd be the most famous drug lord; he was a smuggler—the drug was basically brought to him."

"And you?"

"I wouldn't run if my dad were alive. I wanted something along the lines of normal. Not that the media ever made it possible; they've wanted me to run ever since ... ever."

He reaches out to sip on his wine, then sets it aside and turns back to me. I sit back and am aware of the excited nerves going through me as he lifts his hand to touch me.

"But we cannot live in a country where our presidents get murdered and we never find out who's responsible. We're greater than that, smarter than that. We've forgotten what it means to be an American—the Constitution doesn't say 'I, all for me.' It says 'we the people.' Everyone is out for themselves now, and that's not what we're about." He says it with the certainty of someone who never settles for less than the best.

He reaches out for me and my tummy tumbles. "So it's not just about me." He kisses my cheek in a way that's almost brotherly. "Remind me that if I ever can't keep my hands off you in front of the team," he whispers before he kisses the back of my ear, his eyes sparkling. "By the way, you smell divine."

I smile and meet his gaze.

Exhaling and lifting my face closer, I slip my hand over his chest and press my lips to his.

Matt groans softly, his body tightening under my fingertips, his hold firming around me as he sucks my tongue, his hunger palpable, unleashed. The shadow of stubble along his jaw tickles my skin.

"I want your wanton little noises tonight," he murmurs quietly into my mouth, meeting my gaze as he slips his hand under my top. "I want you soaking me to the wrist." He plunges his tongue inside and cups my breast, flicking my nipple. "I want you coming undone for me, so fucking undone you'll think you're breaking."

"Yes," I breathe, moving my arms, holding him close as I shift beneath him and pull him over me on the couch.

"You're not too tired to come, are you?" He strokes his fingers over my pussy.

I mewl.

"Don't worry, baby, I'll give you what you need. I've got you. Just relax, let me give it to you," he says softly, dragging his lips along my face, my neck.

I moan softly and slide my hands up his hard arms.

"You're gorgeous. God, you're gorgeous. I just want to be in you. I want to be looking at you, like this. Writhing and noisy. You're so sweet, baby, nobody knows there's a sex bomb lying underneath those little business suits. Only me."

"Yes, you, Matt," I agree, shifting beneath him as he unzips his pants and pulls himself out, and then he sheaths himself and fills me, and I'm lost in this, in him.

We move things to the bedroom an hour later, cuddling naked in bed. "I like it here," I say.

"You're the first good memory this place has had for a while." He brushes my hair back and smiles at me. "I'm glad I brought you here." He kisses me, the sweetest kiss I've had in my life, and no matter how exhausted I am, I can't sleep. Like him, I don't want to miss a moment of this—even a second.

This isn't a childish crush anymore. I love him. I love Matt with my whole being. I breathe him, breathe for him.

I breathe to help him win—even if that means I won't ever, ever feel his arms around me like this again.

I wake to a husky voice. "Charlotte, we're leaving."

I stir. "What time is it?"

"Five. We need to get going." He strokes the top of my head and nods to a fresh cup of coffee. "In case you need it. Did you have a good night's sleep? Or should we call it a nap, it was so brief?"

I smile and nod, and I don't expect him to kiss my mouth because we're in a hurry. But he does, his eyes proprietary as he eases back and pats the side of my butt. "All right, rise and shine, beautiful."

I fall back in bed, squeezing my eyes shut, and I bite back a smile before I push myself out of bed.

RAIN OR SHINE

Charlotte

seem to be great at organizing the field team as well as all of Matt's engagements perfectly, but I seem to be really bad at things most normal people are good at.

I can't sleep.

I can hardly eat.

I'm high from him, from the looks, the stolen touches, the secret lust, watching him at rally after rally, speaking firmly and from the heart to crowds calling out his name.

It's been eight days since we were at his dad's place by the beach, and I'm still affected by the intimacy we shared.

I'm in love with him; there's no doubt about it. It's not just sex, not just a crush. It all became clear during our time together. Being with him in his secret space was special—as special as the night Matt came to dinner with his father. I feel guilty for caving to my desires, potentially putting his candidacy in jeopardy when I know this man would be *so* good for the country. But I yearn for more time with him.

Attempting to put some space between us, I told Carlisle I'd ride the bus with the campaign team to New York, but Matt simply sent Wilson to my hotel room to tell me what time he expected me at the airport.

I climbed into the plane along with Hessler, Carlisle, a famous political strategist named Lane Idris, Matt, and Jack. I was grateful Matt's grandfather was busy running his real estate business from Virginia and wouldn't be flying with us.

I listen to the men talk politics and observe Matt watching, thinking about their suggestions. When the talk turns to other subjects, Matt turns to me and eyes the book on my lap.

The book I'm reading is *Democracy in America* by Alexis de Tocqueville.

I love it because it's not about how perfect democracy is, but rather how imperfect it is. Like everything in life, democracy needs to be balanced.

Strange to be thinking about balance when I've never felt so unbalanced in my life.

We spend the short flight discussing politics and democracy.

I learn Matt's favorite book is *The Righteous Mind*, which examines why conservatives, liberals, and libertarians have different opinions about right and wrong, most based on their gut feelings. He calls it an eye opener on all our curses and virtues, and says a candidate must bring people together.

When we arrive in New York, I do a good job of acting cool and collected, until Matt tells me he's heading out for a bite with Hessler and asks me to come along.

"Sure," I say, as calmly as I can.

But when we stop off at the local campaign office first, I make a detour to the restroom and pull out my makeup kit, making sure I look amazing. Just because I'd never really gone out with him, and it feels like this is the closest thing to a date we could ever have.

Matt asks his driver to drop us off in Nolita so we can walk a bit before arriving at the restaurant in Chinatown. We're trailed by four security guards as Hessler, Matt, and I make our way along Mott Street to the Peking Duck House, a restaurant he fondly recalls coming to with his parents on special occasions.

There's something so vibrant about the New York streets. And Matt fits right in. He drew a lot of attention in the other cities we visited, but New York is used to celebrities. Amidst the hustle and bustle, everybody is doing their own thing—and Matt Hamilton isn't Matt Hamilton today. He's just a hot guy casually dressed in jeans and a V-neck T-shirt, walking next to a girl who's having trouble keeping her cool. It's nice to be able to walk next to him without attracting the attention of everyone passing by.

"This is incredible," I say, smiling as I take in everything around us.

Hessler is smoking to my left; Matt's got his hands in his pockets, a look of thoughtful enjoyment on his face as he studies my profile.

"Are you hungry?" he asks.

I groan and clutch my stomach. "Extremely so. You?"

"I've definitely got my eye on something tasty," he says with a wicked sparkle in his eye. And he leans over to whisper, "As always, you look amazing."

I feel my cheeks warm at the gruffness in his tone. I look down at my low-cut black lace camisole, short black flouncy skirt, and black high-heel sandals.

He smiles at me, amused by the blush rising up my cheeks as he raises his arm over my head and catches the door

Hessler just opened. At the move, I catch the delicious scent of his Bond No. 9 cologne.

As Hessler walks toward our table, Matt softly brushes his fingers over my exposed back, just under the fall of my hair. The gesture is simple, a little proprietary, and so unexpected that an intense ribbon of heat shoots down my spine.

I can't believe how turned on I am by the time I take a seat. I get wetter every time Matt moves his hand under the table along my thigh, his fingers caressing the inside of my legs under the hem of my skirt.

He occasionally removes his hand, but never for long.

I can see him scanning the restaurant, confirming his touch is private—only for us.

We have the most delicious lunch while I enjoy hearing Matt and Hessler talk about their interests outside of politics. Hessler is an avid golfer. Matt grew up playing baseball and still closely follows the Mets, his favorite team.

Hessler leaves early to smoke before heading to the rally in Washington Square Park. Matt picks up the check while Wilson and the three other security guards wait for us outside.

I watch raindrops start trickling along the windows as we wait for his credit card to be returned. By the time we're outside, it's pouring. Matt tells Wilson and the other guards to stay twenty feet behind us. My heartbeat picks up as I anticipate the alone time.

I smile at the guards as we walk past, and I pull an umbrella out of my handbag. Matt holds it above our heads as I curl against his side and we begin walking up the street.

The rain is coming down so hard that the umbrella provides little protection. I begin laughing and point toward a deserted covered fruit stand. "We should get under that awning."

"Nice ploy." He shoots me a smirk and a knowing look—as if I'm intentionally trying to steer him off to the side.

I open my mouth to set the record straight, but before I can, Matt firmly pulls me toward him and tenderly presses his lips to mine. His hand slides around my waist, down to my butt, gripping me tight against him.

He lowers the umbrella a bit, shielding us from prying eyes. He tightens his grip, his mouth hungrily devouring mine.

The moment is electric, mind-blowing—his mouth as wet as the raindrops on my hair, sweet and minty and hungry. His shirt wet, plastered against his sculpted chest.

His tongue moves over mine. I deeply inhale the scent of his cologne.

Delicious. Intoxicating.

Then, as if stirred from a beautiful dream, I suddenly come to my senses.

"Are you crazy?" I whisper and pull free, my voice barely audible through the pounding rain.

He grins, eyes dancing. "Yes."

I laugh, and he's smiling, but his smile doesn't last long.

He pulls me back against him and rests his forehead on mine, his eyes searching my features. "Tell me how I can satisfy this country when I feel so lacking? Tell me." He squeezes me, silently asking for an answer.

I know what he means.

He means that he has me, but not openly, and I have him, but not for long. What we have satisfies our physical cravings, but we're left wanting more.

Matt gingerly tips up my chin as he lowers his face to mine. First he nuzzles my nose and strokes his thumb across my lips. He presses gently down on my bottom lip to open my mouth. My eyes slowly drift closed and my mind goes blank as he tenderly presses his lips to my cheek. I inhale deeply, and so does he.

"How do you not get bothered by it? The press following your every move? This is the first time we've been outside without being followed," I say breathlessly.

"I grew up with dozens of lenses surrounding me—they were never far away. I grew blind to the extra eyes, and most days I don't mind being watched." He glances at my lips, then returns his gaze to mine, and quietly adds, "But sometimes they're so close I feel like I have no space to breathe." He smiles down at me and lifts the umbrella. "Let's go—we have a rally to attend."

"Washington Square Park. I still can't believe we secured the permit—although it's probably because your family owns a good portion of New York."

He smirks. "Maybe it's because I'm charming."

"Oh, I wouldn't bet on it," I lie.

The rain barely stopped in time for the rally—but that didn't deter the crowds. On the contrary. They filled the park, and even the surrounding streets were packed.

He kills it at the Washington Square Park rally.

After rousing the crowd to a "HAMILTON! HAMIL-TON! HAMILTON!" we head back to the hotel in several cars. I ride with him and Carlisle. The city is alive, bursting with light and night noises as we approach our hotel.

I'm silent and in awe. I'm in New York with the hottest man I've ever seen, riding in the back of a luxury car, heart thumping in excitement and a hot little tingle between my thighs because of his nearness, and because he's got his hand resting just where he can brush his thumb over my thigh—and lounging in his seat as if that hand belongs there.

I suppose I should take it off, but I like the way it feels too much to do that.

It excites me, true. But it also relaxes me. I'm taking in the Village, Midtown, and then, Fifth Avenue all along the east side of Central Park.

"We're getting good media coverage," Carlisle announces.

"Good," Matt says.

I smile, so proud of him today.

Rain or shine, the Hamilton team campaigns.

That night, I wait for him to message me through the secure campaign phone that the coast is clear, and when he tells me he's coming over, I unbolt my door and pull him into my bedroom.

I'm still deliciously sore from the fuck he gave me last night—*fucks*, actually, and there were three: one slow and gentle, one fast and primal, and a very wet and passionate one in the shower—when I get to the New York field office the next morning. Carlisle and Hessler summon us all together, as they frequently do. We're briefed in an eight-by-eight room, crowded with all of us. Matt stands in the corner, leaning against the wall, arms crossed as he lets his managers do the talking.

My eyes meet his across the crowd. It's only a glance. That's all we give each other. But it's enough to make my tummy go crazy.

"Let's run down what's been going on," Carlisle begins.

I slide my eyes back to Carlisle and focus on the run-down.

Shit is getting real and we're going to need to bring the big guns to every event, and be aware that our *competition* will be aware of our every move.

President Jacobs, sixty-five, conservative, a peacemaker, a bit too weak-spined.

Gordon Thompson, fifty-nine, radical, a bit too war-loving.

Carlisle shoots us all a dire look and then looks at me a little too brazenly. "Just to be clear, we are working with the best independent candidate the USA has ever seen. No third-party candidate has ever won. This will be unprecedented. Matt Hamilton was born for this; we all know it. Not always the favorite one prevails in politics. It's the one who wrangled more support in his campaign. So it's up to us to make his supporters multiply like freaking Jesus did the bread. Okay?"

Everyone nods.

My throat closes and guilt starts creeping up my throat. I nod vigorously.

Carlisle nods, appeased.

"Let's get our candidate back to the White House where he belongs." He gives a final nod, and we all scatter. I head to the door of Matt's office with his itinerary in hand.

"Good morning, Charlotte," he says as he enters and waves me inside.

"Good morning, Matt."

The moment I shut the door, Matt lifts me up to the desk, and I gasp in surprise but hang on to his shoulders for support. The possibility of getting caught makes me scan his office— then I realize we're not at headquarters, that this office has no windows. Walls mean privacy for us, and I go loose and pliant in his arms, wet and instantly ready.

He reaches under my dress to pull down my panties. His eyes meet mine and hold them in his roiling, stormy gaze as he takes my mouth with his and starts rubbing my folds with his fingers. I gasp, and he smothers my gasp beneath his lips, my arms clenching around his neck, and his hot mouth and expert fingers giving me what I need.

"Matt."

He holds me on the desk and my knees are weak as he opens my thighs wider to make room for him. Need burns fiery bright as he starts to enter me.

He pauses. "God, I don't have a condom."

I grab his jaw. "I'm protected, on the pill. I'm clean."

"I'm clean too. I've never ..." He trails off as he looks at me, cups my breast in his hand, caressing, kisses me, then pulls his mouth free to roam down my neck, to suck on a nipple through the fabric of my dress. I'm thoughtless, arching up.

Matt helps me stand, then flips me around and lifts my skirt over my ass, kicking my legs apart.

I swallow back a moan when I feel him drive inside. He leans over me, nipping the back of my neck. "God, you're heaven," he says, hands on my hips as he drives into me from behind. I *do* moan this time; he reaches out and covers my mouth. I lick his palm, and he thrusts inside me again.

I mewl into his palm again. He pounds me as hard as he needs. As hard as I crave. He drowns my cry of release with his palm and buries his own growl in the top of my head.

We don't speak of it when we're done. I just laugh nervously, and he smiles and pats my back, righting himself until he looks as perfect as ever.

"Charlotte," he says before I leave.

"Yes?"

"If I win, I want you in the White House. Working there." He drops behind his chair. "I'm on my best game when you're around—let's just put it that way."

"Are you blackmailing me? Emotionally?"

"I'm asking you."

"You're asking me with that demanding look that means you're demanding."

"Then I'm demanding-slash-asking you."

I frown.

He stares at me, shifting to prop his elbows on the desk. "If I'm elected, I'm going to do everything I promised those people out there I'd do. I need the best team possible; a president can only accomplish what his support system allows. I want you in the White House."

"I've never had ambitions to work in the White House," I say. "It's not a place that I want to have a career. It's more like the kind of place I found exciting to visit and loved worshipping from afar."

And I don't think I could bear how hard it would be to see you every day and remember ...

His eyes look frustrated. I'm sort of afraid he's going to push it—I don't want him to. He's too tempting to me. Being with him is too addictive. I want to be mature and realistic about this. About us.

So before Matt can insist, I steal out and get back to work, bringing my attention to our end goal: giving our country the chance to join the strong, charismatic leader we've been waiting for.

MORE

Charlotte

We're in San Francisco now.

It's noon as we all gather in our makeshift local campaign offices when Carlisle drops a newspaper on Matt's desk. On the bottom of the front page are two pictures—of Matt smiling down at me and helping me out of the car to our hotel.

The caption beneath them both reads, **Is Love in the Air for Matthew Hamilton?**

He doesn't read the article. Instead he's got his cell phone out, putting it on speaker and speed-dialing as he skims the rest of the news. A male voice picks up, stating his name and the name of the newspaper that happened to have posted that picture. Matt greets him and immediately gets to the point.

"Who took those pictures?"

"Not me, Matt, honest to god."

Matt runs his hand over the back of his neck and sighs, frowning at the phone.

"We're running a campaign here, not a season of *The Bachelor*. Let's keep our eye on what's important, all right?"

"Sure thing, Matt. And hey, thanks for the book you sent last Christmas. My wife keeps it on the mantel as display."

"I'm glad, Tom. And thanks for the coverage."

He hangs up and looks up at me, then at Carlisle, then he resumes reading the news, calmly sipping his coffee while I struggle to look inconspicuous.

We have a meeting with two dozen of our campaign team members next.

For the entire two and a half hours, the team is scribbling notes with pens inscribed with Matt's campaign logo, and then they're all standing as he rises to leave and starts shaking hands, thanking them. I'm surprised that many of the male team members approach me to say goodbye as well.

Matt falls in beside me as we exit the conference room.

We leave the building and walk two blocks to our hotel. Usually there are other team members trailing behind, but today we seem to be headed toward the hotel on our own. My heartbeat picks up.

Matt is supposed to shower and have a quick lunch before he accompanies Carlisle to meet Senator Lewis, who has a large amount of delegates and support in this state. I'm hoping to take a shower as well and maybe a nap; the previous long night is weighing a little on me. It amazes me that it didn't seem to weigh on Matt one bit. He looks better than ever, though the truth is that he is always active, buzzing with calm, steady energy.

Silence engulfs the elevator as we ride to our floor. Matt shoves his hands into his pants pockets and looks at me.

The fact that we were kissing heatedly recently in public, in New York City, is suddenly the only thing I can think of.

He asks me if I'd like to go up to the top terrace of the building for ten minutes.

I nod. It's nearly sunset when we step outside. The large terrace has beautiful views of the city, especially the horizon, orange with the fading sun's glow.

We stand there and take in the scenery for a moment.

We're quiet for a while, the kind of quiet where you don't really need to say anything, where just being in that place at that time is enough.

"We're on the home stretch now." He smirks, then glances meaningfully at the elevator behind us and shakes his head. "This little escape is enjoyable but not private enough to suit me. I mean to keep seeing you as much as I can. Alone, Charlotte."

My cheeks warm at his words. I grab my hair as it flies with the wind.

"I'm pretty sure as we head to election our moments will become more and more fleeting," I admit, laughing.

"I won't allow that to happen." He plunges his hands into his pockets. "I want to spend my every free moment with you —and I want you to spend yours with me."

I feel shy all of a sudden. "You need your sleep," I whisper, shooting him a chiding look.

Lightly smiling, he reaches out to brush the back of his thumb along mine. "I've got news for you, Miss Wells—my off-schedule hours are mine to do with as I please. And I intend to do *you* every one of them."

Oh god, my sex just sort of gripped really tight.

He's so sexy when he talks like this to me.

I'm flushed, uncertain about continuing to play this game, especially when it's getting close to voting day, when the camera eye will keep zooming more and more on him as he continues making news and racking up voters.

"I'd like that. But I don't know if it's a good idea to keep taking risks … We're ending this soon." I chance a shy glance at him. "Aren't we?"

He drops his hand, his jaw tightening. "I watched my mother take a backseat to the country. I can't allow you to do that too," he says.

"Maybe I don't mind taking a backseat to the president …" I trail off, suddenly realizing what's coming out of my mouth.

"That's not happening. Ever." His eyes flash, and I'm taken aback by the steely determination in his words and voice.

I quickly try to explain. "Look, the needs of *one* woman shouldn't come before a whole country. I wouldn't expect—"

"You don't need to be anyone's afterthought. Not even the country's. I'm not doing that to you—don't even ask me to. Not me, not anyone." He looks at me, then rakes his hand through his hair. "God. You've still got so much ahead of you, you've got so much to offer, you don't deserve eight years—four at least—" He trails off, his eyes dark, as if he hates remembering.

"It wouldn't be hell to me if I spent it with you," I whisper.

We're interrupted when one of our team members appears on the terrace. We step back a little from each other when we hear the elevator ting and then Hessler comes over, instantly charging forward to talk business with Matt.

Matt's smile fades, and he pops open a button on the sleeve of his shirt and folds his cuff as he listens. Getting down to the dirty job.

I spend more time listening than the five minutes we spent alone together just now, and then I quickly excuse myself.

I notice the steely frustration in his gaze as I leave, the way his jaw clenches as if he's keeping himself from saying something.

NEWS

Charlotte

I hardly slept. I kept wanting to go to him, I kept sort of hurting, remembering how Matt got ticked off just thinking of me in the same situation his mother once endured. I kept thinking of him wanting to spend more time with me, and I kept checking my calendar, crossing another X on another day with him that I won't ever recover.

I also got a call from my mother, and if I hadn't already had enough on my mind, that phone call also had me tossing and turning all night.

She's concerned about the rumors and concerned I might be harming this campaign more than doing it any good.

"Half of the press is speculating about you two," she warns. "Are you sure you don't want to consider quitting while you're ahead and Matt is the country's favorite, and come back to Women of the World?" she asked.

"I'm sure," I told her, but last night, as sleep eluded me, the kernel of doubt she planted sat like a ton of bricks in my gut.

This morning I'm rushing to get ready. The TV is set on the local news, and I'm half listening—when I hear my own name being said.

I freeze in the bathroom, where I was applying makeup.

Disbelieving, I walk out to the bedroom and stare at my face on the TV screen—a picture of me from a high school yearbook, another of me standing discreetly behind Matt at one of the events.

A big red circle is around Matt and me in that picture. Next flashes an image of me from my social media that the campaign staff had actually asked me to take down; I'm in a bikini, pictured with Kayla, Sam, and Alan. Did the press gain access to it through other posts on my friends' sites?

It's a shock to see my image on the TV. My personal images out there. True, social media is public. But on TV?

I set the lipstick aside on the nightstand, my eyes widening as I listen.

They're now speculating about me? *Just* me?

"Think there'll be a romance …?"

"Maybe, Carl. Her Georgetown colleagues describe her as being a sweet, hardworking girl who always did the right thing."

"President Lawrence—or as they called him, 'Law'—Hamilton and Senator Wells had a friendship dating back to their years in the army, so maybe it really is just a friendship between Matt Hamilton and Charlotte Wells. Time will tell."

I flash back to the last night I spent in Matt's arms. The hotel room becomes tiny, claustrophobic. I'm reeling like a drunk, and the kernel of fear my mother planted seems to grow a thousand and one limbs.

Really, there are other news stories to be told.

I skim the channels. On another station, they're talking about Gordon having a deal to funnel supporters from the Republican candidates who lost their bid for the presidency.

Another has a story about President Jacobs and his latest executive order.

I flip to another channel, which is showing Matt speaking during one of his engagements. "Our country is on the brink of transformation." And the crowd, drunk on him, is swept up in the moment.

I frown, march into the hotel closet to search through the clothes I packed, and pull out my most powerful power suit that says I mean business—and that's all I mean.

I'm grateful the rest of the day focuses on what matters. The campaign.

Even more grateful to find that Matt had decided to cut the speculators' wings, flat out.

Matt's comment on the issue of our relationship on TV that evening: "Miss Wells is an old family friend, and more important, she's perfect at her job. Thank you." And with a nod and a grin, he leaves them all whispering and tittering.

Feeding them crumbs … but for how long will it be enough to satiate their appetites?

DEBATE

Charlotte

I ride to the first debate with Hessler and Alison, and arrive at the event just in time to watch Matt get out of the car right in front of us, the cameras swarming him like bees to honey. I know that physicality is important in debates and speaking engagements. Matt doesn't have any problem with that. He walks straight in, his jacket in his hand, a trail of us behind him.

"What did you do to prepare for this this morning?"

"What's your plan—how are you going to win the debate tonight?"

"No preparing. I was born for this." His lips curl wickedly and he then nods formally at the reporter.

We head into the debate hall for the walk-through, preparing, seeing the stage and taking in his position to the right of the center, where President Jacobs will be.

There's excitement in the air, the vibration so charged, you can feel the anticipation. Matt looks calm, but he's got his game face on.

I know that this is not a moment to change plans or re-think strategies; it's a moment to feel confident, calm, and steady.

Carlisle, too, looks relaxed. He knows Matt does well in this kind of setting. He has an innate strength for connecting with audiences and voters, even reporters.

Before the debate even starts, Alison is taking pictures as if it's her last camera.

I watch him stand there, composed and powerful, his every word measured and smooth. I know he's improvising it all; his speeches are very conversational, frequently making people smile even when he's not trying to be funny. He's simply natural and charming when he meets people, treating them as equals—something many politicians pretend to do but actually don't. Matt doesn't have a politician's bone in his body.

And maybe that will be what ends up making us lose this race. He doesn't want to do things Carlisle assures us had worked for his father's campaign, such as exchange support for future positions in the government. Matt won't sell out. He wants people to work in high positions because of their merit, not because he needs their backing.

He's the only candidate fully funding his own campaign. All the money from fundraisers has gone to support some of the causes he holds important—I was surprised when I got a phone call from my mother, thanking him for his donation to Women of the World.

The heat is on. Sweat beads along my brow as the candidates take their positions.

Matt is speaking about women's rights, and looks at me briefly before the topic veers to equal rights for all. I can't believe how turned on I get watching him talk about his vision, his plans. It stimulates me in every way—mentally, emotionally, and physically. He speaks of what I hope my country's future will be like.

Gordon goes on and on, blaming the Democrats for our problems, blaming everyone but not really providing solutions. He talks tough, but his body language says otherwise; he keeps his shoulders to his ears and speaks in a bit of a supplicating tone.

The moderator keeps coming back to Matt.

He's got a more confident and assertive body language, his voice firm. The alpha stance is appealing, and Matt is a very likable candidate, his voice steadier and more forceful. People want someone who takes charge, who's going to fight for what they believe in. They also want someone who can keep his cool—someone authentic when he speaks, as if he didn't memorize the speech.

He looks with respect at the other candidates, listening to what they argue about without rolling his eyes or sneering— like Gordon does.

Gordon listens with disdain to what Matt and President Jacobs say, openly showing his hatred. Matt doesn't interrupt his opponents; he's silent, eyes focused and intent as he listens, a presidential air already about him. I love how he keeps pushing back at Gordon's sexist comments.

"How can Matt Hamilton here," President Jacobs scoffs at the name, "be commander in chief when he never served in the military for a day, while I served four years?"

"Matt?" the moderator asks. "Would you care to respond to President Jacobs?"

Matt smiles at the president as if he hadn't just been insulted, then he looks at the public and speaks squarely to them. "Anyone who knows me knows this is one of my biggest frustrations. My wish was to enlist in the navy, and it was my father's request that I do so after I got a law school degree. The summer after I graduated, my father was shot, and I chose to remain here to support my mother, who feared losing me next."

There's complete silence.

"If you're questioning my ability to make a hard call when it's needed or command our military properly, I must remind you, it's *you* who have had ample opportunity to retaliate against terrorist attacks and have balked—"

"Are you suggesting the United States go to war?"

"War, no. I don't believe in an entire race paying for the wrongdoings of a few. But I do believe we have more muscles to wield than what we've wielded so far."

They speak about immigration, taxes, and then, of course, the issue of Matt's lack of a First Lady is addressed.

"You're breaking with tradition! The White House dignitaries need a hostess," President Jacobs rants.

"Who will I be to deny them?" Matt grins, and the audience laughs. Once the laughter subsides, Matt sobers up and he leans into the microphone. "Throughout our presidencies, there have been a number of formidable women who have served as First Lady without being married to the president. Harriet Lane acted as First Lady during the presidency of her uncle, James Buchanan, and there have been at least twelve others who have served in a similar fashion. In that capacity, I have incredible women on my team, ladies with class and passion and more humanity than many of us put together."

He looks into the center camera.

"I also happen to have a living mother, who not only served as First Lady before, but continues to this day to be one of the most beloved."

There's applause.

"So you'd have a nontraditional First Lady? In such a modern age?" Jacobs asks.

He shoots Jacobs a look. "First you criticize me for not having one, now you criticize because I think there are advantages to having one? The First Lady is meant to be more than a pretty hostess on the president's arm. I'd rather surround myself with capable people who deserve the part."

People fall silent as they absorb that, but the tension is high.

Carlisle is frowning at me as if he hadn't expected this part of the debate at all.

He quickly recovers when he sees the reaction in the room.

Soon, the candidates deliver their closing statements, with Matt's statement last.

"Debates are about divisions, about differing points of views, but there are some universal truths that cannot be denied. The universal truth of cycles—spring, summer, winter, fall; the universal truth of gravity; and a universal truth that we've discovered from the first moment our ancestors appeared on earth six million years ago—man adapts.

"Man has used his brain to outwit predators who are stronger, faster, more numerous. Man has learned to tame some of those predators: wolves became our friends, animals were bred for food. Man learned to farm, feeding millions where before they would feed less than a fourth of that; man invented shelter, clothing, weapons, writing, trade, architecture that defied their physical capabilities, and now, a network and infrastructure that connects us all. Planes, translation, the internet. We're more interlaced than we've ever been.

"So why are we still divided?

"We live in a world where there is still racism and poverty. We live in a country where there is still unequal opportunity for us all ... a world where millions of our children continue to go uneducated. I'm for the possibility of every American finding fulfilment in his or her life—making a difference for others and for themselves."

I can't get my oxygen back. The statements from Gordon and President Jacobs seem lame now. Focused simply on little pieces of what Matt just reminded us is actually a whole living, breathing world.

We're in Matt's hotel suite in Dayton, Ohio. The good news is that not only is the first debate over with, but Carlisle is thrilled. The media coverage influencing voters really seems pro-Matt.

"I'm too old for all this excitement," Carlisle says, sighing exhaustedly but happily.

I bring him a hot coffee. "At your age, most men run for president." I smile and chance a glance at Matt, noticing he felt the quip coming his way and is smiling to himself.

The press has speculated endlessly on whether he's too young to be president. And yet tonight he was the only man on that stage.

Carlisle chuckles at my jab at Matt's age. "I already put one in the seat and I'd be happily at my consulting firm if it weren't for this one." He jabs a thumb at Matt as he heads to the window.

"He lured you out," I say.

"He lured *you* out," Carlisle counters.

I smile.

"He's the one," he says with firm conviction. "If I can't get him to the White House ..."

"He'll run again."

"Girl, I've got a heart condition. One more is all I can take." He pats his stomach as if his weight is to blame for his heart problem, which could be right, and waves me off with his hand.

I head toward Matt and stand next to him, and we stare out the window for a moment. I don't know that we'll ever get close enough again that his breath mingles with mine. So I just stand as close to him as I can without getting burned.

MRS. HAMILTON

Charlotte

We're making a pit stop in D.C. once more. Carlisle and Hessler are meeting with a couple of delegates tonight, and they asked me to accompany Matt to a dinner with his mother and grandfather.

"That old prick will at least hold his tongue with someone he considers a stranger around," Carlisle tells me.

"You hate Mr. Hamilton?" I ask him as we head to the poll-review meeting this morning.

"I admire the crap out of him. I just want him off Matt's back; we've got enough on our hands. Do you realize in getting the lead in the polls at this stage we're accomplishing something that's never been done?"

"Does Matt know that you want me there?"

"Of course he does. He's the one who suggested it."

"Oh."

My heart sort of tumbles, because I'm suddenly pretty sure Matt orchestrated this whole thing to his advantage in the first place.

Carlisle nods in dismissal and I hurry to finish making sure we have the polling result copies for every manager and director of the campaign who's to attend this morning's meeting.

I get a kick of excitement at the thought of meeting a woman who's been adored by the media for years.

"I might be less apprehensive to meet a queen than your mother," I tell Matt that night as he leads me into his house.

It's the first time I've seen Matt's mom in person, and I'm awed by her beauty and class. The one and only Eleanor Hamilton. She's as polished and elegant as Matt is; his dark eyes and hair come from her. My own mother has always admired her—everybody does. She and Matt are the embodiment of strength under adversity.

"Charlotte, it's nice to meet you at last." Her voice is soft and warm as she takes my hand. "I can see why everyone is so taken with you."

I laugh but feel spots of warmth on my cheeks when she looks at Matt.

The décor in his home is modern and elegant too. Wood floors. Pristine taupe rugs with a hint of matte gold thread in delicate scroll patterns. Soft taupe wallpaper and fine art. I hadn't really noted it the first time I'd stopped by—intending to end whatever it was we'd started.

Well, look how that went.

A cold sliver runs down my back when I hear Matt's grandfather.

"Matt." He slaps his grandson's back and ignores me.

Matt takes me by the arm and brings me one step forward, his voice stern and low. "Charlotte, Grandfather. You've met quite a few times on the campaign trail."

"Ahh, yes, Charlotte," he says dryly.

"Sir." I return his nod with one of my own.

"I'm giving her a tour," Matt tells his mother.

"First time here? I don't believe it," his grandfather says.

Matt ignores him and leads me down a wood-paneled hall facing a window with a view of D.C.

To its right, there is a great room with a view of the White House.

"Wow." I have trouble finding my voice, my eyes wide as I take in the majesty of the presidential home, illuminated in the night. "Must be hard to believe you lived there once."

I feel him shrug beside me, his voice low. "Actually, it's harder to believe this is my view now. And sometimes still hard to think I'll never see him again."

I cannot help from asking, "Did you ever want to know why that happened?"

"I ask myself that every day. Come."

He leads me to the bedroom; the view from the terrace is sweeping and endless.

"All this represents freedom and hope," I say, signaling to D.C. "How can you still believe in justice after that?"

"You just do." He opens the glass door. "You can smell it in the air."

"Ever tried to find out?"

"I've tried to. Why—why and if on orders. I think about it constantly. I dream the scene, over and over, but I don't want to live in that place." He points at his feet. "I want to live in the now." He points out the window. "And that is where we're going. That's where my head's at for now." I can tell by his expression that he's being pulled into his memories. "Those first few months, I was consumed with it. Investigators mysteriously disappeared or were replaced by a new team. My mother couldn't sleep without medical aid. Her worst fear is to lose me too. Her hope was that I'd be a lawyer."

"And yours?"

"My hope?" he asks, seemingly surprised I even have to ask. "Our hopes change, don't they? As our paths unfold. Now it's to do what he wanted me to do—something for the country."

I hear voices out in the living room. "Why doesn't your grandfather like me?"

"He doesn't like anyone who gets in his way."

"I'm not in his way; I try to steer clear of him as much as I can." I laugh.

Matt's lips twitch sardonically. "You're more of a threat to my candidacy than any of the actual candidates."

"How can that be possible?" I signal at myself. "I'm no one, have *no* political aspirations."

He taps his fingertip to the bridge of my nose, which I seem to be scrunching. "You're distracting."

"A tenth of what you are, at the most!" I cry.

He laughs.

We head back out to the living room and have a drink with Matt's grandfather and mother. I notice the conversation is strained; I think the fact that Patrick and Eleanor's agendas are so opposite right now is one of the reasons why the tension feels so thick in the air. I can hardly draw in a good breath.

Even Jack—who's been lounging by the fireplace in the living room—seems to be a little more alert, his head tilting as if he's trying to follow the conversation.

Matt seems to be used to it, though, and once Patrick leaves for the night, I relax a little. Excusing myself to the restroom, I leave Matt alone for a moment with his mother.

I hear them talking as I return. "I see the way you look at that girl and wonder why run, why not settle down?" his mother is asking him.

Matt sighs and stands to gaze out the window. "If I don't run, Dad's death will have been for nothing."

"No, it could *never* be for nothing," his mother says passionately, heading over to him.

"It could be for nothing if we don't change and everything stays the same," Matt tells her with a sigh.

He hugs her to his side and kisses her forehead, and she rests her head on his shoulder.

There's a very tender, powerful mother-and-son bond. She looks older and frailer when next to him; his strength is striking compared to her fragility.

In one interview, Matt's mother confessed that the day of the shooting, she thought she'd lost them both. How devastating for her! How afraid she must be now, the shooter never having been caught.

President Hamilton's assassination went on to be an unsolved mystery, like so many political murders before that.

After such grief, though, Matt's mother is still so refined. There's a strength beneath the silk.

Her clothes rustle as she returns to take a seat on the living room couch. Then there's confusion in her voice as she stares at Matt's back. "You had a tough life there, giving your father away for the betterment of the people. Hardly any privacy, no normalcy even when I tried so hard to give it to you. Why do you want to go back?"

"Don't *you* want to go back?" he asks her, looking confused as he turns and walks to take a seat next to her. "Tend to your tulip beds? Galas were your life. You were the finest First

Lady this country ever saw. Don't you want to fill that front fountain with ducks again? Come home on Marine One to the South Lawn of the White House all lit up for the night?"

Her eyes water and she lightly pats the corners to keep them dry.

"I want to see the ships Dad had on the walls of the Oval Office hung up there again. I want to be on the other side of Dad's desk, make the calls that he could never make."

"Matt!" she says.

"It was your home for seven years." He waits a moment. "The White House is not just the White House, Mother; I see that now. The White House is the world. Help me change it."

"I know what you're thinking. Every widowed or bachelor president has had a relative acting as First Lady. I heard you at the debate. But Matt, I cannot act as First Lady anymore." She stands up, then puts her hand on the top of his head, like she probably did when he was a boy. "Please rethink this. The White House *is* only the White House. Out here, you can have a *life*."

She looks at me as I step inside the room quietly, unsure whether I should stay quiet or let them know I'm here. "I know you want one," she tells him, still looking at me. Kissing his forehead and grabbing her glittering designer clutch bag, she smiles radiantly at me, like a queen getting her bearings. "So nice to meet you, Charlotte."

Matt scrapes his hands down his face as she leaves, and for a long moment, I sit in Matt's living room, letting him collect his thoughts.

"Charlotte, could you reorganize things and get me a few days off? I need to be by myself. I need to think."

I start at his request, not expecting it. "Of course. Of course, Matt."

He glances at his watch. "We should probably take you home. The media will be counting exactly how many minutes you remained at my place after my mother left."

I stand quickly.

"Wait. Not so fast." He takes my hand and tugs me down again so that I take a seat next to him.

My heart starts pounding wildly in my chest.

"Ever since I saw you walk through the door of the campaign kickoff, no one else is worth thinking about. From the moment we started talking, I knew I wanted you around." He tugs me closer. "I want a kiss right now."

With effort, I lift Jack by the paws and he licks Matt's lips, and Matt laughs and wipes his jaw and mouth, petting the top of Jack's head as he shoots me a look. "Correction, I want *your* kiss right now."

I know better, but I can't resist teasing him, so I lean over and kiss his jaw, feeling the warmth of Jack's head between our abdomens as he settles on Matt's lap.

"Don't kiss me like you'd kiss your father. Kiss me like you'd kiss your secret lover. Like this." He holds my face in one hand and presses his mouth to mine. He parts my lips with his.

Slow kissing.

The kind that curls your toes and makes every sense acute.

I respond, taking his jaw in my hands, feeling its muscles flex under my palms as he moves his mouth over mine, feeling the shadow of beard on his skin. He says, "Hmm," and deepens the kiss as I kiss him softly back.

My mouth feels wet and swollen and tingly when we ease apart. "Come here," he gruffs out. "Jack, scat," Matt orders.

Jack heads to his spot by the fireplace and I somehow end up on Matt's lap, and we kiss again, deeper, heavier, our breaths starting to labor.

Did he stop, or did I, I wonder dazedly a few seconds later.

His hands are on my hips and he's looking at me with dark eyes.

"I find it drastically inconvenient that I think about you at the most inopportune moments. How am I to govern a country when I can't control my own thoughts of *you*?"

"*Every* moment you think of me can't be inopportune. There have to be some good ones."

"True." He frowns as he thinks about it. "In the shower, and most definitely in my bed."

I squeeze my eyes shut. "Don't put that idea into my head."

He chuckles. "Like it's not already there."

I'm blushing.

I love when his full lips soften with humor and a smile spreads upward to light his eyes. But then his square jaw tenses visibly. He leans forward and moves his mouth over mine, devouring. His mouth slows, becomes softer and yet firmer.

He withdraws, leaving my mouth burning with fire.

I feel raw, vulnerable, and I don't want him to see. So I close my eyes and kiss him softly. His lips leave mine to nibble my earlobe, and then as I try to catch my breath, his tongue comes to graze mine, playing, tasting, stroking.

He tips my chin up and forces me to meet his gaze. "I would not mind waking up to your face every morning." I can see by the crinkle of his eyes that he's smiling. Smiling as he looks at me, but then his smile fades, and I know what he's thinking.

He doesn't want a wife. Not someone long term. Not at the White House. I want to tell him I'm willing to try, that I'd be willing to stand behind him, support him, not ask for more than he could give. Instead I'm afraid I'd be lying, that I really would have no idea what I'd be getting into, that I might resent him and ache for his time and his attention, his love and comfort, things a normal man would readily give the woman he loves.

And so I tell him, "You've got so much on your hands, there's no room for me in your bed."

We're a perfect couple, in the most imperfect situation.

He won't be a man who'll be there to always kiss me goodnight. Not as the president.

If I could wish one thing, I'd wish to hear him tell me he loves me.

And he never will. He can't.

Hearing the passionate way he talked to his mother about returning to the White House, I see it clearly: he has a mission, a calling, and nothing will stop him.

Have you every loved someone so much it hurt like *hell*?

I hadn't until now.

I slide from his lap and we sit there quietly.

We met eleven years ago, almost twelve now. In the years in between, it feels like he never left me or my mind. And I wonder if I was ever in his. For a moment at least. Until he saw me again at the campaign kickoff.

There is no need to speak. My knowledge of him is deeper now than when we started campaigning. And he knows me.

He knows I'm afraid of heights and yet I can't seem to keep from following him to high places. He knows I have a weakness for children and animals and am as protective about my privacy as he was when his father was president and he was thrust into the limelight.

He knows maybe I bear this situation just because I want to be near him and because he's right: I love my country and I want to do whatever I can to make it a better place, if not for me, for the children and animals I love so much.

GONE

Charlotte

I rearranged his schedule so that he can take three days off. It's been known the Hamiltons have a huge mansion in Carmel and I imagine him there, regrouping, sunbathing in the buff, maybe meeting up with his friends, clearing his head from everything, when I get a text early Monday.

Taking one more day off. You'll have to shuffle some more things around.
M

I reply:

Count on it.

I sigh and set my phone aside, worried.

After the debate, Gordon and Jacobs have been attacking Matt relentlessly. We're getting closer to voting day, and he's lost two points in the last polls—courtesy of a relentless campaign against him from both parties. President Jacobs accuses him of being a philanderer with no family values, no wife.

Gordon accuses him of being a playboy, listing dozens and dozens of women he's had affairs with, claiming his phobia of commitment is a measure of his inability to stick with one thing. If he can't commit to one woman, how can you expect him to commit to an entire country?

Funny, this coming from a man who's had four wives.

And in that list of women, of course, he mentions me. Charlotte Wells. How ridiculous it is for Matt to consider bringing an inexperienced twenty-something-year-old to the White House.

I wonder if Matt has seen everything, and what he thinks. I picture him saying, "People will think what they want to think," and leaving it at that. But I can't feel the same. I feel a shudder of humiliation when I think of two things.

Of what people believe. Of what my parents will be exposed to if Matt and I continue playing with fire.

And of losing to two men who don't deserve the seat I believe my candidate deserves.

My thoughts are racing dangerously as I open my computer and stream the news.

Pictures of me and Matt running ...

Of Matt buying me shoes ...

Of Matt looking at me during campaign events ...

I keep waiting, dreading someone will have a picture of us kissing in New York. But it doesn't pop up. I keep watching, but it still doesn't appear.

I can't take the guilt and the worry that it will, that it'll all get fucked up in one second.

I shut the news tab, my throat tight as I open a new computer file. My fingers are trembling, but in my heart, beneath the pain, I know this is what I need to do.

I head to Carlisle's office that evening. I take a seat and slide the paper across his desk. The letter is facing him, but he doesn't read it; his eyes are fixed on me.

"My resignation," I say quietly.

He reads it over, his expression opaque, then he lowers the paper and turns it around to face me. "Are you certain about this?" He sets a pen on the side, so that I can make it official and sign it.

I stare at it and my throat starts to close as I read my resignation letter.

Matt had a lot of thinking to do. And I hadn't known that, in his absence, so would I.

"I couldn't forgive myself if he lost the election because of me," I tell Carlisle.

"I know Matt. I've known him since he was a teen aiding us with his own father's campaign." He presses his lips together. "He won't accept your resignation," he adds.

"He *has* to. You need to make him see reason. Carlisle, we're so close to winning; we're talking about the difference he could make not for one person, for millions."

"I know, I know, dammit." He sighs, jams his hands in his pockets, and looks at me. "But he wants what he wants. He wants you in the campaign. We all do." He nods. "We'll field whatever comes our way; you won't be a scapegoat. Matt won't allow it—he's told me so himself."

I swallow. "I'm not worried about me, I'm worried about him."

"That's *my* job, girl." He stands and pats me on the shoulder. "Don't think just because Matt is a nice guy, he's not willing to get down and dirty with them if he needs to."

"That's not what he stands for; that's not what he believes in."

Carlisle leans back and eyes me narrowly. "I misjudged you, Charlotte." He smiles at me, and nods again as he finally accepts my resignation letter.

"Thank you; that means a lot coming from you. I've learned a lot these past months." I hesitate at the door, but then return to give him a hug. "Thank you for taking a chance on me, inexperience and all."

"Well, you're only inexperienced once, and now you're no longer." He smiles at me with the most fondness I've seen yet as he takes my letter from his desk and slips it onto the top of a pile in the right drawer.

"We'll handle it discreetly," he says. "Rhonda can be scheduler. We'll say you decided to continue working and making a difference at Women of the World."

"Thank you, and don't worry about me talking to the media," I say as I head to the door, suddenly overwhelmed with grief. I pack my stuff only after everyone leaves the building so there are no questions asked of me that I can't answer.

I can't believe I'm quitting on him. I can't believe I won't be able to stay and see this through. Everything I wanted to do has now been reduced to the fact that I do better by quitting? I'm disappointed that I let my own selfish emotions get in the way. But I can't regret the time I spent with him.

I head to Matt's desk and remove the pin that I always wear. The pin commemorating my favorite president, one I'm waiting for his son to replace. I set it on his desk and hope he knows it means …

Well, that it means I'm leaving because I care.

That night, I do what my mother has been aching for me to do. I pack a bag and head over to sleep at my parents' place. When she comes into my room, there's a long silence between us.

"Do you want to talk about it?" she asks softly.

I shake my head. A tear slips down my cheek. I quickly wipe it away. I shrug and look out the window, holding back the other tears.

She quietly comes over and embraces me in her warm arms. "You're doing what you need to do. Politics are not for the faint of heart," she reassures me. I know that she knows I fell in love with him. She saw it coming and warned me from the start.

"I know." I nod. "I know, which is why I never really wanted to dive in until … well, until him."

"You did the right thing." She squeezes my shoulder. "So many careers around politics have been ruined by scandal and —"

"I need your help. Please. What do I do? I just don't … I don't want to be in love with him forever."

"Nothing, Charlotte. You go on as if nothing happened. On Monday, you go back to Women of the World. You smile, you think of others, you forget about this, you forget about him. Did you two …"

I can't speak it out loud, how powerless I was during moments when all I wanted was Matt's arms around me and nothing else.

During one of our more comfortable talks during all these months of campaigning, Matt once told me a lie marks you forever with the public. You cannot lie, not ever. Twist the truths, maybe, play around with words ... but a lie, never.

I left so he wouldn't have to lie about me.

When my mother leaves, I take an extra-long bath in my old bathroom, then I climb into my warmest pajamas and get into bed. The same bed where I first fantasized about Matthew Hamilton.

I'm so confused, I feel heavy, as if the world's hate is already on my shoulders.

"Here, kitty," I call to my cat.

Doodles is a ball of white fur curled up on the windowsill. She doesn't move from her spot.

"What? Are you going to give me the silent treatment because I was away for so long? Oh, come on, Doodles, I need a hug right now."

No response.

I hug my pillow, and eventually feel my cat join me in the bed in the middle of the night, when I'm still awake, staring out that same window.

Mother thought it best I wait it out a week before returning to work, just in case any press comes knocking on our office doors. She wants to protect me from that, and I want to protect Matt from that, so I agree.

That night, we're having dinner—my father, my mother, and me.

"I think you should move back in with us for a while. Until all this settles down."

"There's no dust to settle." I shake my head firmly at my mom. "I'll go back to my place tomorrow."

By the time we reach dessert, I check the time again.

"Is there somewhere you need to be, Charlotte?" my father asks. He sounds terribly exasperated.

"Not me, Matt," I absently answer as I head over to the television in the living room. "There's this speaking engagement tonight. I'm sure it'll be televised."

I grab the remote on top of the TV and skim through the channels. Carlisle appears onscreen, standing there instead of Matt.

"Apologies, friends and supporters, tonight Matt needed to cancel. I'm here to answer any questions you might have …"

He cancelled?

I'm shocked.

He never cancels. Even when he had a headache, he'd just pop the Advils I'd set on his desk.

I drop the remote and watch as Carlisle begins to answer questions. What if something's wrong? I want to call Carlisle, but he's clearly busy. If I called Hessler, would he tell me? What about Mark or Alison—would either of them know?

I grab my phone and quickly skim my contacts, my hand shaking.

"Come and have tea with us, Charlotte," my mother calls.

The doorbell rings and my mother turns. "Jessa, darling, can you see who's at the door?"

Jessa rushes from the kitchen to the front door, passing the dining and living rooms as she does, then she comes back to where we sit. "It's Mr. Matt, miss."

My mother's teacup clatters, my father raises his head, and I don't think I'm breathing.

"Well, don't stand there, show him in," my mother urges.

I'm in the middle of the living room, while my parents sit frozen at opposite ends of the dining table, when Matt appears. I don't think I'm breathing when I see him. I just didn't expect to see him anytime soon. And suddenly it just hurts. My eyes hurt. My chest hurts. All of me hurts.

I feel as if something is squeezing around my heart, and it takes my every conscious effort to keep my parents from noticing.

Matt is wearing a black sweater and black pants, his hair wet from the rain outside, and he's never looked so hot. So sexy. So in control.

His eyes meet mine, and after a brief crackling stare, he slides them over to my parents. "Senator Wells," he says.

My father's chair screeches as he stands. "A pleasure to have you in our home, Matt."

He greets my mother, and she embraces him fondly. "You're just in time for tea or coffee," she says. "Would you like some?"

"Thanks. I'm actually here for Charlotte." His eyes are hooded mysteriously, to the point where I can't read what he's thinking.

"That's what we assumed," my father says with a nod. "Thank you, Matt, for the opportunity you gave her, campaigning for you; we've never seen her dive into anything with so much passion."

"It's *her* I came to thank for her support," Matt says. His eyes slide in my direction and he drinks me up as if the mere sight of me provides a shot of vitamins to his soul.

I blush crimson at the thought as my parents' footsteps trail up the stairs. I drop down on the couch, and Matt takes a seat across from me. My parents' house seems smaller with him inside. As small as it felt when his father and the Secret Service were here, except now it's just him.

Matt.

Doodles is swishing her tail, eyeing us. "What's her name?" Matt stretches out his hand, palm up, and Doodles goes to him, just like that.

"Doodles."

He lifts his brow and smiles, scoops her up, and sets her on his lap.

I feel nearly devastated by the want to go replace Doodles on his lap and kiss him, but the noise coming from the upstairs bedroom reminds me of where we are, of my parents in the house.

And suddenly I miss Jack as much as I miss Matt and his touch. I miss touching him when I can't touch Matt, curling my hand into the fur of his head and feeling his big ol' dog weight on my lap, so trusting, like there's nothing I could ever do wrong in his eyes.

Apparently he shares that with his master.

Oh, god. Matt. Why is he looking at me like that?

Why is he here? "You shouldn't be here," I say breathlessly. "You know you shouldn't be here."

"But I am." He sets Doodles at his feet and leans forward, a gleam of determination in his eyes.

I have to battle for restraint to keep from heading straight to him and saying …

Saying what?

"How did the thinking go?" I ask in a quiet voice.

I don't want my parents to hear us. I don't want anyone to hear us. It seems that my times with Matt are always stolen, and very few of those times do I have him alone like this.

I treasure our times alone.

"I went to see my father." There's a trace of sadness in his eyes. "I always pay him a visit at Arlington National Cemetery when I need to feel grounded." He's stroking my cat with his big hand but his eyes don't leave me, not for a second as he talks. "Then I went to our house in Carmel. Just to be alone for a while."

"Things get so hectic, I know," I say.

When he speaks again, his voice is warm. "I was supposed to concentrate on the campaign and I kept thinking of you." His smile is as intimate as a kiss. "You can imagine my disappointment when I came back to D.C. to find you gone."

"It's for the best; you know it."

His smile suddenly gains a spark of eroticism. "Actually, I don't."

"Matt, Gordon and Jacobs are after anything they can get on you."

"And trust me when I say I won't let it be *you*."

I exhale, then hug my arms around myself.

"Why did you leave?" he asks.

I try to keep my voice level. "I thought it was for the best."

"Never. That's the last thing I wanted when this began." His eyes keep holding mine, a muscle working in the back of his jaw. "I don't want you gone. If anything, I want you closer to me."

I flush harder and try to push any talk about the connection between us aside. "The polls, Matt—"

"Two points lost are two points I can gain back. *We're* gaining them back. You'll pile up my schedule even if I don't sleep."

I laugh, but he doesn't. He leans forward, his thighs stretching the material of his jeans and his shoulders the cotton of his sweater. "Come back to the campaign."

"Charlotte," I hear Jessa say as she brings a tea tray from the kitchen, "your mother wanted me to bring this." She sends a beaming look in Matt's direction, flushed as if she were nineteen instead of sixty-three.

"Thanks, Jessa."

"Thank you," Matt says warmly, reaching out for a cup and taking a sip.

She seems to flush even more as she heads back to the kitchen.

"My mother will be worried about a scandal. You need to go, Matt."

I stand and tug at his hand, forcing him to release the cup, set it down, and he catches my fingers as he comes to his full height. "Can I count on you?"

His nearness suddenly engulfs me. Every atom of my body is awake and buzzing with the heat of his so close, the feel of his eyes on my face, expectant, warm as the sun and just as bright.

"Always," I croak.

His hand and mine are linked and burning.

He smiles at me, a dazzling smile, and squeezes my fingers, looking down at me with the most adorable expression on his face. "Thank you."

He releases me and pets my cat one last time before he walks to the door, and I walk with him.

"Thank you for coming. I'll bring my things back tomorrow," I say.

"Tomorrow is the gala—" he begins, and I cut him off.

"I'll be there too," I assure him, pushing him out the door before he can kiss me. Even a kiss to the cheek would devastate me, and I'm afraid of yielding to the impulse to do more.

He's smiling, amused as he watches me slam the door shut.

I close my eyes and inhale, hating that I know the same thing I knew then: that he can never really be mine. But to quote him back, that hasn't stopped me from wanting him.

GALA

Charlotte

Tonight's gala seems to be the grandest and busiest of all the galas we've held. We're at the grand ballroom of The Jefferson Hotel.

The White House is so close, you can practically feel its power churning and surging, surrounding you. I glanced at its white columns as I arrived, and not for the first time I wondered what Matt's life was like there. If there was any normalcy at all.

The ballroom is glittering tonight, everyone who is anyone is attending—from huge industrialists to prominent artists, musicians, doctors, and teachers—and yet my attention is focused on spotting only one person. *The* one.

I'm in a white dress and my eyes drink in the luxurious decorations surrounding me in my search of the one thing I most want to see.

The figure of the man that has my heart pounding like this.

"Charlotte!" Alison launches herself and hugs me. "A vision in white—I approve!" she happily says, then leans back and lifts her camera. *Click.*

"Alison, come on!" I groan, and she tugs me into the crowd, where I say hello to my team colleagues. No one even hints at noticing or knowing that I'd left, and I'm sure it's due to Carlisle's expert hand at damage control.

I keep searching for Matt across the room with a pounding in my heart and a knot of nervous anticipation in my stomach. It feels like forever until my eyes snag on the tall, dark figure of a man—and they stay there, absorbing everything that is Matt Hamilton.

Dressed in a pitch-black suit and black tie, his hands—long-fingered and tan—keep shaking those of the people who walk up to greet him. The outlines of his shoulders strain against his suit jacket. He stands among the crowd, wickedly handsome, his face animated as he speaks to them about something he's clearly impassioned about.

Our country, I know ...

And then his eyes lift and he spots me across a sea of heads. The touches of humor around his mouth and eyes fade as our eyes lock.

The intensity of his gaze hits me like a punch. His stare is so galvanizing, it sends a tremor through me. The harder I try to hide the way I feel about him, the harder it hits me. I glance away, anywhere, really.

That's when my eyes fall on a couple wading into the ballroom. My *parents.*

My eyes widen in surprise.

My mother spots me and gives a light queen-like wave in my direction. My father's eyes are on something—someone—else.

I'm so surprised my father agreed to attend, it takes me a few blinks to make sure he's really here. Being a Democratic senator, it's a huge testament to his support of Matt. Huge.

As I approach to greet them, I see Matt do the same. His walk is all confidence and vitality. "Senator Wells," he says, as he greets my father. His handshake is firm and swift, full of grace and virility.

God, his voice. How can you even miss someone's *voice*?

A warmth fills my stomach when I see the genuine respect in both men's eyes as they greet each other.

I thought perhaps my dad being here meant he was supporting *me* as I venture into the world of politics, where my parents had always wanted to see me. But as I watch them, I know my dad is not only supporting me—he wants Matt to win.

To realize my father finally supports Matt—to know that Matt, his campaign, his touch with the people, has won him over like his own father did all those years ago—makes my admiration and awe of Matt grow.

I'm dying to talk to him, but it's impossible with him being the center of attention. The center of everything. I step in to greet my parents as well, and I feel Matt's eyes on me as I do.

For some reason, he shifts his stance to stand closer to me as he's greeted by the mayor of D.C. and his wife, and instinctively I remain where I am and let him introduce me too.

Conversation swirls around us, and all this time, I'm only aware of the low, dull throb inside me. Matt stands casually beside me, an almost imperceptible tension emanating from his body.

He takes advantage the moment he's free from the attention of others to look at me.

"That's quite a dress."

The room blurs around me as I lose myself in those espresso eyes.

I want to flat out go up on my toes and kiss him, do what a girl does with a guy she loves, tell him I missed him, want him, thought of him. I want to put his hand on my body. That's all I want. Just his hand on my body, even if it's just a light touch.

He reaches out to press his fingers into the small of my back to guide me away from someone who wants to pass. The move puts us in view of a group of chatting men, and one of them calls out happily, "Matt!" and walks over immediately.

"Ahh, yes, Congressman Sanders." He greets the man who approaches with a firm shake of his hand. They start chatting and in between exchanges, he glances at me for three seconds. I meet his gaze and am aware of the excited nerves going through me.

I go up on my toes and say, "I want my pin back," before brushing past him to say hello to someone else. When I look at him minutes later, he's smiling at something someone says as our eyes meet. His smile falters for a minute as heat steals into his eyes, but he manages to keep it in place even as he looks at me.

The look in his eyes tells me exactly what he wants to do to me, how he wants me. Every female part in me feels it. Knows it.

Matt will be fucking me senseless tonight.

SECRET MEETING

Charlotte

Wilson drives me to a home in Washington, D.C.

He pulls over in front of a beautiful two-story brownstone, and because the Hamiltons' empire consists of a vast billion-dollar real estate corporation, I assume it belongs to Matt. I walk up the steps as Wilson opens the door and lets me in.

"He's upstairs," Wilson says.

I follow the stairs and head toward the streak of light coming out of an open door.

Across from the door, Matt looks out the window. Black pants cover his long legs, topped by a shiny black belt and a white button-down shirt with the top buttons undone, and he holds a glass of wine in his hand. He turns when he senses me —how could he not?—and slowly sets the glass aside with a clink.

I shut the door behind me, and I'm lost in the swirl of bronze in his eyes. It's like I'm in a subspace. No thoughts or reason, only need … just heat and desire and him.

Shadows dance across the room, playing with the candlelight.

Matt clenches his jaw as he looks at me. His eyes glow like fire in the night and he starts walking toward me with such single-minded purpose that I do the same.

"Tomorrow, this never happened," I say urgently.

He catches me by the ass and lifts me, my legs curling around him as our lips smash together.

A part of me wants Matt to tell me that it could work between us, that though I'm a normal girl and he's a man in extraordinary circumstances, we could work it out. But he's not a man you get to keep. So at the same time, I want his assurance. I know it's impossible. I know this is all we've got—the few moments I'll have alone with him when he's just Matt. The man I've fallen in love with.

"You don't get to quit me," he says, those dark of his eyes intensifying. "You don't get to walk away from me. Next time you do, all you'll have to do is look behind you to find me at your heels."

He lowers his head again, opens my lips with his, and our tongues collide.

"You can't have it all, Matt," I breathe into his mouth. I'm kissing him wildly now, without restraint, biting his lips a little as I fist his hair.

His eyes are heavy-lidded as he peels free and starts unbuttoning his shirt. He looks hot as heat itself, his lips red from me.

My heart lurches as he spreads open his shirt. I see an expanse of tanned, smooth skin and muscles. He shrugs off his shirt, his shoulders and biceps flexing with the move.

I'm fumbling as I quickly unzip my dress. I shrug it off and let it whisk down my legs.

He pulls off his belt and sends it away with a clatter, and before he can remove his slacks, I'm back on him and we're kissing.

We're kissing without restraint, wild, our hands and mouths all over each other. He groans between his wild, fierce kisses, "I can't even find the words to describe how perfect you are." He holds my face and kisses me, and I hold his jaw and kiss him back, then push him away and ease toward the bed.

He follows me. "I've missed those blue eyes. I even missed the way you scrunch your nose at me."

I scrunch my nose.

His eyes laugh silently, and I laugh out loud, but we go sober.

I've missed his eyes too.

My calves hit the bed and he reaches for me, his hand curling around my waist as I grab his shoulder to brace myself.

His chest jerks with a breath, as if my touch singed him. He's smiling as he pulls me flush to him. My torso touches his and fire streaks through my veins.

A tremor runs through my nerve endings as his fingers spread on my back. Plastered against his chest, my nipples have turned hard as rubies.

I want him to take my bra off and bare them to him.

I want him to take them in his mouth and taste them.

I want him so much, I burn for him, in my veins and my heart and between my legs.

He slips his fingers into my hair and exerts just the right amount of pressure to tug my head a little closer—even as he leans his head to mine. A muscle tics in the back of his jaw as he presses his lips to my cheek, dragging them down my jaw, my neck. His breath is warm on my skin as he whispers, "Perfection."

Before I know it, he's worked off my panties and is pulling off my bra. Shivering when the air brushes over my skin, I lean back on the bed—naked. Letting him look at me while I look at him.

His body could be in a centerfold—and yet it's real. It's here, and it's all for me.

One last time …

He's over me the next instant, hungry. So hungry.

He suckles my nipple and draws my legs apart with his hand, caressing the inside of my thighs as he heads upward.

I've never wanted to devour another human being the way I want to devour him.

I kiss his jaw and rock my hips to coax him to touch me. He complies, first stroking his finger along the folds of my sex. I can hear a wet, slick sound as his index finger trails up and down, up and down. Then he eases the tip inside me.

"God … *Matt*."

"Say it again. Say it again just like that," he says, kissing his way to my other breast and taking the nipple. Sucking. Licking. Laving. Tasting.

My voice cracks. "Matt."

He grabs my hair and keeps me in place as he drags his mouth lower, his shoulders flexing, the candlelight making love to his muscular chest as he starts kissing me between my legs. He runs his tongue along my folds and I groan, his tongue dipping inside of me.

I move urgently beneath him as he works my body into a frenzy, works *me* into a frenzy.

The pads of his thumbs stroke over the tips of my breasts, caressing my nipples. I groan deep in my throat again. He curses low in his throat, eases back, and strips the rest of his clothes off fast—never taking his eyes off me.

God, his cock is so thick and long, so *huuuge* ...

He crawls over me and I'm panting, our eyes holding.

His fingers curl around my hip, holding me still. And then with a slow but powerful rock of his hips, Matt thrusts inside me.

I nearly come when he drives all the way in, every inch of his cock caressing every inch of my channel. I gasp, clutching my limbs around his body as my sex clings to every inch of him.

We're not speaking. Leaving unspoken the fact that we are stealing, flat-out *stealing* this moment, and we both seem to want to savor it with our every sensation. Sight, sounds, touch, taste, scent.

I move with him as he drives forward purposefully. I'm writhing and twisting, kissing and touching him as much as possible even as Matt kisses and touches me. Exquisitely does what any living, breathing, red-blooded man would do with a girl like me.

My eyes hold his, cling to his, widening as I take him inside me—long, hard, pulsing with life. He won't take his eyes off me. They're heavy and so male, and looking at me as if I'm some living *Mona Lisa*, a breathing Statue of Liberty. There's not enough air in the world to fill my lungs right now. He's breathing just as hard.

He rocks his hips and keeps entering, watching me. My body contracts with aching need, and every time I feel him rock—so hard, so big, so close—I get wetter and wetter, absorbing everything. The soft sucking motions of his mouth on my nipples arrow down to my sex, which keeps squeezing around him.

I run my fingers up his chest and let my own mouth wander, tasting, tasting, tasting. He's warm, sweaty, and salty. He groans and thrusts back inside, pulling my head back, watching my neck arch, and he tells me to keep making those sounds, that they're driving him crazy.

I'm the one who's losing my mind now. I'm loving the way he groans, looks at me, feels, tastes, as we move without control.

He drives into me again, deep and hard, his hands holding me by the hips, our hips rocking, our bodies arching, and our mouths twisting around each other.

"Are you with me? Charlotte, are you with me?"

I answer him with a whisper, just "*yes*" as my body thrashes in orgasm.

He presses a kiss to my earlobe, tensing his body as he comes as well.

We're breathing hard as we turn on our sides, facing each other. He props himself on one arm. I don't have the energy to do that. But in our eyes, we're both communicating.

"Matt ..."

"Hey." He takes my chin, sober now. "Don't think about it. We're being careful."

I close my eyes.

Rolling to his back, he exhales and stares at the ceiling. "When this whole campaign started, I had no idea." He looks at me. "No idea about you, C."

"C? Do you want me to call you M?"

"No, but I look forward to having a major hard-on the day you call me Mr. President ..." He rolls back to his side and touches between my legs and I really can't complain anymore.

"God, Matt ..."

"I'm a man. I'm flesh and blood. And I want you. Have you been sent here to torture me? Sent by Jacobs or Gordon to ruin me?"

"You're the one who's got it in his head to be torturing *me*. Making me travel with you, always so close to you. What do you think it does to me? It makes my job difficult."

"But it's not just about me, Charlotte." He glances at the window. "*That*—from the moment I decided this is what I want to do above all else. It's not just about me." He cups my face, some silent torture in his eyes even as he moves his finger inside me.

"I know." I swallow, and my cheek burns under his warm palm as my hips rock involuntarily. "So take your hand away. The more I stay here, the more dangerous it becomes."

He moves his other hand to the back of my neck, whispering as he rubs his thumb over my clit, "I will, after you kiss me. Tonight is about you."

I close my eyes, raising my head. His breath bathes my lips. "You make me want to be the best version of myself I can ever be." He licks my lips.

I kiss his mouth. I kiss his mouth and then roll him over and drag myself down his length. Lower. And lower. Kissing a path down the line of silky dark hair that travels down his chest, the smooth skin above his navel, and then down to the thickening mat of hair that leads to his cock. I take him in my hands. Full. Thick. The crown of his cock swollen to the max and dripping with desire for me.

I lick the drop.

Matt is watching me, a predatory look in his eyes as he cups the back of my head and tugs me closer—closer to his cock, until I grip the base with my hands and take him into my mouth.

MORNING

Charlotte

I slip into a comfortable gray sweatshirt that belongs to Matt as we have coffee very early the next morning. I'm curled up on the couch while Matt stands by the window, one hand holding his coffee as he stares thoughtfully outside. He wears only pants, and I can see a streak of nail marks down the back of muscled arms.

Did I do that?

"Are we still set to leave for the last campaign stretch on Monday?" I hear myself ask.

He turns to me then, his expression thoughtful. "All set." He pauses, his voice gruffer. "Do you realize how difficult it is to give the last of the campaign my all when I know that if I win, I lose you?"

"You'd run again. If you lost."

He clenches his jaw.

I quickly blink back the tears and strengthen my voice.

"Matt, I was on the sidelines for months, looking at a thousand and one strangers, and I realize we all have something in common. You. You're like a part of this country's history. You represent a painful moment, and the strength to go on and thrive. You inspire people just by being who you are. Matt."

I walk over to him, and he sets his coffee mug aside. He takes my hand and lifts it to his lips, kissing my fingertips. "In so many ways I ran for you."

"What?" I laugh incredulously.

"Thinking you and people like you are out there. Deserving more."

"Then give us more."

His gaze slides to the window, face etched with thought. "How much more is enough? How many monsters will need to be slayed? How many dissident voices will need to be quieted?"

"I don't know, but you'll figure it out along the way."

Matt clenches his jaw and lowers our hands, squeezing my fingers.

"Matt, if anyone is worthy of anything, it's you. If anyone is worthy of leading our country, it's you. Who do you want it to be? Thompson? Jacobs?"

"God, no, fuck, no."

He turns to me, and I meet his gaze head-on, knowing this is goodbye. Knowing this is the last morning I let myself wake with him, and seeing in his eyes that he knows it too—even if he doesn't like it.

I inhale shakily. "You're two points away from the lead. Go out there and get it, Matt. Because you know what? I won't be helping you next year." I scowl then and push at his chest as if he'd bullied me into saying it.

He laughs then, grabbing my wrist and drawing me against the flat planes of his chest as he looks at me. "What'll you be doing then? Next year?"

He watches his hand as he strokes his fingertips along my cheek, making me breathless. I swallow. "In a year? I'll be living the American dream, because you'll be my president."

He clenches his jaw and whispers, "Come here," wrapping both his arms tightly around me as he lowers his head.

"You cannot kiss me again, not anymore," I halfheartedly protest.

But as I speak I go up on tiptoes and let him kiss me, slow, a goodbye kiss. I tremble when I think of it being the last time I feel his lips on mine.

"Are you crying?" His voice is a murmur.

I blink back the tears proudly, but he's faster than I am and wipes them away.

"Charlotte ..." His voice seems both surprised and protective. His eyes darken as he looks at me and he strokes a hand down the back of my head. "Fuck me, this isn't goodbye. I could lose. I could fucking lose."

"No!" I take a step back, putting some distance between us. "Matt, I want you to win this presidency."

Determination flashes across his features. He fists his fingers into his palms, then growls, "And I want to win this presidency, Charlotte."

I nod then, in this moment, both of us coming to an understanding. We both worked each other out of our systems for the last time. It's over with. Done with.

So I step into his embrace and we just hug. Knowing this is goodbye. Not a goodbye as in me leaving the campaign again. But goodbye to ... what could have been.

Politics aren't simple, they are messy; there is always deceit and something lurking underneath. This time it is the fact that I love him, and I think he might have, in another time or

place, come to love me, but you cannot do two things at once
…

My mother says, sadly, that she doesn't think there has ever been a truly happy First Lady in the White House or a president capable of making one happy. He holds the most powerful office in the land but it's so consuming, love has no place in the White House.

Almost in a brotherly way, in the same way he kissed me when I was eleven, Matt kisses my cheek. He wraps his arms around me and I inhale him, closing my eyes, curling my hands around him, forcing my tears back because though a part of me wants to keep him, I want him to win, too.

There's no time for this. We've got an election to win.

Everywhere we go, everyone seems to be watching Matt and whether he looks at me, smiles at me, or so much as stands close to me. Carlisle has been sending me looks, warning stares to avoid giving Gordon and Jacobs fodder. Still, Hewitt, as press manager, is playing the card of childhood friends, and Matt is so stubborn and secretly mad for giving the public such access to his private affairs. He has been blatantly using the press manager's expert handling of the situation to keep me close and keep looking at me as much as he pleases.

Which in turn both pleases and distresses me.

We travel to Des Moines, Iowa; Manchester, New Hampshire; Milwaukee, Wisconsin; Charleston, South Carolina; and one afternoon, we even go visit a tree called the President.

We stand before it, close to the wood sign that identifies it, in the middle of the giant forest of Sequoia National Park in California.

The tree is over three thousand years old, and the most amusing thing is the smaller sequoia trees surrounding it are called the Congress Group: two dense stands of medium-sized sequoias that represent the House and Senate.

"If you win and your ego starts getting too big, one trip here and it'll be squashed back down. I've never felt so tiny next to a tree." I look up its tall, gnarly trunk to the top, where its leaves rustle in the breeze.

Standing here, I marvel at how many people I've met and all the landscapes I've seen. I've been taken out of my D.C. bubble to see the colorful quilt that makes up our country.

It's incredible, touring all the states, each unique in its own right, each having its own growth spurts and challenges. You don't know America until you step back and really look at it.

It makes me want to see more of the world—to travel, do everything, see everything, be touched by everything and touch it back in return.

It helps me remind myself the reason I'm staying away from Matt ... even when Matt still effortlessly carves time to spend moments alone with me.

BACK IN D.C.

Charlotte

We arrive in D.C. early the next day. My machine is flooded with phone calls.

My mother would love for me to spend the night home.

Kayla, Alan, and Sam want to see me.

I look around my apartment, then scroll through my phone contacts.

After denying it all. After everything. One night.

Tomorrow we vote, and that's that.

But I cannot leave it at that.

I would like to tell him that I love him, but this is not something you do to someone when you know he may have such a hard, demanding path ahead. This is something you might do if he didn't, if the public chose someone else, and maybe then he's free ... to choose *me*.

But I don't want to imagine anyone not choosing him, denying what he has to give. I also am human and no matter how much I want to make a difference, I want things for me too. Those things have narrowed down until all I am aware of wanting, every second of the day, is him, in any way I can have him, even if it's just a tiny piece.

Tonight I could have him whole, all of him. And I want him—I want to hold nothing back, except the words. But I can tell him with every kiss that I cannot help the way I tremble, the way being touched by him makes me feel like the only thing in the world for me is him in those moments.

I sit down and think of him, and before I can think better of it, I text him and ask if I can see him.

I don't know what it is I want, but I know I cannot go to his house, nor could Matt come here. He's too closely watched, and I'll be too tempted, and it won't be fair. It needs to stop at that last night we shared, but I'm no longer going to be his campaign scheduler. After tomorrow, I'm not sure where to go from here, and if I'll ever see him again.

We meet at the Abraham Lincoln Memorial. We sit by the steps, gazing out at D.C. as the wind whips through my hair and stings my cheeks.

"You could really win tomorrow," I whisper.

"I know."

"I want you to."

"Do you?" He studies my features.

Silence. I shiver. "What's done is done, what isn't done isn't done, I guess." I shrug. "We did all we could, didn't we?"

"That's right."

Before I know it, he shrugs out of his jacket and drapes it over my shoulders. "Charlotte," he says softly, "we wouldn't be here without you."

"Yes, we would," I assure him.

We wait for a young couple to walk past us, then he inches his hand close to mine, on the steps, under the fall of his jacket, and drags his thumb over the back of mine. "If I lose, I want you to go out on an official date with me."

I drop my head and suddenly feel more emotional than I've ever been, a whole year of campaigning both for him and against my feelings for him hitting me hard. I don't want him to lose, but I hate yearning for it, just for this second. "That's really unfair." My voice cracks.

My face is suddenly wet. I don't know why I'm crying; I just am.

"The chances of you losing are this big," I say with my fingers.

I'm sniffling now, and I stand and tuck his jacket closer around my shoulders so I can hide my face inside the collar.

He stands too, stepping closer, his voice tender. "Show me my chances again," he says.

I clutch the jacket closed with one hand and lift the other, making the space between my fingers slim.

He takes my fingers in his hands and widens the space between them just a little. "I'd say more like this." He smiles down at me, trying to cheer me up, and I love him all the more for it, because the smile doesn't reach his eyes at all.

"I love you. I love you and your silly glasses," I say, widening my fingers as much as I can, and then I add, laughing and crying, "I can't even use my arms to show you."

One second his smile is there, the next it's replaced with a look of fierce emotion. His eyes roil with it—with something I'd never seen in Matt's eyes before. Impotence.

I start to leave, ducking my head into the jacket to hide myself from another group of passersby. I hear him start after me before they stop him.

"Holy shit, Matt Hamilton!" the guy says. "I mean, sir … it's a pleasure, a real pleasure."

I hear Matt greet them, but I can feel his eyes on me as I slip my arms into the sleeves of his jacket and use it as a shield against the cold and leave.

I take the train to my apartment. The first thing I do when I arrive is splash cold water onto my face. I'm drying it when I hear a knock.

Dropping the towel, I open the door, and Matt stands on the other side. His hands are at his side, his eyes a little wild.

I gasp. "Matt!" I glance around the hall, relieved to find it empty. "What are you doing here? My neighbor could see you —"

One second Matt is on the other side of the door, the next he's shutting it behind him and the back of my head is in his hands, and his lips come crashing down on mine.

ELECTION DAY

Charlotte

The next morning I wake up alone in bed. Across the floor, only a few feet from the bed and next to my clothes, is Matt's jacket.

His jacket—Election Day!

I leap to my feet and turn on the TV as I hurry to change. Thirty minutes later, I'm in line at my polling place. I watch the line of voters and wonder who each is voting for. Had voting ever been this exciting? There's a charged anticipation in the air, or maybe it's just me, my fingers itching when I finally slide behind the privacy curtain and stare at the voting sheet.

For one second, my chest hurts. I know what I'm losing. I know what I'm choosing. But the urge to see him win overcomes my own selfishness, and I mark an *X* next to his name.

I stare at the ballot for a moment.

I missed voting for the last president when I was stuck home with the flu. It's the first time in my life I actually vote, and the eleven-year-old who promised to help him if he ever ran for president can hardly believe that today, I'm standing here and voting for *him*.

I feel an odd sense of loss as I exit and yet distract myself as I try to make sure no one is following me when I take the train, then walk a few blocks to The Jefferson Hotel.

Detouring to the lobby restroom for a moment, I pull out my makeup kit. I carry only lipstick, blush, and mascara, but I dab a little of each on my face.

I didn't need to add blush. A red tint stains my cheeks, and my eyes look a little rounder, very dark, and very shiny. *Oh god.* It's almost as if I'm afraid to go upstairs, walk into the room, and have everyone see right through me.

Exhaling for courage, I step out, take the elevators, and head to Matt's suite.

The last time we were in D.C., we hosted a fundraiser at the ballroom of this hotel. A lifetime ago and at the same time, only yesterday.

I knock on the door and when Alison opens it, my eyes fix on a tall, large figure standing by the window across the room with his hands in his pockets. He's the one farthest from the door, and there are dozens of people between us. But it doesn't matter; space doesn't matter.

He sees me; I see him.

His gaze looks very male as our eyes lock. It's as dark as it was last night, and it makes my stomach constrict painfully. Warmth spreads all over me as I step inside. Will he be able to tell that he flusters me?

Of course he will.

I greet everybody as I walk into the suite, leaving him until last.

"Matt." I smile at him, excited the day has finally come.

"Charlotte."

He returns my smile, but the way he says my name sounds gruff.

He doesn't look frazzled like the rest of us. He looks like he just left the spa and wellness center on one of the lower floors.

God, I envy his ability to keep his cool.

But one year is enough time to get to know somebody and I know that hungry shadow in his dark eyes too well, and I know that his mind is working full speed.

Maybe speculating on the exit polls as we hear the newscasters in the background, as the seconds tick by, and the minutes turn to hours into what feels like the longest day of the year.

As I sit on one of the couches next to Alison and Mark and alternate between watching Carlisle smoke and glancing at the TV, I am acutely aware of Matt and where he sits and breathes, and every inch that he physically occupies in this room.

Out of the corner of my eye, I see him lift his eyes and smile a satisfied smile, and it makes me squirm and remember more than that.

He's back to reading something, Jack's head on his lap, Matt's hand on top of Jack's furry black head. I remember that hand last night …

We locked the world out when he closed the door.

I remember him backing me into my bedroom, his hands easing off his jacket, slipping under my shirt. Possessive and firm, that's how his touch felt. His kiss. I needed him so much that when he stripped me, I wanted to rush, clawing at him as I stripped him too. But Matt wasn't in a hurry.

He kissed me and tenderly *shh*'d me as he lay me down on the bed, and he took me in in the moonlight that came in through my window as he caressed me.

I melted into a pure white-hot need as he kissed my mouth, my cheeks, nibbled a line down my throat. His mouth moved around and over the peaks of my breasts, all over my stomach, to the insides of my thighs, and then it spent a long time between them.

His tongue drove inside me with slow, deep flicks that seemed to be what he needed to quench his thirst.

His hands held my thighs open as I convulsively tried to close them shut, the feelings too intense.

Hot and firm, he used his lips and suctioned with just the right amount of pressure to unravel me.

I unraveled.

I felt like I was cut from one string into a thousand. I came against his mouth with his hair between my fingers, but even then, he seemed hungry. His eyes, as he came up, glowed dark brown as he stroked his fingers down my face and captured my mouth in a crushing kiss that curled my toes.

I remember that hunger. How it built and built and didn't diminish. Not after an hour, naked under the sheets with him, nor even after another hour.

And I remember the sound I made after he made me orgasm with his fingers and then, finally, slipped his hands into the nook at the small of my back and clenched my bottom as he drove inside me. I groaned his name. And I remember the way he smiled against my mouth, a smile of relief, and then moved, groaning my name, telling me I'm classic, so classic.

I remember how we did that, all night.

Him, whispering things so gruffly I didn't understand what he said, only heard the hunger and tenderness in his voice and the rake of his teeth on my skin as we got rougher, more desperate, our breaths faster.

I remember it all, today, of all days, and I feel my cheeks start to burn bright red as I try to push it all out of my mind.

Amazing how I can forget sometimes what I dreamt, my apartment keys, my cell phone, but not a single detail about him.

Things from the past come to the surface. Holding his jacket for him, accidentally sipping from his coffee cup, spilling my folders at his feet and him kneeling down to help me.

I lift my gaze to find him reading the daily copy of the *Washington Post*. He's wearing his glasses.

When he lifts his gaze and looks at me above the gold rims, his eyes darken and my breasts suddenly feel sensitive under my bra. I lick my lips and they feel extra sensitive after being kissed by him all night.

Matt's gaze falls briefly to my lips, and I can't help but drop my gaze to his mouth, which looks full and firm. Suddenly all I want is to feel it again, firm and hungry, his tongue ravenous against mine.

I don't know how I'm going to do it.

How it will be possible to fall out of love with him.

But that's what I need to do. Because this was only temporary, because that date he proposed won't be happening.

I need to forget him and I need to put as much of an effort into the task as I did into his campaign.

Still, he's staring at me across the table with those dark eyes that look both warm and tender.

With a jolt, I remember his jacket strewn across the floor of my apartment along with my lingerie.

The thought of someone seeing that I have it in my possession makes me worry, and my eyes widen and I leap to my feet.

Matt frowns and pulls off his glasses, standing instinctively as if to help me.

"I forgot I have something for you," I say.

I can see he doesn't like the idea of me leaving this suite, but I don't give him time to stop me as I hurry to the door.

"Stay away from the paps and if they question you, you know the drill," Carlisle says behind me.

"'No comment,'" I assure him as I swing open the door.

My eyes meet Matt's, and I feel that familiar skip of my heartbeat. I close the door behind me, the nerves about today's results multiplying by the second.

I keep my head down to avoid any paparazzi, which I thankfully manage to do as I head to my apartment to get Matt's jacket.

Once I reach my building, I hurry inside and spot it in the same place I left it.

My heart does that flip again.

I walk toward it slowly, almost as if I expect it to bite me like a cobra. But that's not really why suddenly time seems to slow down—it's because I suddenly don't want to take it back.

I want to slip his jacket around me one more time. I want to wear it and hug myself and pretend that my arms are his arms. I want to tuck my face back into its collar and breathe in his scent.

The urge to do this is so enormous. I stifle the impulse with a lot of effort, calling back my professional side, the side that knows last night was not just unplanned, but a mistake.

So I take the jacket in my hands and fold it neatly into a department store shopping bag, then I head back to The Jefferson Hotel, determined to be professional and to put last night behind me as our farewell.

YOUR NAME IS CHARLOTTE

Matthew

There's a calm I didn't expect as we wait for the popular vote results to come in.

Charlotte brought me my jacket a while ago. Hell, I didn't want it. I wanted a piece of me with her. I can't shake her off and when it comes to her, I'm selfish enough that I don't want her to shake me off either. Her concern for others keeps mystifying me. She's been more concerned about a scandal than I have all this time. More concerned with making sure that the man the country sees is the one *she* makes me want to be.

She's in my veins, this girl.

Nobody would guess that I sit, watching and waiting, lifting my eyes to find her watching the screen, twirling her hair on one finger, biting her lips, sometimes looking back at me— nobody would guess how much I want every inch and piece and breath of hers.

The suite is flooded with the most integral members of my team. Carlisle of course, as well as our chief strategist, our communications director, and some field operatives.

There's a buzz in the air. Carlisle chain-smoking, oozing tension.

And here I am, calmer than I expected, my mind divided in two equal parts: one wondering about each vote, each state, each poll result; the other fixed on the woman across the room who was in my arms only hours ago.

A part of me wants to draw her aside and say something that will appease us both, but even I know there are no such words. I'm running for the most powerful office in the land. Ironic that I can't promise something as simple as my love to her.

My mind drifts as I imagine what I'd do if Jacobs or Gordon beat me in this election. I picture heading to the Senate, working my way back to the race, dividing my attention between work and the woman I'm obsessed with. But when I'm back in the race again, what then?

Both my mother and I lost my father the day he became president. I don't want Charlotte to lose me. I don't want to lose the spark in her eyes whenever she looks at me, full of admiration and respect and desire—the spark that inevitably dies when you keep hurting those who love you, even if unintentionally.

It can't work, I tell myself. *You've known it and you still couldn't keep away. You still want to hold this girl and never let her go even as that's exactly what you prepare to do with every piece of news filtering into the room.*

It streams on the TV and on live podcasts some of my team members are playing on their phones.

"Matthew Hamilton's win requires every young voter out there, every minority, every woman, to come out and vote, and the turnout has been unprecedented today ..."

"Early returns have been astounding ..."

"Hamilton leading in Texas. Alabama. New York. People want change and they want it now."

"They're saying you've got Ohio," Carlisle says.

"Yeah?" I lift my eyebrow, a kick of restlessness settling in my gut. One I can't run out of my system right now. I scan the room for Jack and whistle him over. He leaps on the couch and sets his head on my lap. I stroke his head absently as Carlisle skims through the channels, remote in one hand, cigarette in the other. He stops on one.

"That's right, Roger, the Hamilton campaign pulled off an impressive feat this year until, well, that incident where Hamilton failed to appear and give comments on the rumors—" the anchor is saying, and I grab the remote and shut off the TV, glancing at Charlotte in silence.

It bothers me to have the media speculate about her, and today I have no patience for it.

Her crystal-blue eyes look at me and pink crawls up her sweet cheeks. *There'll be no kissing the pink away from those cheeks.* And suddenly the feeling of impotence bothers me too.

The room falls silent as I toss the remote aside. Carlisle lights up another cigarette by the window, and I soon leave Jack on the couch and join him. I can almost hear the clock ticking in my head when Mark barges inside.

Tick, tock, tick, tock.

"Turnout was unprecedented," Mark begins.

She looks at me helplessly for one second, and my eyes meet hers, the excitement in Mark's voice crackling in the room.

"You've won enough states to secure the electoral college vote."

A chorus of gasps and exclamations follow the declaration.

"Holy crap!"

"OH MY GOD!"

"Fuck, I knew it!" This last remark from Carlisle.

The second it takes my mind to process what I heard, I am with my father. He's standing in this room wearing that proud grin he used to when he talked about me, and he's telling Charlotte, *He's going to be president one day ...*

My eyes seem to have a will of their own as they slide unerringly to lock on Charlotte.

She's looking down at her lap, with a smile on her lips and a single tear on one cheek as she stands to face me. It seems to take her a moment to fully realize what she heard too. She's the sexiest thing I've ever seen as she wipes the tear away, leaps like a girl, and clasps her hands together. Her pulse flutters, and my mouth wants to be right on hers, I want my hands on her, I want myself in her.

She keeps a distance and allows the others to come and congratulate me first. Hugs and cheer, and claps, Carlisle booting up the TV for even more confirmation, and I look at the screen, strongly resolved to take care of what I've been given. America is mine.

I'm being engulfed by Carlisle, hands shaking, everyone congratulating.

"Matt! Now's the time for champagne."

Someone is bringing back the bottle I made them remove earlier.

Charlotte hangs back, and it isn't until everyone in the room has had their say that she steps forward, her voice betraying nothing.

"You're this close to being president, Matt," she says, showing me with her little fingers.

I smile and think to myself, *Not as close as I was to telling you I loved you back.*

She's the last to hug me, and when I pull her small frame into my arms, she pulls back hastily; Charlotte making sure I hugged her for the same length of time I hugged each of the others.

It's not enough.

I hug her with my damn eyes as she lets go. She gathers her things and tucks a glorious strand of red hair behind her ear, and then walks away.

I've never been so aware of the price I paid for my victory.

*To be continued in **COMMANDER IN CHIEF**...*

DEAR READERS,

Thanks so much for picking up my new WHITE HOUSE series. Matt and Charlotte's story consumed me from the start, and I've been working nonstop to bring you the sequel, COMMANDER IN CHIEF, by early next year. It's been a fabulous experience for me, different, exciting, shining with hope and bursting with passion. I cannot wait to share the continuation of Matt and Charlotte's fiery romance.

Thank you for your support and enthusiasm for my work XOXO,

ACKNOWLEDGMENTS

I can hardly believe this book happened. I began it last year and worked on it sporadically, sometimes thinking it would be a pet project just for me. At other times, I was too consumed by it to care about what would happen. Then I finished, and was so eager to jump into *Commander in Chief*, that I just couldn't keep it to myself.

This book is for Amy, who is all kinds of amazing—the best agent, advisor, and friend. I am so blessed to have her on my team, as well as all the other amazing people at the Jane Rotrosen Agency.

I also could not have done this without my family's love and support, and so many other people who have contributed in small and big ways to supporting my writing.

Huge, huge thank yous to my editor Kelli Collins and Sue Rohan for her expertise, Gwen Hayes, my copy editor Lisa, my proofreader Anita Saunders, and my betas Nina, Angie, Kim J., Kim K., Jenn, Monica, Mara, and CeCe.

To the fabulous Nina at Social Butterfly and the entire team at Social Butterfly PR, you ladies are truly phenomenal.

Thank you for being as excited about my books as I am and for all that you do.

To Melissa, thank you for everything, and to Gel, for the incredible support and promo material.

Thank you to my foreign publishers for translating my stories so that they can be read across the world.

To Julie at JT Formatting and my cover designer, James at Bookfly Covers, you did an amazing job!

Bloggers, I am ever so grateful for your support and enthusiasm for reading. You always make my day when you choose to share and promote my work from among so many other amazing stories to share, read, and review. Thank you!

And to my readers. You are always in the back of my mind, every time I'm writing. I get to parts that make me smile, or do *other* little things to me, and I think to myself, "I wonder if they'll feel this, just like *this*." It is always my aim for you to, so I am always grateful to be given the chance to coax you into my world.

Thank you for your support and your love. Thank you to everyone who picked up, shared, and read this book.

ABOUT

New York Times, *USA Today*, and *Wall Street Journal* bestselling author Katy Evans is the author of the Real and Manwhore series. She lives with her husband, two kids, and their beloved dogs. To find out more about her or her books, visit her pages. She'd love to hear from you.

Website: www.katyevans.net
Facebook: https://www.facebook.com/AuthorKatyEvans
Twitter: @authorkatyevans

Sign up for Katy's newsletter:
http://www.katyevans.net/newsletter/

OTHER TITLES BY KATY EVANS

Manwhore series:

MANWHORE
MANWHORE +1
MS. MANWHORE
LADIES MAN

Real series:

REAL
MINE
REMY
ROGUE
RIPPED
LEGEND

CPSIA information can be obtained
at www.ICGtesting.com
Printed in the USA
W11s1606011116
196LV00003B/530/P